FIRE OF WRATH

Book Six

Salvaggio's Light

An Epic Contemporary Romance Serial
By C. L. Cattano

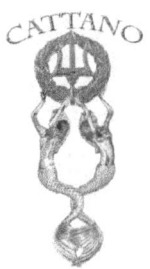

VAGARY PUBLISHING

Fire of Wrath
Book Six
Salvaggio's Light

A Vagary Publishing Book
Copyright © 2017 by C. L. Cattano

Cover Art, Title Page Art and Typesetting Copyright © 2017 by Chynsia Hinesley

Published by:

www.vagarypublishing.com
inquiry@vagarypublishing.com

VAGARY PUBLISHING

Rogena Mitchell-Jones, Independent Literary Editor
RMJ Manuscript Services LLC *www.rogenamitchell.com*

ISBN: 978-1-947852-03-7
First Edition

WARNING

It is suggested readers of this story be adults over the age of eighteen.

This dramatic romance series has many scenes describing sex as well as intense emotional scenes and acts of violence.

This is a serial story with themes that flow from one book into another with lots of twists and turns. Reading this series from the beginning is highly suggested, or the reader may not be able to follow all of the storylines.

Go to the Salvaggio's Light Facebook page to join other readers who are talking about the series.
www.facebook.com/SalvaggiosLight/

Join the C L Cattano mailing list and check out my website at www.clcattano.com

Acknowledgments

I WOULD LIKE to thank everyone who has worked on and read the Salvaggio's Light serial up to this point, especially those who have reviewed, commented, and contacted me publicly and privately. Your encouragement and constructive criticism is appreciated. This next part of the serial was particularly difficult to write (and I think you'll see why when you read the next few books) and it has even been hard for my proofreaders and editor because of the dark turn the story is taking. I just want to assure you the darkness is a necessary part of the arc for the characters and the story, so I hope you stick with me until it passes so we can be together at the end.

Dedication

For Marie — who dreams of me.

Salvaggio's Light

An Epic Contemporary Romance Serial

Coming Soon

"Through me the way into the suffering city,
Through me the way into eternal pain,
Through me the way that runs among the lost."
—Dante Alighieri, The Divine Comedy

1

Just minutes later...

SIRENS SCREAMED AS three ambulances arrived at the emergency room entrance of L. A. Medical Center. Paramedics poured out of the vehicles and rushed to get their patched and bloodied patients out and into the hands of the waiting medical staff. Two gurneys carried immobile patients hooked to IV's and strapped to boards, the third carried Flynn Ogden, who was restrained and escorted by the police. Paramedics, doctors, and nurses shouted symptoms and instructions as the patients were briskly wheeled into the hospital emergency room.

Flynn cried out as he watched the other gurneys with their blood covered passengers pass by. "Is she okay? I didn't mean to," he cried. "Please, someone tell me if she's okay!"

"Calm down, sir. She's being taken care of," said the paramedic as she pushed the gurney. "We need to concentrate on you."

"What do we have?" asked the emergency room doctor as he looked over Flynn.

"Looks like a broken arm, and no other injuries," said the paramedic. "He's a suspect so the police will be following him inside."

"Take him to x-ray," the doctor instructed the nurse.

"Don't let her die!" Flynn cried desperately to the doctor as he was whisked away. "I'm sorry! Please, don't let her die!"

2

IN THE EMERGENCY waiting room, Letty Carver had been waiting for what seemed like hours, distraught with fear and worry. Letty had just pulled into her apartment parking space when Katheryn called and relayed the tragic news about Eden and Flynn being rushed to the hospital. She advised Letty to get there quickly. Letty held Bronte affectionately. She was glad she had taken the baby home with her after court. Ephraim and Julia paced anxiously around the waiting room. Other than knowing Eden and Flynn were rushed to the hospital, they weren't exactly sure what had happened. Abby had gone to the nurses' station to find out news of their condition and when the two could be seen.

Abby walked in the waiting room upset and crying. "The police are going to take Flynn." Abby sniffed. "I heard them say he has a broken arm but is going to be okay. Katheryn and Stacey are going with him to the police station as soon as they release him. Jude is going too. They're going to question him. I couldn't get in to talk to him."

"What about Eden?" Letty asked as she held Bronte protectively.

"I don't know," said Abby as she shook. "I could hear Flynn screaming for them not to let her die," she said shakily. "I saw her being wheeled out of the ER to somewhere." She paused and ran her hand down her face. "She was covered in blood and looked bad." A wave of tears gushed down her cheeks. "She could be dead and they won't tell me anything about her."

"Did you tell them we have her baby, and we have to know how she is?" asked Letty upset at the lack of information and cooperation.

"It didn't help." Abby shook her head. "They want to know who her next of kin is or where Rafe is because she's on record from the pregnancy as being her decision maker, and she still has power of attorney. We have to find her!"

Julia looked at everyone's hopeless expressions and pulled out her phone. "Oh my god." She sighed. "I'll call Daddy."

"We have to find Rafe." Abby was distraught. "They won't give information to anyone but her, Julia!"

Julia took a deep breath ignoring Abby and put the phone to her ear. "Daddy? Yes, yes I know. I'm not in the office. Listen, we're looking for Rafe. Yes, Rafe Salvaggio. No, no, I'm not meeting her without you. We need to find her because there's been an accident with Eden," she said distressed. "Yes, Eden Kingsley, Rafe's," she paused then forced the word because she wasn't sure if it was true anymore, "girlfriend." Guilt wavered over her because she wanted Rafe to leave Eden, but not like this. "Yes, she's been hurt, and she's at L. A. Medical Center. We've been here for hours, and they won't give any information to anyone but a relative or Rafe. I'm not sure where she is. No one can find her. Actually, all we know is Eden was assaulted. I don't know all the details. We need your help finding out details of her situation or with finding Rafe. Okay, okay. Thank you, Daddy. Bye." She hung up and looked at everyone. "He's going to make some calls. He knows everyone."

"Why are you calling your father?" asked Abby. "What can he do about this from New York?"

He's here," she revealed slightly embarrassed. "He came to see me this weekend to check up on the office and me. He wanted to see if I was still thriving here or if I wanted to go back to New York. He checks in every few years. He knows everyone and has a few detectives on the payroll, so he'll find out where Rafe is for sure."

"You were with your father, and you ignored all my messages?" Abby asked in frustration.

"He was very demanding on my time," said Julia defensively, "but he bought me these boots," she said and showed the boots to everyone. "If you had left a better message the first time you called, I might have been able to get away."

"I didn't know anything else when I left the first message!" Abby said frustrated.

"Well, when my father requests my undivided attention, he gets it," she said innocently. "You know how it is."

Abby's temper sparked as she looked at Julia in anger because she now knew Julia had ignored her for a pair of boots.

"I just hope he can help us," said Letty gravely.

3

MASON ESSEX SAT alone at his table in a small café near the courthouse. He drank the last of his iced tea then sighed heavily because his plan was screwed. *Fucking Jake,* he thought. Since Jake went and got himself shot, he had to think of some way to get things back on track. The police took Jake's SUV with the surveillance equipment and the tracking device he installed. Mason had planned to plant evidence in it after Jake went home. He wanted Daniel to find it under the passenger seat because he knew Daniel would take the evidence to the reverend, but now everything was a bust. It was so frustrating when things went off course.

The door to the café opened, and Mason looked up to see two people walk in, a man and a woman, both wearing suits with white shirts. It was apparent to Mason they were law enforcement of some kind. He dismissed them since it wasn't unusual for law enforcement to be hanging around courthouse cafés. The door opened again, and Daniel walked inside. As soon as he spotted Mason, he made his way to his table.

"Hey," said Daniel as he sat down.

"Hey," replied Mason with a frown. He wasn't in the mood for a social call.

Daniel leaned close. "I saw you were in here, so when those two came in, I thought I should warn you. They're FBI."

"What?" Mason asked suspiciously. "How do you know?"

"Our guys found out. They weren't exactly hiding who they were," said Daniel. "They were asking around about the shooting."

"Oh," Mason said as he nodded. "Makes sense since it was on government property."

"But it's not Federal property," explained Daniel and arched his eyebrows. "It's a County courthouse."

"What are you worried about?" asked Mason with a frown. "Jake didn't shoot anyone. He's the one who was shot."

"I know," said Daniel as he nodded, "but they were all over his car."

"Hmm," grunted Mason. He knew the cops took the SUV, but he didn't know the FBI was searching it. They would definitely find the tracker. He was glad he always wore gloves when he did installs. He did it mostly so he wouldn't get his hands dirty, but the side benefit was no fingerprints. "Why do you think they were interested in his car?"

"I don't know," said Daniel nervously as the FBI agents walked out of the café with their orders, "but I don't like it. Another team went to tell the reverend, and I know he won't like it."

Mason looked at Daniel and almost smiled. Instead, he pulled his mouth into a frown and furrowed his brow, hoping he looked distraught and worried. Mason put his hand to his head and rubbed his temple. "Oh, no," he groaned softly. "Please, no."

"What?" Daniel asked on alert.

"I think we may have a big problem." Mason sighed heavily.

"What?" Daniel insisted.

"Not what. Who," Mason groaned.

"Who?" Daniel asked again confused.

Mason nodded. "Jake." He looked at Daniel's bewildered face. "The reverend asked me to put a tracker on Jake's car," he explained. "He didn't say exactly why, but he wanted to put him under a stress test. I felt I had to give him some of the information from the review. I didn't give him the confession, though." He stopped and looked away then back as he leaned in close. "The confession was missing from my computer," he whispered.

"Missing? How can it be missing?" asked Daniel.

"Exactly what I wanted to know," said Mason with frustration. "So, I installed cameras in my office." He got out his laptop pulled up the video of Jake breaking into his office. "This is what was recorded."

"Shit," Daniel exhaled.

"I showed it to the reverend," Mason confessed. "I had to."

"Of course, you did," Daniel agreed. It was clear Jake had gone off the deep end.

"When I was in Jake's car, I found this," Mason said and pulled an envelope out of his messenger bag. "I saw it was copies of reports. I knew he shouldn't have them in his car. This with the information the Kingsley woman had," he added with a shrug, "it seemed too much of a coincidence."

"Coincidence? I don't understand," said Daniel with a frown.

"Well, she got the information from someone, and now Jake has confidential information in his car. It seems very strange. Why was it there? Who was he going to give it to? What was he going to do with it?"

"Oh, right," Daniel said as he nodded his head in understanding. When he pulled the papers out of the envelope, a USB drive dropped out and landed on the table. "I wonder what's on this," he said and picked it up.

"Let's see it," said Mason. He took the drive and plugged it into the computer. "Looks like documents and a video," he said and clicked on the video.

Jake's face appeared, and they both recognized the day the video was made—the day Jake made his confession for Mason to record.

"It's his confession," said Daniel with surprise.

"No," Mason shook his head, "I mean, it is a confession, but this isn't right. He confessed to having feelings for the woman and failing his Mission. There's no mention of any of it in this video. It looks like it's been all edited out."

"Why would he edit it?"

"I don't know. I didn't even know he knew how," said Mason acting surprised.

"He's a graphic designer and does all kinds of things on the computer with video and websites," Daniel reminded him.

"Yeah, but he calls files *tapes*," said Mason. "I thought he was too old to know how to do this stuff."

Daniel gave a nervous laugh. "Young people aren't the only ones who know how to use editing software, even if our generation uses outdated words."

"I guess," said Mason with a frown. He opened the first document. "What's the old timer word for informant?"

"Snitch," answered Daniel as he looked at the document and anger grew inside him.

"I think we know why the FBI was at the courthouse," said Mason.

"Jake fucking invited them," Daniel growled.

"Maybe," said Mason as he looked at the documents. "It's not definitive. The letter doesn't say 'Dear FBI' or anything. Maybe this was something he was using to protect himself from re-programming."

"Don't be so naïve, Mason," snapped Daniel in frustration. "Look at the facts. Jake's been fucking up a lot. You were right about him having feelings for the other woman, the companion, and I think he was trying to get out by going to the FBI."

"Seems extreme," said Mason and bit the inside of his cheek to keep from laughing. Daniel was hooked.

"Think about it," Daniel said vehemently. "The FBI was there for a reason. Jake had this stashed in his car. They were searching for something in his car. I think they were searching for this," he said tapping forcefully on the papers. "I think Jake was planning to deliver this to the FBI."

Mason acted as if he were thinking about it for a moment. "Daniel, he deleted the Mission review file. I have no confession anymore, and I don't have anything to back up my suspicions about his possible feelings for the woman. I don't know if I can take any of this to the reverend." He paused for a moment. "I can tell him about finding this information in Jake's car, but even if I do, it's deniable. Jake can say it was never in his car, and I can't prove him wrong. If I tell the reverend about this, I can't say for a fact Jake was delivering it to the FBI."

"I thought you told the reverend about the Mission review."

Mason shook his head and sighed. "I didn't tell him we did the review. I just told him my suspicions because the file was gone. If I tell him I did a review and didn't turn it in, I could be severely disciplined. Possibly demoted. I was doing you guys a favor by not turning it in, and now it may come back to bite me in the ass." He looked at Daniel with worry. "I knew Jake was pissed, but he was failing the Mission. I wanted to push him and make him get back on track, even if it meant him hating me. I had no idea he was really so obsessed with the companion and talking to the FBI. I couldn't know he was going to be breaking into the building, stealing equipment and information, and deleting things from my computer. I'm so fucked if the reverend finds out."

"Don't blame yourself," said Daniel and put his hand on Mason's shoulder, feeling fatherly to the younger man. "You're young and were trying to help. I think your intentions were good, and in a way, you did make him refocus. Unfortunately, he was lying to all of us and getting ready to sell us out."

"What do we do now?" Mason asked trying to sound desperate. It was amazing the things he was getting away with today just because he was young. "Jake has put me in a bad position, and the reverend may think you might have known about his plans since you were on the Mission with him. We're both screwed. Well, you may not be as much, but I definitely am if all this comes out."

Daniel looked at Mason and could see he was just a scared kid who was trying to impress everyone so he could get a promotion. Jake hated him, but it was probably because the kid was so close to the truth. He also knew Mason was a favorite in the Stewards. Helping Mason out could be a good move, especially if the reverend made Daniel share the blame for what Jake was doing. "What if we worked together," he asked pointedly.

"What? What do you mean?" asked Mason with feigned surprise.

"I mean, I help you, and you help me," said Daniel firmly. "The way I see it if we stick together the reverend and the Council will believe us over Jake."

"The only way you could help me is if I wasn't involved at all," groaned Mason shaking his head. "You'd have to take all this to the reverend and tell him you found it. You have to tell him you made similar observations about Jake having feelings for the companion without him knowing we talked. It would mean you would have to lie to the reverend," he said and closed his laptop and pulled out the USB drive. He tossed it onto the middle of the table. "I can't have you lie to him."

"Mason, you still have a lot to learn," said Daniel with a short laugh. "Sometimes, we Soldiers have to do things, like lying, for the greater good."

"Even to the reverend?"

"Even to the reverend," Daniel nodded. "Listen, Jake could take us all down. What's worse? Me telling this lie or letting Jake get away with what he's doing?"

"What we suspect he's doing," said Mason trying to act fretful.

"Damn it, Mason! Open your eyes," Daniel demanded harshly. "If we don't report this, even if it's just a suspicion, and it turns out to be true," he stopped himself before his voice got too loud. He took a breath and started again. "The FBI is a serious problem. Lying about finding the information is meaningless if it saves us so we can continue our work."

Mason rubbed the back of his neck then packed his laptop. "If you do this, I need to be out of town or something," he said acting nervous. "Maybe I need to go visit my mom."

"Great idea," said Daniel relieved Mason was giving in to his reasoning. "I'll take all of this to the reverend and talk to him about Jake. I won't mention you at all." He picked up the envelope and started putting the reports back inside and grabbed the USB drive from the middle of the table.

"Fine," said Mason as he stood up. "I guess I can't stop you, so I have no choice except to trust you."

"We're on the same side, Mason," Daniel assured him as he stood. "We're Soldiers, and we have to look out for each other and for everyone in the church."

"Okay, okay," said Mason softly. He looked at Daniel. "Then thank you, I guess."

"I think we'd make a great team," Daniel confided with a smile. He wanted to make sure he could keep working with Mason. Then maybe some of the kids 'favorite status' would be directed his way. "Maybe after this, I can help you with more things, and you can teach me about surveillance and stuff."

"Sure." Mason shrugged halfheartedly. "I better go. Give me the day before you go to the reverend."

"No problem," said Daniel. "I can tell him I found all this in Jake's car earlier today but only looked at it after I got home. I can say I forgot about it in all the commotion."

"You're okay for an old guy," said Mason and held out his hand.

Daniel laughed and shook Mason's hand. "You're okay too."

The two walked out of the café and Daniel went one way while Mason went the other. As soon as Mason turned the corner, he couldn't help laughing to himself. It was so obvious Daniel wanted to do anything to save his own ass. It was such a relief to Mason to know by tonight, he would be on a plane out of the country. But first, he needed to stop by his apartment. He had to make another copy of the information he gave to Daniel. Then he would make a stop at the hospital to have a little chat with Jake. Afterward, the plan would have to take on a life without him because he would be gone.

4

IAN HAWTHORN WALKED through the lobby of the Wilshire Hotel. He was there because of a call from the local detective he had contacted after speaking with Julia. Rafe was one of his favorite clients, and he thought of her as a daughter, so he was glad it only took about two hours to find her. He would do anything he could for her when she was in need. He passed the hotel desk and saw a familiar face waiting for an elevator.

Approaching the elevator, Ian called out. "Rafe? Rafe Salvaggio?"

"Yes?" answered Rafe as she looked up surprised. "Ian!" She smiled as she said his name. "It's nice to see you. Ian, this is Greer Noble. Greer, this is Ian Hawthorn, Julia's father and my financial broker extraordinaire," she said as she pushed the button for the lift.

"Nice to meet you," said Greer with a smile.

"It's nice to meet you, Ms. Noble," said Ian and smiled back hesitantly. He was a bit confused about why it was so hard for Julia and her friends to find Rafe. "This is very awkward, Rafe," he said as he turned back to her, "but it seems I'm to be the bearer of some disturbing news."

"Really?" asked Rafe with concern as the bell for the elevator rang indicating the doors were about to open. "What is it?"

"I just spoke with my charming daughter a while ago, and it seems everyone is looking for you," he revealed but kept how he found her to himself.

"Well," Rafe frowned as she looked at him, "I'd appreciate your confidence," she said as the elevator doors opened. "I really don't want to be found right now."

"I see," Ian said uncomfortably. "Well, this makes things all the more difficult." He looked from Rafe to Greer and back to Rafe, wondering if she was having an affair. It was none of his business he decided. "You see, I was informed Eden has been in some sort of accident, and they need you just down the street at L. A. Medical Center."

"What? An accident?" Rafe asked apprehensively as Greer held the door to the elevator open. "Do you know what happened?"

"Actually, I don't know all the details, but it sounded rather urgent," Ian reported. "Julia wanted me to make calls to the hospital and other helpful parties because they won't release information to anyone, but you or a family member. She sounded distraught and mentioned something about a possible assault."

"Shit!" said Rafe. She looked at Greer in shock. "Greer, I should go," she said as Greer held her arm.

"Wait," voiced Greer, "you should take my phone. Call Beth if you need me to help."

"Thank you," said Rafe as she took the phone. She left her own phone behind to avoid the calls she knew she would get from everyone about leaving Eden. She was again grateful for

Greer's helpfulness and gave her a quick hug. "I'll let you know what's happening as soon as I can. Thank you, Ian!" she called as she rushed out of the hotel leaving Ian and Greer at the elevator.

5

AFTER BREAKING SEVERAL traffic laws, Rafe Salvaggio strode determinedly into L. A. Medical Center and up to the emergency room reception desk.

"I'm Rafe Salvaggio," she stated, obviously agitated and blunt. "Where's Eden Kingsley? Jayne Eden Kingsley," she inquired.

"Just a moment," said the nurse as she typed on her computer. "Oh, just one moment. I'll page the doctor," she said and dialed the phone.

Abby rushed down the hall at the sight of Rafe. "Rafe!" she called. "Rafe you're here!" she screeched as she hugged her. "Thank god!"

"What's happened?" asked Rafe brusquely. "Where's Bronte?"

"Bronte's with Letty in the waiting room," said Abby quickly. "She's been with Letty since you disappeared. Rafe, we aren't sure how Eden is or what exactly happened," she said and started to cry. "She was covered with blood when she came in. She..." she sobbed. "She might have been shot."

Already concerned because of Abby's sudden tears, Rafe paled and staggered back against the ER desk as she took in Abby's words. *Eden might have been shot.* Her heart jumped in her chest, and a wash of red swept over her eyes as she saw her friend Brettito's pool of blood on the street and on her hands. Her vision cleared and Rafe looked at Abby. "What?" she cried out, fighting to keep control of herself. "When? How the hell did this happen?" she demanded.

"Ms. Salvaggio?" said the doctor as he walked up behind Rafe.

Rafe turned quickly, her heart racing. "I'm Rafe Salvaggio," she answered and took the hand the doctor offered. "How's Eden? Where is she? What happened?" she asked as she shook his hand.

The doctor looked at Abby then at Rafe. "Will you come with me please?" he asked and led her to a private area.

6

FLYNN OGDEN WAS taken into custody at the Los Angeles Police Headquarters. Katheryn Hardam was talking to the investigator while Stacey and Jude were waiting in one of the interrogation rooms for her.

Katheryn entered the room. "They're bringing him now."

"Can we stay?" asked Jude.

"This is supposed to be client and attorney time, but you can stay for a few minutes," she said sympathetically.

A burly officer escorted Flynn into the room. "Hi," Flynn said sadly. He sat down and put his cuffed and banded hands on the table. The cuffs wouldn't fit around his cast, so they had to use a zip tie to connect the encased hand to the cuffs on his good wrist.

"Can you remove those?" Katheryn asked the officer.

"Sure," grunted the officer. He removed the cuffs but left the band around the cast. "I'll be right outside. Knock when you're ready," he said and turned to Flynn. "You will remain seated at all times," he said officially and firmly. "If you move from the chair, I will have to restrain you or take you back to your cell. Do you understand?"

Flynn nodded. "I understand." The officer left and locked the door from the outside. Flynn looked at Katheryn with red-rimmed eyes. "Is Eden okay?"

"We don't know how Eden is right now, Flynn," said Katheryn gently. "As soon as I know something, I'll let you know."

"What happened?" asked Jude with concern about her friends. It was hard to imagine Flynn doing something leading to his arrest. Plus, not knowing what had happened to Eden coupled with Rafe missing was unbalancing her.

Flynn fidgeted with his cast. "He... he... attacked her. I tried to stop him but," he looked up, "I couldn't, so I had to shoot him. She can't," he swallowed, "she can't die," he said shakily. "When I pulled the trigger, they were so close together," he said desperately wanting to cry again but he couldn't because he had cried himself out of tears.

"Jesus, Flynn. When did you get a gun?" asked Stacey in shock.

"I've had it for a while," confessed Flynn. He looked at Katheryn. "I have a license to carry it."

"Well, at least something has gone right," muttered Katheryn knowing it may be the least of his worries. Her client didn't look good on paper or in person. His pallor was drawn, he looked ragged, and he might even have been dehydrated.

"What will happen if they both die?" asked Stacey with morbid interest.

"Stop, Stacey!" demanded Flynn in misery. "Eden can't die!"

Stacey looked at Flynn with squinted eyes. "What about Jake?"

"I don't care if he dies," spat Flynn getting agitated. "He deserves to die!"

"Flynn," Jude chastised. "No. If he dies, you could go to prison."

"I don't care!" Flynn declared defiantly. "At least he'll never be able to hurt anyone again!"

"You're not sorry you shot him?" asked Stacey in disbelief.

"Why should I be sorry?" asked Flynn fiercely. "He attacked Eden! I'd shoot him again in a second!"

"Okay, enough," said Katheryn firmly. "Calm down. Flynn, I need you to tell me everything you told the police." She looked at Jude and Stacey. "I think you two should go now."

7

IN A SECLUDED area inside the L. A. Medical Center, Rafe Salvaggio, pale and anxious, watched as the doctor looked at his chart. The doctor saw the patient's paperwork was in order and looked up at Rafe very seriously to discuss his patient's case.

"Doctor, is she," Rafe started distressed, "is she okay?"

"First, just let me tell you we believe she'll be fine," said the doctor solemnly. "She had been knocked unconscious when the paramedics got to her, but she's resting comfortably now. All of her vital signs are good and strong."

"Was she shot?" asked Rafe fearful of the answer.

"No." The doctor frowned as he looked at the chart again. "She has no gunshot wounds, but she was badly beaten and has contusions on her head, face, arms, and knees. She also has some bruising on her face, back, chest, shoulder, neck, and legs. She's fortunate no bones were fractured or broken."

"Who the hell did this to her?" Rafe asked as she ran her hand over her face, angry someone had hurt Eden but relieved that she wasn't shot.

"You'll have to talk to the police about whose responsible, ma'am," the doctor informed her.

"Well, can I see her?" Rafe asked wanting to see for herself if she was okay.

"Of course. Come with me," said the doctor and led Rafe down the hall to the elevator. "She's been moved into a room, and we need to keep her overnight for observation because of the head trauma," he said as the elevator took them to the second floor. "She'll probably have some difficulty speaking until the damage to her esophagus heals, and she'll be restricted to limited mobility because of the damage from the assault."

On the second floor, the doctor led Rafe to Eden, who was lying in her hospital bed asleep and hooked up to an IV. They had cleaned her up and bandaged her cuts, but the bruises on her face and neck were angry reds, purples, and black. They had dressed her head, wrapping it to protect the cut on the back of her head.

Rafe took in the blond hair showing through the bandage and the contrast of the bruises on her pale face. She touched Eden's hand, seeing the scrapes and cuts from fighting off her attacker. She watched Eden breathe for a moment, and then her head began to throb with the pain from holding in her anger.

"The paramedics reported her clothes were torn, so we were required to do a rape kit," the doctor said solemnly behind Rafe. "The results haven't come back yet, but I'll let you know as soon as I get them."

The doctors words caught Rafe off guard. She was speechless as she looked at the doctor in horror.

"When she arrived," continued the doctor, "she was going in and out of consciousness, but no other injuries were found. Her body has been through a lot of trauma from her assault. When she wakes up, she'll be in pain and discomfort, but we can help with medication as needed. We need you to fill out some paperwork."

Rafe looked at Eden sadly then squeezed her hand gently. "Can I send someone in to watch over her?"

The doctor nodded. "Yes, of course."

"Okay," said Rafe as she released Eden's hand, "let's go do the paperwork."

8

RAFE SALVAGGIO WALKED into the ER waiting room with a clipboard full of paperwork to complete. Everyone stood to meet her as she walked over to Letty who was holding Bronte. She kissed Bronte then sat down as the others moved closer, and Letty sat in the chair next to her.

"How is she?" asked Abby frantically. "Was she shot?"

"No," said Rafe sharply. She took a deep breath to calm herself. "She wasn't shot, but someone beat her very badly. She's asleep now, and I have to fill out this paperwork." Distressed, she put her face in her hands for a moment. She looked up at everyone who had been desperately waiting for news. "They," she said shakily, "they think she may have been raped."

"Oh no, no, no, no, no," said Abby distraught as she rushed to Rafe's side. She and Letty put their arms around Rafe.

"Where the hell have you been, Rafe?" Letty asked upset. "How'd you know to come?"

"I," Rafe hesitated not knowing if she wanted to tell anyone where she was staying. "I've been at the Wilshire," she said relenting. "I saw Ian Hawthorn there."

"No way!" said Abby astounded and cross. "We checked all the hotels. We didn't see your car! Did you check in with a fake name or something?"

"No," said Rafe as she frowned. "I used my private garage to park my car in until yesterday. I didn't check in." She hesitated. "My room is under Greer's name.

"Greer!" Abby screeched in outrage. "Rafe, how could you? We've been looking all over hell and back for you for the last three days! We left a hundred messages!" She looked at Rafe through squinted eyes as another question niggled at her brain. "Why the hell do you have a private garage?"

"I'm glad my father found you, Rafe," said Julia remaining cool and calm like a proper British boarding school alum. "Apparently, you've been lied to about a few things."

"I know I've been lied to, Julia!" snapped Rafe angrily.

"I'm calling Katheryn," said Letty. She pulled out her phone and dialed.

"No, not by Eden," Julia tried to explain, "by Jake. I don't know all the facts but—" she was cut off abruptly.

"But," Letty cut Julia off, "Katheryn does, and she'll be here soon. Then she can explain everything."

"I guess everyone's been lying to me," said Rafe her emotions a swirl of hurt, fear for Eden, and anger.

"Why didn't you answer your phone?" demanded Abby. "You always answer your damn phone!"

"I didn't have it with me," said Rafe as she rubbed her temple.

"What? Why not?" asked Abby angrily.

"I didn't want to be found," said Rafe forcefully. "I didn't want to tell you where I was or explain anything to anyone."

"What about Eden?" Abby screeched.

"Eden has all the explanation she needs."

"Why didn't you come to me? I'm family," Letty said sadly. "I'd have helped you."

"I just didn't," said Rafe defensively. "I didn't want to deal with Eden or anyone." She looked at Letty and the hurt on her face. Letty had been there for her the last time Eden left her and took good care of her. "I guess I should have let you know," she said sadly. "Eden has just been going through the motions and keeping up her lies to all of you until today when she could leave without anyone the wiser. I didn't want to deal with her or Jake anymore!" She sighed doing her best to hold back her tears. "She's leaving and taking Bronte. She's going to be with Jake," she revealed to all of them.

Everyone just watched her and saw her deep pain as she told them her version of the truth.

"I," Rafe looked up and fought for words, "Greer suggested I see today through to hopefully have some closure. I'll stay to help her until Jake gets here for her, and she can change her paperwork. I'm thinking about leaving with Greer in the morning on a trip."

"This is just so wrong!" moaned Abby in distress. "Rafe, you have to stay. Don't do this because—"

"Abby, don't," said Letty cutting her off as she gave her a look reminding her of their promise to Katheryn.

"Please," Rafe said as she looked at the paperwork, "will one of you just go sit with her while I do this?" She started filling out the paperwork. "She's been moved up to room two thirty-one."

"I'll go," said Abby. Upset, she stormed out of the waiting room angry she couldn't spill everything.

"I need to talk to the police to find out what happened and who did this to her," said Rafe sadly. "After I fill this out, we can all go up to the second-floor waiting room."

Letty looked at Ephraim and Julia. She put her hand on Rafe's shoulder. "Rafe," she said anxiously, "it was Jake." She nodded as she spoke. "He did this to her."

"What?" asked Rafe in disbelief and confusion. "Jake?"

"We don't know anything more," said Ephraim. "Katheryn was with Flynn at the police station, but she's on her way here now."

"Katheryn? Flynn?" Rafe looked at everyone and wondered what the hell they were talking about. "Someone better tell me what the hell is going on!"

"Rafe," said Letty as she looked sadly at her, "we promised we would let Katheryn tell you, and she knows more than we do right now anyway."

"This is just too much!" growled Rafe as she signed the paperwork furiously. "No one can fucking tell me anything! This is a bunch of bullshit!" She got up and walked out of the waiting room.

"You should have told her something," said Julia shaking her head.

"We can't, we promised," said Letty sadly. She looked at Ephraim and Julia. "All hell is about to break loose."

9

TURNING IN THE paperwork at the ER desk, Rafe Salvaggio was reeling from what Letty had told her. She had a thousand questions, and no one would talk to her. She had no idea why Jake would do something like this to Eden. She knew he really didn't love her, but Eden loved him. Why would he hurt someone who was going to be with him and who loved him? Whatever the reason, it pissed her off. Eden may have chosen to leave her, but she certainly didn't deserve this. She looked up and saw Eden's doctor approaching.

"Ms. Salvaggio?" the doctor said as he approached.

"Yes," she answered and turned toward him.

"I just wanted to update you on those test results," he said reservedly. "Will you come with me?"

"Of course," said Rafe and followed the doctor to a more private space.

The doctor looked at his chart then up at Rafe. "The results show there was no evidence of penetration or semen," the doctor informed her. "There is also no evidence of contact," he explained, "skin or hair follicles."

"So, she wasn't," Rafe hesitantly.

"No," the doctor shook his head. "Her clothes were torn, and they found her attackers skin under her nails from fighting him. We aren't classifying it as rape at this time, but it could have been attempted rape. We won't know for sure until Ms. Kingsley wakes up and can tell us more."

"Oh, okay," Rafe whispered with relief still not sure why Jake would do this to her or attempt to rape her.

A police investigator turned the corner and approached the doctor. "Doctor, is Ms. Kingsley awake yet?" the investigator asked.

"No, I'm sorry, she's still sleeping," said the doctor. "If you need anything just let the nurse know," he told Rafe and left to answer a page.

"Who are you?" Rafe asked, wondering who this man was and why he was asking for Eden.

"I'm Investigator Sharp, LAPD," he said and showed his badge and ID. "You are?"

"Rafe Salvaggio." She shook his hand. "I'm here representing Ms. Kingsley as her power of attorney. What happened?"

"I can only give you the basics because we don't have all of the facts in yet," he said and took out his notepad. "According to one of the assailants, Andrew Flynn Ogden, Ms. Kingsley was being attacked by an assailant, whose name I can't release at the moment."

"I know who it was. It was Jake," Rafe said venomously, "her boyfriend. Did you catch him? Is he in jail?"

"No, ma'am," Sharp hesitated then made a note in his notebook. "So, he was her boyfriend. I actually thought this might be a domestic violence case since it happened outside family court. It looks like I was right. Anyway, this Flynn character fired two shots hitting the assailant and just barely missing Ms. Kingsley."

"Flynn shot him?" Rafe asked shocked.

"Yes," Sharp cleared his throat. "The paramedics thought Ms. Kingsley was shot at first too. Her assailant fell on her when he was shot. It turned out it was the assailant's blood on her, and she wasn't shot. We still aren't sure of the status of her assailant, but he lost a lot of blood. The crime scene people say less than an inch saved Ms. Kingsley's life."

"An inch," Rafe said softly as she put her hand to her head, unbalanced by what he had said and she began to shake. "What," she cleared her throat. "Do you know why he attacked her?"

Sharp shook his head. "No, sorry. We don't have a motive yet. But assailants are either being held or will be held and questioned. The Ogden suspect was released from the hospital after they re-set his arm and was arrested. He's at the station now." Sharp looked at Ms. Salvaggio and could clearly see she was shaken. She had stopped responding and asking questions. "Listen," he said, "why don't I help you back to the waiting room?" He took her arm and led her away gently. After delivering her to the door of the waiting area, he left to continue the investigation.

Julia watched Rafe as she made her way into the room and then just stood as she stared after the detective stunned. "What is it?"

"An inch," Rafe whispered, "the bullet," she swallowed and rubbed her temple, "the bullet missed her by less than an inch." She looked at Julia in confusion. "Flynn shot Jake," she said shakily. "He almost killed Eden." She walked over and sat down because her legs were unsteady. "Why would Jake hurt her? She was going back to him."

Letty and Ephraim looked at Rafe with worry. A marked change had come over her since she was last in the room with them. Now the dark stain around her eyes was in sharp contrast to the paleness of her face. As Rafe leaned over with her head in her hands, Letty and Ephraim fought the urge to break their promise to Katheryn.

10

INSIDE THE DIMLY lit L. A. Medical Center hospital room 231, Abby Van Falkov was watching and worrying over Eden Kingsley. The door was closed, muffling the sounds from outside the room. Abby looked at Eden's bruised and bandaged body. She did not know whether to be angry or sad. She couldn't believe Eden had been keeping such a huge and dangerous secret from everyone. She could have been killed. Abby choked back her tears for her friend. She regretted being so mean and angry with her.

Abby tried to reconcile in her mind what she thought she knew about Jake and what he had done to Eden. She never would have imagined he would be capable of hurting someone, let alone Eden. Before all this happened, Rafe thought Jake loved Eden. She thought he was a jerk sometimes, but he seemed like a decent guy and never seemed violent. Even Eden was doubtful he was violent when she mentioned he was following her after their break up.

Knowing he was part of some fanatic religious group was even more disturbing. She thought about everything Katheryn had told them and was still reeling at the news that Jake was part of the organization causing all the problems with the adoption, and it was the reason Eden ended her relationship with him. She thought Eden was lucky Flynn had been there to help her. Theories of why Jake had done this to Eden ran through her mind from love obsession to religious fervor to orders from his religious nut bosses.

As everything tumbled through her mind, the image of Rafe's haunted face pushed its way in, and Abby shook her head in misery for her friend. She was glad Rafe showed up, but Abby knew everything Katheryn had to tell her. It also seemed if Rafe was with Greer, it meant things might not go as smoothly as Eden might hope.

Eden was on the brink of waking and becoming restless with pain in her body and her dreams. She moaned in pain. "Rafe," she mumbled hoarsely in her sleep.

"Eden, wake up," said Abby softly as she held Eden's hand. "Eden, we found Rafe."

Eden's eyes fluttered open slowly, and she tried to focus. "Rafe?"

"It's Abby. Everything is okay," Abby told her as she rubbed her hand gently avoiding the I.V. needle attached.

"Abby," Eden tried to talk, and tears fell from her eyes. "I hurt everywhere," she said raspingly.

"The nurse will be here in a bit," said Abby as she pushed the nurse call button. "Everyone is here. Rafe is filling out paperwork, and Letty has Bronte."

"You found her," she said, her voice raspy. She tried to figure out what hand she could use to wipe her tears. "Does she know about everything?"

"Not yet," said Abby as she used a tissue to gently wipe the tears from Eden's face. "Letty called Katheryn."

"Hello," said Nurse Lindy as she walked in briskly. "I see you're awake," she said with a smile.

"She's in pain," Abby told her helpfully.

"Well, it looks like I can take care of her," said Nurse Lindy as she looked at the medical chart. "I'll be right back," she said and left the room.

"Flynn," said Eden softly, "what happened to Flynn?"

"He's at the police station," Abby told her. "He has a broken arm but he's going to be okay. Katheryn's going to help him."

Nurse Lindy walked in with a medical tray. "Okay, I have something for your pain," she announced. "It won't cause drowsiness. We want you to stay awake as long as you can," she said as she put the medication through the IV. "There you go.

You should start to feel the effects soon. I'll be back to check on you later."

"Eden, why did he do this to you?" asked Abby burning with curiosity after the door to the room closed. "Everyone's freaking out. We thought you were shot, but thank god, you weren't. They told Rafe he might have raped you."

Eden closed her eyes and shook her head slowly and carefully because of the pain. "He didn't," she said croakily, "he was angry," she swallowed with difficulty, "wanted to know... where I got the information... about him."

"Oh my god!" said Abby agitated. "What'd you tell him?"

"I didn't tell him anything," she whispered. "I don't know who sent it to me." She looked up at Abby in misery. "I..." she swallowed with difficulty, "I want to see... Rafe. I need to see her." She started to cry again, and Abby hugged her as best as she could through the tubes and wires. "I thought she... went to Greer."

"She's here," Abby reassured her and made the hard decision not to say anything about Greer—yet. "Don't worry."

"She told me she... still loves her," Eden said raspingly as she sobbed into Abby's shoulder.

"What? When?" said Abby in disbelief.

"When you guys got her stoned." She coughed and tried to get moisture to her throat. "She told me. Abby, after Katheryn talks to her," she started shaking, "she may go to her. I have to... talk to her," she said as more tears fell. "I don't want her to go."

"Oh, my god," Abby whispered to herself as she turned away from Eden so she couldn't hear. "Rafe, what are you doing?"

11

RAFE SALVAGGIO WAS pacing the floor angrily. She hadn't had any luck getting any information out of anyone and was working hard to control the fury building inside. The group had made it up to the second-floor waiting room where they were waiting for Katheryn. They nervously watched Rafe pace and were relieved when Katheryn and Jude walked into the waiting room.

"Rafe, I'm glad to see you," said Katheryn as she walked up to the pacing woman. She could feel the tension in the room.

Rafe stopped pacing and glared at Katheryn. "What the hell is going on, Katheryn? No one is telling me anything!" Rafe was fuming.

Katheryn looked around the room at everyone. "Would you all mind giving us some privacy?" she asked politely though they all knew it was not a request.

"We'll go see Eden and then maybe go to the cafeteria to get something for Bronte," said Letty as she took Bronte from Ephraim and everyone followed her out except Julia.

"Rafe, can I stay?" asked Julia tentatively. "I'm just as behind as you. I understand if you don't want me here."

Rafe stopped pacing and looked at Julia. "Maybe you should stay," she said looking at her suspiciously. Julia had sent her father after her, so she was helping Eden. Maybe if she let Julia stay, she would see she should help her instead and would finally have someone on her side for a change. "It seems like I'm the last to know anything as usual. It may help to have someone else here."

"I'll just sit over here out of the way," said Julia and sat in a chair at the end of the couch.

Katheryn sat down, opened her briefcase, and looked at Rafe. "Sit down, Rafe," she said firmly. "I understand Eden is going to be fine."

"Fine?" Rafe snapped furiously. "Katheryn, they told me Jake did this!" She pointed toward the hall and Eden. "He beat the shit out of her! The bullet missed her by less than a fucking inch! I don't think there's anything fine about it! What the hell is going on? Why does Flynn have a gun? Why would Jake do this? She was supposed to be going back to him!"

"Rafe," Katheryn said calmly as she shook her head, "she wasn't going back to him."

"What?" Rafe looked at her with disbelief.

"She wasn't going back to him," Katheryn said decisively. "She wasn't leaving you."

"Oh, my god." Rafe shook in misery. "Are you sure?" She watched Katheryn nod. "How do you know? What's going on?"

"Rafe, I'm going to tell you exactly what's going on," said Katheryn firmly. "Some things are going to be hard for you to hear or accept, but you have to know everything I'm telling you is the truth."

"I'm already confused, Katheryn!" Rafe threw up her hands. "You're telling me something happened in the last two days to make Jake want to do this to Eden? Was it because I left? Was it because she wouldn't go with him? She changed her mind? Is this my fault?"

"Just listen, Rafe," demanded Katheryn. "Everything I'm telling you, Eden knows. We've both known most of this information for a while. We didn't know withholding it was going to be harmful. In fact, Eden was sure, if you knew, it would hurt you and your relationship with her. It was a major factor in why she chose to withhold the information and asked for my confidentiality."

"Just tell me what the hell is going on, Katheryn!" said Rafe getting angrier at her stalling.

Katheryn laid out the contents of the envelope Rafe had given to Eden three days ago on the coffee table. "First, all of this evidence you've gathered against Eden is tainted," she explained. "Jake lied to you and turned Eden's fears and confessions to him into proof of his lies."

"Tainted? What do you mean? I don't understand," said Rafe trying to be calm.

"I know you don't understand," said Katheryn. "There has been no reason for you to know or understand anything differently than what you do, based on the information you have. I also need to tell you I believe Jake was using a listening device to eavesdrop on you. They found one in his SUV. So he might have gotten the information he used to convince you about Eden by listening to your conversations."

"What are you saying, Katheryn?" Rafe asked at a loss.

"Rafe, the reason Jake was lying to you is because he is part of the group who found Eden in the beginning and then filed the injunction against your adoption of Bronte," Katheryn explained.

"The one Eden found to file the injunction?" asked Rafe confused.

"No, they found Eden." Katheryn paused hoping Rafe understood what her words meant. "Remember the computers the FBI took?" Rafe nodded, and she continued. "We think this group found Eden in a chatroom. They gathered information on her and targeted you both."

"Chatroom?" Rafe rumbled as she shook her head and became more agitated. "I still don't understand, Katheryn. You said your source told you they might have got information on me by hacking into my computer. Now you're telling me they definitely did get information, but it was on Eden's computer? When? How? If it was Eden's computer, why did they have to take mine?"

Katheryn sighed and took a breath. "This is going to be difficult, Rafe, so just stay calm and listen. They had to take all the computers to be sure they didn't miss anything. Do you remember just before you and Eden split the first time and before your father died, she asked you to go to therapy with her?"

Rafe looked at Katheryn. She remembered everything, but she wasn't sure why they were talking about it. "Yes, Eden said she wanted to make sure we were good."

"The things she confessed to you after Bronte was born, about the feelings she was having for men actually started back even before then and before your first break up. All of this started sometime back then when she first started visiting and talking to people in chatrooms."

Rafe shook her head and looked at Julia for help in her confusion. "I don't understand. Are you telling me she..." Rafe couldn't continue the thought as a sick feeling ran through her. "What does this have to do with anything?"

"The people she talked to in those chatrooms may be part of the group who filed the injunction," Katheryn revealed.

Katheryn let her words sink in and took a breath to prepare for what she had to say next. "Apparently, at least one of the exchanges was sexual," she explained cautiously, "and it's one of the ways they find what they call 'Charges' or people they watch and monitor with the intent of 'rescuing' any innocent children born into immoral lifestyles, according to their doctrine. "

"Doctrine," Rafe echoed still trying to understand.

"Yes," confirmed Katheryn. "Once they gained her trust, they were able to obtain remote access to her computer and were listening and watching her, both of you, at times."

Katheryn could see the shock and building anger in both Julia and Rafe at the information, but she pressed on before Rafe could interrupt. "It wasn't long before the group found out

Eden was pregnant, and later, she had Bronte. They confirmed everything by watching her via her computer. They saw she was still dealing with the feelings she should be with a man while she was living with you. They sent Jake to be a convenient outlet for her feelings, to get her away from you and the life they disagreed with. Shortly afterward, Eden moved out again." Katheryn reached into her briefcase again and laid out the information Eden received on Jake. "Eden received this information anonymously and immediately broke it off with Jake. She has not been in any type of relationship with him since then."

"Why," started Rafe as she looked over the information, "why didn't Eden tell me about this? Could we have used this information and stopped the injunction sooner?"

"This information proves Jake is scum, but it wouldn't have helped with the injunction at the time she gave it to me," Katheryn told her. "I've worked very hard researching other cases they've been involved with just so I could get the attention of the FBI. It's been difficult because the group uses litigation only as a last resort. The FBI has just recently gotten testimony from Eden, and they're analyzing her computer. They're pulling a case together against them. We knew Jake was part of the organization, but we had no proof we could show linking him to your case," she paused, "except he dated Eden. Eden chose not to tell you at the time because you two were barely getting along, and she didn't want things to deteriorate."

"She didn't want things to deteriorate!" Rafe boomed heatedly. "I think she would be better off if she had told me. At least I wouldn't have beaten the shit out of her!" she fumed as she pointed at herself and shook her fist in anger and frustration. "What was she thinking?"

"She was thinking she wanted you to be Bronte's other parent," said Katheryn sharply. "She felt you had enough doubt in her, and she didn't want to add to it. There was no reason to think we needed to tell you about Jake until she found out he had been talking to you, and he was the reason you stopped wanting to be around her."

"So why didn't she tell me he was part of this group when she found out he talked to me?" she asked crossly.

"She thought it was a one-time thing. It seemed to be the pattern for all the things happening," Katheryn said calmly. "Eden was going through a lot of personal issues herself, as you may recall." She met Rafe's angry stare with her own unflinching glare. When Rafe looked away, Katheryn knew she understood they were talking about Eden's anxiety problems. Even so, it didn't look like Rafe was allowing the excuse to temper her anger. "When you agreed to spend time with her, she didn't want to give you a reason to change your mind about it, and the very mention of Jake set you off."

"Is this part of what she was hiding from me?" asked Rafe trying to process everything. It all seemed to be never-ending. "The thing she always needed more time and patience for before she could tell me?"

Katheryn nodded. "I believe it was."

"This is fucking unbelievable!" Rafe fumed as she stood up in a rage.

Julia and Katheryn could feel the heat of Rafe's anger as it radiated from her. Julia shifted uncomfortably in her chair but remained silent.

"So, let me get this straight!" Rafe seethed as she paced the room and emphasized her words with her flailing hands. "She has feelings for men. She gets a cyber fuck leading Jake to her, for a real fuck, in my bed by the way!" she growled and pointed to herself. "Her digital fuck leads to her moving out—again! She finds out Jake is part of this fucked up group and breaks up with him. Then an injunction is filed, but she decides not to tell me about Jake because she doesn't want things to deteriorate." She looked menacingly at Katheryn. "Then she begs me to spend time with her and almost convinces me she loves me! Did I leave anything out?"

"She does love you," said Katheryn trying to maintain calm for Rafe's sake. "Sit down."

"It doesn't look like it from where I'm standing!" Rafe scoffed. "Do you realize what I was going through every day with this shit?" She picked up the picture of Eden kissing Jake with the children in the park. "So you're telling me this is a lie? Katheryn, this looks real to me! What the hell does this picture have to do with the injunction?"

Katheryn remained calm under Rafe's blistering rage. "I'm trying to tell you, Rafe," she said calmly. "Jake was doing anything he could to make your situation unstable and to tear down your relationship with Eden so it could be a tool to use for the injunction and stop the adoption. We believe it was his job for the group. He followed her to the park and used his son to get close to Eden. She didn't kiss him willingly. She was tricked. She didn't know someone was taking pictures, and she certainly didn't know he was still talking to you."

Rafe stood up and paced the floor again, extremely agitated. "I don't understand how she could keep this from me!" She looked at Katheryn distrustfully. "You knew about Jake, and you didn't tell me? I thought you were my fucking lawyer!"

Katheryn held back her own temper at Rafe's attack. "I did warn you about the group. You were very well aware of them," she said calmly. "Eden was my source and, to the best of my knowledge, I used the information in the best way I could to help you and protect Eden. She didn't have proof Jake was still talking to you, and it was Eden's decision not to tell you about Jake. I had no idea it was happening, and I know if either of us had been made aware of what was going on with you, we would have given you this information about Jake."

"He was talking to me, Katheryn!" Rafe barked as she stood over her. "We had nice little chats once or twice a month! If I would have known he was part of all of this—" She threw up her hands. "This is just too much!"

"Sit down, Rafe," said Katheryn as she looked at Rafe sternly. "There's more."

"There's more?" Rafe laughed despairingly then sat down and crossed her arms. She looked over at Julia. "I just can't wait for this," she said with blistering sarcasm.

Katheryn pulled out a piece of paper. "Eden has been dealing with Jake herself. This is a short list of things she's reported to me that she knows Jake was part of, or she suspects he was part of. But again, she has no proof to take to the authorities except her word against his." She looked at Rafe and began to read the list. "Jake vandalized Eden's car slashing the tires and spray painting it with graffiti, he followed her around and harassed her at a distance."

"Stop!" Rafe snapped, and then she leaned forward and snatched the paper from her to look at it. "He did all this, and she kept it a secret?" She threw the paper back at Katheryn. "Did she have a fucking death wish? She told me her car was getting a paint job! It seems to me she got off lucky today. He could have killed her! She was a fucking inch from dying!" she reminded them and couldn't get the thought of it out of her mind.

"Again, Rafe, she couldn't prove Jake was doing it—"

"Fuck proof!" Rafe screamed cutting her off. "She didn't have to bring me proof if she was afraid! Even if it were just in her imagination, I would have made sure Jake never bothered her again! I would have shot him myself!" she roared in anger.

"This kind of reaction would have been more for them to use against you and hurt your chances with the injunction," said Katheryn calmly, "which is another thing Eden wanted to avoid." She looked at the list again. "He also wrote the letters in the package begging her to come back to him. She suspected he filed the abuse charges, took photographs of you on the beach they used for one of the amendments, and reworked the uploaded lecture so it could be used on another amendment. And he gave the information to the reporter who wrote the article, and then took the picture given to you."

"She fucking told me she didn't remember who she told those things to!" Rafe said incredulously. "Now you're telling me Jake is responsible for the article too?"

"I am," said Katheryn and took a deep breath knowing the next part was going to be explosive. "Also," she paused and looked up at Rafe, "he attempted to take Bronte twice," she said, "once from you and once from Eden at the park."

Rafe leaped from the couch shaking with rage, her fists clenched. "He was trying to kidnap her!" she exploded. "I... I..." she started, but her anger stole her voice. "I'm so furious!" she blazed when she got her voice back. "Why the fuck didn't she— you— or anyone tell me about this? Bronte's life was in danger!"

"She didn't tell me until recently," said Katheryn holding her hands up in surrender. "I only learned about it after you left."

Rafe looked at Julia in disbelief. "Julia, she told us Jake just wanted an excuse to talk to her!" she fumed.

"I remember," said Julia in shock.

"What if I had given Bronte to him?" Rafe shouted as her anger still burned. She ran her hands through her hair trying to cool herself as she was sweating from anger. "I had the police at my house when she came to me from the park telling me some man tried to take Bronte! She could have told the police right then and had him arrested!" She looked at Katheryn in agony. "My god, Katheryn, I'm beginning to question her fucking sanity!"

"Frankly, at the time, I don't think she was very stable," Katheryn admitted. "She was scared, and she was on her own. Then after your crisis at the school, she started taking Xanax. I think she only had Flynn to confide in, and she convinced him to keep silent. I believe it was then when Flynn purchased his gun."

"Confide in?" roared Rafe livid. "Katheryn, these things aren't something you keep secret from people, especially if you have to go out and buy a fucking gun! It's kidnapping, its Bronte's life," Rafe screamed, "her daughter's life!"

"Precisely," said Katheryn calmly. "Her daughter's life," she paused deliberately. "She thought she had it under control, and it didn't happen again."

"Is that supposed to be a slap in the face?" Rafe seethed and gave Katheryn a menacing look. "The fact Bronte isn't my daughter? You do realize I'm very aware of the fact Bronte is *her* daughter!"

"Rafe, don't go on the defensive with me," Katheryn commanded. "It wasn't a slap in the face. But it may very well have been what she was thinking."

"But Katheryn, she didn't tell the police she knew who the men were in the park!" Rafe fumed. "She was the one guilty of bad thinking!"

"I agree with you," Katheryn nodded, "but there's nothing we can do about it now. Let's just be thankful Bronte is okay."

"What if Eden had Bronte with her today?" Rafe said hotly as she shook her head in disbelief and sweat ran down her back from the heat of her anger. "Eden would be beaten up, Bronte would be missing, and who knows what else because Eden couldn't tell me one little fucking thing!"

"Again, I agree with you, but it's not what happened," said Katheryn flatly and put the papers back on the table.

"I'm beginning to think maybe they do belong together," Rafe said scathingly. "They were both lying to me."

"Rafe, she put herself at risk by allowing me to expose the fact she had damning information on Jake," Katheryn revealed. "Her risk, combined with my research, and the threat of an FBI investigation, helped stop the injunction. Eden wanted to fix the problem she believed she was responsible for, and she did. The injunction has been dismissed, and the adoption is on the docket. Those are some facts you should remember."

"She shouldn't have kept it a secret from me," Rafe insisted scornfully. "I could have been there," she reasoned. "This may have never happened!"

"Why did you keep the fact you were talking to Jake a secret?" asked Katheryn accusingly.

"Because I thought he was just a rival for Eden's affection, and I didn't want her to go back to him," she said contemptuously. "He told me she was still punishing me. I thought I could make her love me again! I fucking challenged him for her! I was in a fight to keep her with me! I was doing everything I could to convince her to stay with me and not go back to him and take herself and Bronte away!" she seethed. "I had no fucking idea he was anything more!"

"So you love her," said Katheryn solemnly.

"I've never denied it, and I've never doubted it until this very moment!" Rafe fumed. "Believe me, I tried to stop, but I couldn't do it!" She ran her hands over her face wiping away the sweat from her brow. "After this," she stared at Katheryn ominously, "I just may be able to stop."

"I suggest you think about everything and don't make any knee-jerk decisions," Katheryn advised. "I'll leave this information for you to look over." She stacked the paperwork on the table then closed her briefcase. "You may want to talk to Eden, when she's able, to see if she can shed any light on why she made the choices she made." Katheryn stood up. "The adoption court date is in two weeks. I still have your letter to withdraw the petition. Let me know if you still want me to file it with the court. I need to get back to help Flynn. They're trying to charge him with murder or attempted murder depending on whether Jake lives or dies."

Rafe looked up at her in shock as Katheryn left the room.

12

MASON ESSEX MADE his way cautiously through the halls of the hospital. He knew there were cameras everywhere, so he kept the hood on his hoodie up. He had already passed by the waiting room where he saw Rafe and her lawyer inside along with another woman with long silver hair who he recognized from his surveillance. He turned and went down a little hallway he found would circle around so he could get to the nurse's station without being seen by them. Once there, he listened to the nurses and overheard them talking about the gunshot victim and his room number. Mason knew it had to be Jake and headed toward the room.

He was happily surprised there was no one loitering outside the room, not even a police guard. Slipping into the dark room, Mason gave himself a small smile of congratulations. Now, since he found Jake, all he had to do was carry out the last part of his plan then head for the airport. Mason reached into his messenger bag and pulled out a white beret adorned with a gold cross. Pushing his hood back he quickly put on the beret then stepped further into the room.

Jake was lying quietly in the hospital bed while machines hummed around him and medication dripped into the I.V. then slid down into his veins. Mason went to his bedside and looked down at him. He was pale, and his eyes were closed. Bandages covered his arm and torso.

He knew from what he overheard the bullet Jake took played pinball inside him. It went through the fleshy part of the back of his arm and then went into his torso hitting a rib, breaking it, then redirected downward where it nicked his kidney before exiting. He must have had a great team of doctors because he was out of surgery in just a few hours.

Mason opened his messenger bag again and took out a protective case and a couple of latex fingertip covers. He put the fingertip covers on then opened the case and carefully picked up the USB drive stored inside. He put the case away and put the drive in Jake's hand. He pressed Jake's thumb against the drive on one side and then the edge of his finger on the other side. This way it would look like Jake had held it and opened or closed it. Mason then got the pre-printed 8x10 envelope from his bag, already containing reports and documents, and slid the USB drive inside. He pulled the waxed tab off the adhesive and sealed the envelope. He then pressed Jakes hands and fingers on it before putting it back in his messenger bag.

He knew Jake had been awake earlier. He had overheard the nurses talking. He cleared his throat loudly making his presence known if it wasn't already.

"Jake," said Mason in a normal volume. "Wake up, Soldier."

Slowly, Jake opened his eyes and looked at Mason with hatred. "What..." he started, but the dryness of his throat prevented more.

"The reverend sent me," said Mason in an official sounding voice. "He wanted me to give you some good news." He watched as Jake just looked at him with little expression other than hatred. "We're working on a way to make the best of this situation. He was impressed you took a bullet for the cause. I think he's reassessing his plans for you." Mason smiled with just the corner of his mouth. "Actually, he's already made plans but isn't ready to reveal them to everyone yet. I was there when the plans were made. He asked me to deliver the plans to you. Do you want to know what they are?"

Jake tried to speak, but his throat was too dry. Mason saw his problem, so he got some water in a straw and gave him water a few times. When Jake's throat was moistened, he looked up at Mason. "Fuck you."

Mason chortled. "I said it was good news," he said with a smile. "I'll just tell you so you can get some rest and relax. He's giving you a promotion." He watched Jake's eyes widen. "Congratulations. He now believes your talents are wasted on small Missions. He's giving you a much bigger one. You're going to be a Commander." He nodded his head at Jake's disbelieving expression and gave a small laugh. "He's going to put you in charge of recruiting and training. He said something about you giving the ultimate sacrifice and his vision for you had changed. He sees you as the man who will find the next Great Leader on Earth. You'll work with him directly, and I think you may even become a favorite."

Jake looked up at Mason, unsure what to think. Just hours ago, he had lost everything, and now he was getting everything back plus a prestigious position in the Stewards. "Why?"

"He had another vision," Mason said with only a slight twitch of his lips betraying his lie, but it was dark in the room, so it was easily missed. "He had a vision about you. He wasn't sure what it meant until today's events." He watched as Jake's eyes shifted from side to side probably wondering about the vision.

There was no vision.

Mason was making it all up as part of his plan. This was a quick fix because what he originally planned wouldn't work now. "In the vision, you were surrounded by dark forms, and it seemed like you were betraying the Great Leader on Earth. But really, you were recruiting. The reverend is convinced the dark forms were the FBI suits. He wants you to recruit them. He thinks having someone in the FBI will be crucial to the Stewards and you're in the perfect position to achieve this goal."

"How," said Jake overwhelmed.

"Well, you don't really know very much about what's going on higher up in the Stewards, but the FBI isn't aware of your limited knowledge. When they question you, just cooperate and make friends. This way you'll have the opportunity to see who might be open to recruitment. He has faith in you. We're going to plant some evidence. Some will be true, some false. But it'll be what you can offer them to make them think you're cooperating. Don't volunteer information, just assure them all the evidence they put in front of you is true. We'll do the rest on our end. There's only one catch."

Jake looked up at him hard not liking there was a catch.

"You can't talk to anyone in the Stewards again until you're contacted by us," Mason continued. "Not Daniel, me, the reverend, or anyone else involved with the Stewards or with your failed Mission or this assignment. If you see them, try not to even look at them. You will be a false Judas for the Stewards. You need to convince the FBI you want out of the Stewards and want to help them. You also have to ask for FBI protection."

Mason could tell Jake didn't like the last condition, so he wanted to end the conversation quickly before he started asking questions. He pulled off his beret and unpinned the gold cross then held it out so Jake could see it. "I'm not supposed to do this, but I think this may be the only way you'll get the insignia of your new rank right now." He put the pin close to the gown Jake was wearing so he could pin it on him. "Do you accept the Mission and your new position as Commander?"

Jake looked at the gold cross then at Mason, stunned. He was actually being promoted at this moment, and his head was spinning from everything Mason had said. He hated Mason, but he was carrying out the reverend's orders. This could be his chance to really be someone in the Stewards.

"Yes," said Jake shakily.

"Good," said Mason and pinned the cross to the gown. "I'm putting it on the inside for now," he said as he flipped the edge of Jake's gown over. "This way you can wear it for a while. Later, have the nurse put it with your things. I don't think anyone will know the significance, but just in case, don't let the FBI know anything except it's just a cross showing you're a good Christian." Jake reached up tentatively with his good arm and felt the cross. "Good luck," said Mason and gave him a salute. He put his beret in his pocket then pulled his hood back over his head and made his way out the door.

Jake held onto the gold cross and smiled. He was a Commander.

Mason practically skipped down the hallway to the elevators. He made it to the exit without any problems. He thought he would have to make a trip to the police station, but a detective was standing outside talking on his phone. Mason walked to the bench by the door and sat down to wait for the detective to get off the phone. When he did, Mason approached him.

"Excuse me," said Mason to get his attention.

"Can I help you?" asked the detective.

"Not me," said Mason. "I work for a delivery service and a guy inside asked me to deliver something to the FBI. Are you the FBI?"

"No, I'm a police detective."

"Oh, well," Mason hesitated, "the guy didn't give me an address. Do you know where I can find someone with the FBI?"

"Who asked you to deliver something?"

Mason opened his messenger bag and took out a small clipboard. "The guy's name is Jake Thompson. I was supposed to give it to someone at the courthouse, but I couldn't find an FBI person there. I found out he was one of the people shot today, so I tried to get the package back to him, but they won't let me in his room." He sighed heavily. "I'm not sure what to do now without an address."

"You may have to go to FBI headquarters. I can get you the address."

"How far do you think it is?" asked Mason. "I'm on a bike, so I usually don't go too far from my pickup point. Plus I have a lot of other deliveries I need to do."

"I'm not sure how far it is," said the detective as he looked up the address.

"Aw, man," groaned Mason. "Hey, could I just give it to you? You could probably get it to them faster than I could."

The detective looked up and saw Katheryn Hardam walking out of the building. "There's who you want. She's probably got an agent on speed dial." He motioned to Katheryn. "Ms. Hardam maybe you can help us out. This delivery boy has a package Jake Thompson wants to have delivered to the FBI."

Katheryn looked at the sheepish delivery boy with suspicion. "Really," she said smoothly.

"Yeah, he told me to deliver it to them at the courthouse, but I didn't see anyone who looked like they were FBI. I'm not even sure what they'd look like," said Mason acting frustrated. "I can't give the package back to him because they won't let me in his room."

"Let me make a call," said Katheryn and took out her phone.

"What'd I tell ya?" asked the detective with a smile.

13

RAFE SALVAGGIO WAS pacing in the hospital waiting room processing all of the information given to her by Katheryn, stopping at times to look at the papers she had left behind. Rafe had so many questions that she forgot them as fast as she was coming up with them.

"Julia, I just don't know what I'm supposed to do now," said Rafe agitated. "Why wouldn't she tell me this stuff? Am I so unreachable, even in a crisis, she feels she can't come to me?"

"Katheryn said she didn't want to give you more reasons to doubt her," offered Julia. "What would you have done if she had told you?"

"I don't know," she admitted. "I don't know if it even matters." She looked at her in despair. "Right now, not only am I doubting her, I doubt myself."

"Why do you doubt yourself?" Julia asked with concern.

"Look at me, Julia!" Rafe insisted furiously. "Look at what I've been doing! Even Greer asked me who I believed, Jake or Eden." She sank into a chair. "And I believed Jake."

"But he had a lot of evidence, and most of it was true and confirmed by Eden," Julia pointed out. "It was overwhelming. You challenged him, so you had to have thought maybe," she paused, "just maybe he was lying about her."

Rafe scoffed at her reasoning. "The only thing I thought he was lying about was he kept telling me he loved her," she said sadly. "I definitely knew he didn't." She leaned over and put her head in her hands trying to press out the pain. "I thought maybe he had her fooled, and I could make her see I was the one who really loved her."

"So," said Julia cautiously, "do you still love her?" She knew it was a selfish question but could not help herself.

"Does it matter?" Rafe laughed bitterly. "How can this work?" Rafe stood up and began to pace the floor again. "I don't know," she said and rubbed her neck and temples as her head seared with pain, "I just don't know. I think..." she shook her head slowly, "I think maybe I should just go now."

As Rafe paced, Jude and Letty walked into the room and took in her wild and angry appearance. Rafe's clothes were stained with sweat, her hair forming ringlets of curls where it was damp, her face drawn with anger and pain, and the darkness around her eyes threatened to spill over her cheekbones. She would stop, put her hand on her head or chest, and take deep breaths to try to calm down, and then pace the room shaking with anger as she mumbled to herself.

"Rafe, what are you doing?" Jude asked because she was still in the waiting room pacing. "Don't you want to be with Eden now?"

Rafe ignored her and kept pacing and mumbling to herself.

Jude heard her threaten to leave again. "Don't leave, Rafe," Jude pleaded.

"Why not?" Rafe asked as she looked at the door.

"Because, you love Eden and she loves you," Letty offered. "Why do you want to leave?"

"I do love her, but what kind of love is it?" Rafe asked scathingly. "She can't talk to me, she's afraid to tell me things, she doesn't trust me." She took a breath to calm herself. "How can we have a healthy relationship with all this between us? I'll stay to make sure she and Bronte are okay, and then I'm leaving."

"Rafe, she said she was trying to protect you," said Letty wanting to help.

"Protect me," roared Rafe incensed. "How was putting herself and Bronte in danger protecting me?"

"She didn't know this would happen," Letty insisted.

"It may be better for her if I weren't around," said Rafe heatedly as she shook her head. "I'm so unreachable to her and such a bully, she's afraid to tell me anything."

"She says she loves you," Jude said relaying Eden's words.

"But she doesn't trust me and can't talk to me," Rafe poured out angrily.

"Rafe, you have to start somewhere." Letty braced herself to try to reason with her. "This whole thing is a mess, but you've made it through it. You didn't do it totally together, but you each made it through because each of you has so much love for the other."

Rafe sat down next to Letty. "Right now, those words make absolutely no sense to me," she said trying to be calm. "I'm so tired, Letty." She ran her hands through her damp hair again. "I've been fighting a lie and not even the lie I thought I was fighting. It wasn't Jake lying, but Eden. If she would have trusted me," she said sadly, "she wouldn't be in there now." She leaned back and sighed. "I did this to her. It's my fault. I caused all the fears she has. I really was her monster," she declared as she leaned forward and cringed at the pain shooting through her chest. She put her hand on her heart trying not to cry out in agony.

"Rafe, it's not your fault, it's not true," said Jude distressed at Rafe's emotional state. "You didn't cause this to happen. It was Jake, the group he is part of and their lies, not you."

"But if it weren't for me," Rafe insisted, and put her hand back down shakily, "my actions, Jude," she took a deep breath and looked up at her, "Eden wouldn't have been vulnerable. She wouldn't have needed to make changes or leave me. I think," she breathed shakily, "she'd be better off without me."

"Rafe, don't belittle her and her feelings, and don't be so sanctimonious," Letty chastised her. "She didn't necessarily have her feelings because of your actions."

"As she keeps bringing to my attention and as if I don't know, I cheated on her and hurt her, Letty!" Rafe said hotly. "Because of my actions, she didn't feel safe in our relationship anymore. The reason she left me was to get into a safe relationship, and for her, she thought it was a relationship with a man."

"But she came back to you," said Letty trying to show her there was hope. "She came back because she loves you. So there had to be more to it than just your actions."

"Letty, you don't know what you're talking about," Rafe said scathingly to her.

"Oh, and you do?" scoffed Letty. "You know everything Eden has been going through and how she's feeling about it? You asked her?"

"Of course, I don't know everything, Letty! My failure is part of the point!" Rafe said furiously. "She doesn't trust me enough to tell me anything anymore!"

"Cugina, you two started out with so much love for each other, and it's still there," said Letty as she shook her head in disappointment. "I know I've not been very supportive of her,

Rafe, because I thought she was hurting you, but I know now she really does love you. Don't throw this away. You can trust each other again. You can start working on it now by being there for her and letting her know you'll always be there for her."

"Letty, I've never left! I've never closed my door to her! I've never, never," she choked out, "until Saturday, and I only left because I thought it was what she really wanted!" Rafe informed her as her temper blazed. "I fucked up and I'm sure I'm everything in the article she accused me of being, but I never left! She left!" She raged then stopped and tried to control her temper. "She left, and I really do think she's still gone. I don't think she really has come back to me."

"You kept saying there was always something between you and now the something is gone," Jude interjected hoping to help. "No lies, no Jake, no injunction, nothing. Don't walk away from her now, Rafe. You can fix this. All of us are envious of what we see when we look at you two together. What we see is true love. You can't give up when you have something true."

"She's right. You have to try, or you may end up regretting it," Letty said sadly.

"She's been calling for you," Jude said encouragingly. "We told her you were here and she wants to see you."

"I can't see her right now," said Rafe shortly.

"Why not?" asked Letty upset at Rafe's stubbornness.

"I already said goodbye to her," said Rafe softly. "I don't think I can do it again." She walked out of the waiting room wanting to get away from them and think.

"Rafe, you should go see her," Jude insisted as she followed her.

Rafe ignored her and walked up to nurse's station. "Excuse me," Rafe said to the nurse. "Can you tell me when Eden Kingsley is scheduled to be released?"

"Just a moment, and I'll check," said Nurse Joan with a concerned smile at Rafe's appearance and went to check her computer. She made a mental note to ask her if she was feeling well. It wasn't uncommon for visitors to experience trauma during times of emergency.

Nurse Lindy walked behind the reception counter. "Joan, they're sending an officer up for the gunshot in two twenty-four. They're saying he's the assailant now, and they have to put a guard on him," she informed her.

"I don't know why they think they have to be here," said Nurse Joan annoyed. "It's not like he's going anywhere for a while."

"Yeah, I heard the victim is in two thirty-one. We'll probably have to move one of them," she sighed at the thought.

"Shh, Lindy!" she hissed quietly and rolled her eyes toward Rafe and Jude then walked over to them. "It looks like Ms. Kingsley should be cleared for release by ten in the morning if the doctor signs off."

"Thank you," Rafe said and looked at both nurses. "Thank you very much," she said and walked away before the nurse could say more.

"Where are you going?" asked Jude as she followed. "Eden's room is the other way."

"I'm looking for the restroom," said Rafe as she walked.

"I think it's by the waiting room," said Jude pointing to the waiting room.

Rafe stopped in front of room 224. "Wait here," said Rafe and looked hard at Jude.

"Rafe, you can't go in there," said Jude. She watched anxiously as Rafe disappeared into the room and the door closed. "Oh, Rafe," she groaned, "don't do anything stupid." She paced outside the room and watched for nurses.

Abby was walking toward Eden's room with some snacks and saw Jude. "What are you doing?" she asked inquisitively.

Jude pulled Abby close. "Shhh, Rafe is in there," she said pointing to the room.

"Why's she in there?" asked Abby confused.

"I don't know." Jude swallowed hard. "It's Jake's room."

"Jake? Shit!" said Abby shocked.

They waited for what seemed like ages. Suddenly, Rafe stormed angrily out of the room, moving past them, and headed back toward the waiting room without a word.

"Fuck-a-nurse!" squealed Abby. "Should we check to see if he's still alive?"

"I'm afraid to look," said Jude fearfully.

"Hold this," said Abby and handed Jude her snacks. "Keep a lookout, and I'll check."

"Oh, shit! Shit, shit, shit!" said Jude, worried as she watched Abby walk into Jake's room. She held the snacks close and nervously waited for her.

Finally, Abby slipped out of the room and went up to Jude. "It's okay. He's still alive," she whispered in relief. "What the hell was she doing in there?"

"I don't know," said Jude relieved. "Let's get out of here." They walked away quickly.

"You know we can't tell anyone about this ever," Abby said as she took her snacks from Jude.

"Shit, Abby, you cannot keep a secret!" said Jude panicky.

"Well, I have to keep this one, especially if he croaks or something," Abby said grimly.

"She... she wouldn't," stammered Jude, "would she?"

"It's Rafe," said Abby ominously. "Who knows what she would do. I keep telling you she's a wildling!" She looked at Jude's face affixed with an expression of horror upon it. "I'm kidding, Jude." She forced a laugh. "She wouldn't. I'm pretty sure she wouldn't."

14

RAFE SALVAGGIO WALKED directly back to the nurses' station where she found the two gossiping nurses who were there before. Her visit with Jake only made her angrier. If what she overheard about having to move Eden or Jake were true, she wanted it done now.

"Excuse me," she said sharply.

"Can I help you?" asked Nurse Lindy as she recognized Rafe. "Oh, did you forget something?"

"No," she said flatly. "I heard you talking about moving someone. I think you may have been talking about Eden Kingsley. I just talked to someone and confirmed her assailant is a few doors down."

Nurse Lindy tried to hide her guilty look. They weren't supposed to be talking about patients where people could hear them. "Uhm, yes," she said hesitantly. "Joan, do we know which patient is moving?" she asked the other nurse who was standing behind her.

"It hasn't been decided yet," answered Nurse Joan.

"Well, let me decide for you," said Rafe crossly. "I want you to move Eden Kingsley right now. Move her to a private room very far away from him. If anyone from his hate group comes in and even looks at her, I will have all your asses in court."

Abby and Jude were walking past and saw Rafe. Curiosity led them straight to her. "What's going on, Rafe?" asked Abby.

Rafe ignored them both and looked steadily at Nurse Lindy.

"Well," she said typing on her computer, "I don't know if her insurance will cover a private room."

"I don't give a fuck what her insurance covers. I've signed your form saying I'm responsible for the bill, so give her the fucking room," Rafe demanded.

"Hey, Rafe," said Abby, "calm down." She looked at the nurses. "It's been a day," she said with a grimace.

"I'll calm down when they do what I'm fucking telling them to do," she said hotly.

"We have a private room on the fifth floor available," said Nurse Lindy. "We can have her moved there right away."

"Good," said Rafe tersely. "Do it. Abby, stay with Eden until they move her."

"Sure, Rafe," said Abby she said cringing at Rafe's wrath and just wanting her to take a breath. "Why are you moving her?"

"It's for her safety, right?" Rafe looked hard at the nurses who nodded. "Give me something to make a list of authorized visitors. I don't want you giving out her room number to anyone except the police unless my lawyer or I say that it's okay." The nurse gave her a form, and Rafe began writing names down.

Nurse Joan decided to attempt to help the woman because it looked like her appearance had become worse in the short time she had been away. "Excuse me, ma'am," she said politely. "Are you feeling okay? You look like you may be having a problem. Can we get a doctor to check you?"

Rafe looked at her with a scowl. "Of course, I have a fucking problem," she said harshly. "My friend is in the hospital, and the man who put her here is practically across the hall. I don't need a doctor to fix anything. I just need you two to do your fucking jobs." When she finished, she gave the form she had been filling out back to the nurse then looked at Abby. "Make sure someone is with her as much as possible."

"I will," Abby assured her looking from the nurse to Rafe not sure what to do. "I'll go right now and let her know she's moving. She wants to see you so maybe you could go too," she said trying to be helpful. Rafe gave her a hard look then turned without a word and walked away. Abby looked at Jude and rolled her eyes. "Stubborn." She looked back at the nurse. "Sorry about her. She's just upset," she explained Rafe's behavior. "The woman she loves has been hurt, and she just wants to take care of her."

15

THE EXPRESS SHUTTLE to the airport pulled up to the curb, and Mason Essex was already waiting outside his furnished apartment. It wasn't really his apartment because the Stewards rented it, but he had lived there for the past two years. It was empty now of all his personal belongings. Mason had sold everything he couldn't pack in the maximum amount of luggage his new employer allowed and would pay to have shipped. Mostly, he was taking his sound equipment and computer gear. It was all packed in the metal shipping cases lined up on the curb. Next to them were his suitcases full of clothes and personal items.

The driver climbed out of the van, and Mason helped get everything loaded. "Looks like you're going on a long trip," the driver commented.

"No," said Mason, "I'm heading back home for a while but have to take my work with me," he lied. He didn't want to share anything about what he was doing with anyone. He had gone home before and took his work so the story could be true. Plus it was what he told Daniel he was doing. He couldn't be too careful when it came to the Stewards and who was watching or listening.

"It sucks to have to work on a vacation," the driver commented as they loaded the last of the luggage.

"I'm used to it." Mason shrugged and got into the van with the driver.

The driver pulled away from the curb, and Mason thought about his exit strategy. He wondered if Trouble was going to choose to follow the instructions to his plan. Mason had set Jake up pretty good, so he knew the FBI would have a lot of fun with Jake. Mason would know when he was truly safe from the Stewards when arrests were made, or an article about the Stewards was published. If either of those things happened, then everyone in the Stewards would be on the run, and it would just look to them like he was lucky and got out fast. Even if someone gave his name to the FBI, he had scrubbed all records naming or mentioning him from the Stewards database.

The database was full of all kinds of helpful information. Because of it, Mason now had plenty of money if he ever needed it. Someone, over fifteen years ago, opened a bank account for the Stewards. They put money in it, and then never did anything with it, including sending in updated signature cards. There was a note in the file indicating the account had been closed, but the paperwork had never been submitted to the bank.

The fact no one missed the money was insane, but who knows what was happening fifteen years ago, or even who was supposed to be doing the accounting. The bank was glad to have an updated mailing address and a contact. They had been trying to contact someone about the account for a long time, but it got to a point where they would just try once a year. It was lucky they kept the account open and didn't turn the money over as unclaimed.

It was easy to call the bank and work with them like he was in the accounting department. They were kind enough to let him email a signature page and then send a wire transfer to another account so they could officially close the old one. It was even easier to delete all records of the account from the Stewards database. Now, because of compounding interest over fifteen years on the old account, he had a nest egg of just over two hundred thousand dollars in the Caymans. It didn't seem like a lot, but he was frugal and didn't need a lot to live on. It was just enough to make him feel like if the new job didn't work out, he was secure in whatever he wanted to do in the future.

The shuttle pulled up to the airport's departure entrance and found a place to park. "Well, we made it," said the driver. He got out and opened the back of the van to unload the luggage.

Mason stretched then went back to help unload. They managed to get everything out and locked together for easy transport through the airport. "Thanks a lot," said Mason and gave the driver a big tip.

The driver looked at his tip and smiled. "Anytime," he said and watched the kid maneuver his boxes and luggage inside. "Nice kid," he said to himself and got back into his van.

Inside, Mason checked in his luggage and made his way to his gate to catch his flight to Amsterdam, all with a smile. He had a new outlook on life because of a woman he was supposed to help destroy. He was going to follow her advice and ignore the limits placed on him. He was going out into the world to look at things from another point of view. What he saw so far was amazing. Now he had a new life, a new job, and fresh eyes with which to see the world. He would never forget Rafe Salvaggio.

16

KATHERYN HARDAM WAS at her client Flynn Ogden's side at the L. A. Police Station. They were sitting in interrogation room number three across from police Investigator Kirkland. Katheryn had asked Flynn to let her do all the talking, and she had both guns out, to turn a phrase, to defend her client.

"My client has told you everything he knows and has been more than compliant," Katheryn informed the investigator tersely.

"I agree he's been compliant, but the fact remains a man has been shot, and we have certain procedures we have to follow," Kirkland said unsympathetically.

She looked directly at the investigator. "The charges you're suggesting are ridiculous. My client was quite obviously defending the life of another, and his actions were not only justifiable but excusable."

"Your client has admitted to carrying a gun in anticipation of seeing the victim again and used excessive force in defending his friend," said Kirkland reading from his notes.

"Oh, come on," shot Katheryn with a cynical laugh. "My client's arm was broken. Your so-called victim is two times the size of my client. It would have only been excessive force if he had used a bazooka. My client has a permit to carry the gun and carries it for protection he felt he needed, and it looks like he was right." They looked up at a knock on the door as another investigator walked into the room.

"Sorry to interrupt," said Investigator Sharp and handed Investigator Kirkland a file. "We just got the report from the hospital. He's going to live. We also have the statement from Ms. Kingsley, and it's consistent with the story of self-defense."

"Hmm," Kirkland sighed as he read the reports. "It looks like I need to go talk to the Prosecutor. The crime lab has analyzed the video surveillance tapes, and it does look like your client did everything in his power to stop the assault before using his weapon."

"Well, in light of this, I'll expect you to submit this as self-defense, and therefore, excusable." Katheryn smiled cockily.

"We'll talk to the Prosecutor," said Kirkland stiffly and closed the file.

17

EDEN KINGSLEY HAD been moved to her new private room, and the bed was positioned so she could sit up. She was awake, coherent, and medicated, though still in some pain. The police had finally gone, and she hoped Katheryn was going to be able to help Flynn. Bronte was sitting next to Eden in the bed, and Abby was sitting in the chair next to the bed sharing her snacks with the baby and keeping her from crawling off the bed. Eden was happy Abby had brought Bronte, and as she looked at the baby, she thought about Rafe.

Eden sighed and her eyes teared up as she stroked Bronte's hair. "She's not coming," she said hoarsely.

"It's a lot for her to process," said Abby sympathetically. "It took all of us some time."

"It did, but," Eden swallowed, "you haven't been told everything Katheryn had to tell Rafe. I think it may be too much to ask her to accept." She frowned. "Too much at once."

"Don't give up on her," said Abby as she opened another of her snacks to share with Bronte.

"I won't," Eden whispered. "I just hope she won't give up on me." She looked at Abby sadly. "I love her, Abby. I do."

"I know you do," Abby sighed. "She must love you too. She got you into a much better room than you had." She looked up at Eden and knew her words were no help. "This is so fucked," she said then looked at Bronte abashed. "Sorry."

"I really did just want to protect her," Eden croaked out as tears fell to her cheeks. "She said she was hurting. I didn't want her to hurt, Abby, and now—" She shook her head, unable to finish.

"You didn't know this would happen," said Abby as she held Eden's hand. "Everything has just been so crazy."

Jude walked in and stood next to Eden's bed. "Hey," she said softly. "I told Rafe and the others your new room number."

Eden looked up at Jude. "Is she gone?"

"No," said Jude and shook her head. "Letty's still downstairs with her. She..." Jude hesitated as she thought Rafe looked in almost as bad a shape as Eden. "She says she can't come in."

New tears fell, and she whispered, "Why?"

Jude looked at the floor anxiously. "She says she can't say goodbye to you again."

"Oh," Eden whispered and wiped her tears. She looked at Abby. "Will you take Bronte to her? Will you tell her." She paused. "No, never mind."

"What?" asked Abby as she handed Bronte a snack.

"Please, just take Bronte to her," said Eden and closed her eyes.

Abby looked at Eden then at Jude. She sighed and picked up Bronte and their snacks. "Okay, I'll take her. I'll be back in a bit," she promised.

"Eden, I'm really worried about her," said Jude fretfully.

"So am I," said Eden sadly. "I wish I could have been there when Katheryn was talking to her."

"I don't know," said Jude. "I was watching through the waiting room glass. By the way that she was pacing and yelling and how mad she looked..." She grimaced and shifted nervously. "You should probably be glad you were sleeping. When I left her just now, she looked really rough." She wasn't sure if she should tell her Rafe looked worse than she did when Eden left her the last time.

"I just keep messing things up," cried Eden as tears flowed over her bruised face.

18

MAKING THEIR WAY to the second-floor waiting room, Flynn Ogden and Stacey Randall were happy Katheryn had been able to get Flynn released on bail. Flynn was very worried about Eden and wanted to find out how she was doing. He knew Katheryn had talked to Rafe about everything happening with Eden. He hoped now everything would be better between them. As they made their way through the hospital, a heated discussion was in progress inside the waiting room.

"Why won't you go up and see her?" Letty asked Rafe again desperately. "You can at least go tell her you hope she's going to be okay."

"I've seen her," said Rafe as she paced, torn about what to do next. "I'll send her some flowers from the gift shop," she said hesitantly.

"You saw her while she was sleeping!" yelled Letty angrily. "You have to do more," she said distressed, "more than just sending her flowers!"

Stacey swept into the room with Flynn behind her. "We found you," she sang out with a smile. "Flynn made bail!"

"How's Eden?" asked Flynn as he looked at everyone.

Rafe looked up at Flynn and exploded with furry. She rushed up to Flynn and punched him in the face with all her anger behind the punch. "I thought you were my friend!" she screamed at him.

Flynn fell to the floor and clutched his face with his good hand. "Rafe," he cried in shock and pain. "Rafe," he fought to speak, "I am your friend!"

Rafe seized him by the shirt with both hands and shook him violently then pulled him close to her face. "How could you keep this from me?" she demanded in a fury.

"She made me promise," cried Flynn cringing away and protecting his arm. "I wanted to tell you! I couldn't, I promised."

"You don't keep those kinds of promises!" she screamed in his face. "Not when their lives are in danger!" She shoved him away violently.

Flynn fell to his knees. "I'm sorry," he cried. "I'm sorry!"

Letty jumped between Rafe and Flynn. "Rafe! Stop it! Stop!" she cried out.

"Jesus, Rafe!" said Stacey terrified as she helped Flynn up.

"Rafe, please," said Flynn fearfully. "I couldn't tell you! I promised her," he cried out as he shook. "I knew I had to protect her for you." Flynn looked at Rafe in misery as his face started to show a bruise.

Before anyone could react, Flynn felt Rafe's hands on him again as she seized the collar of his shirt and pushed him against the glass wall then held his face and neck in both her hands. Flynn looked into her face terrified. She looked like a dark avenging angel with blazing eyes full of rage and pain deciding what punishment to reign down on him. He knew everyone was yelling at Rafe to stop, but for an instant, he heard nothing and saw nothing but Rafe. Just as suddenly as her anger appeared, it seemed to disappear, and Flynn saw the pain and remorse in Rafe's eyes.

Rafe put her forehead against his then gave him a chaste kiss on his lips. "Thank you," she said softly, "thank you for saving her." She released him, and Flynn fell to the floor then staggered trying to stand back up. Rafe turned away as tears for Eden burned down her cheeks for the first time today.

Flynn was shaking with the relief that Rafe had released him. Finally, he made it to his feet with help from Stacey. "Rafe," he called after her in anguish thankful for what he felt was her forgiveness. "I'm sorry, I should have told you," he choked out and could not stop his tears of relief.

Stacey pulled Flynn further away from Rafe. "Maybe we should go see Eden. Come on," she said as she pulled Flynn out the door.

"Rafe," Letty looked at her worried. "Rafe, what is happening to you? What are you doing?"

"I really don't know anymore," she said as she wiped her eyes. "I think I need to go."

"What about Eden?" Letty asked as she watched Rafe try to calm herself. "What are you going to do? You have to go see her. Are you going back to Greer?"

"I just—" Rafe breathed raggedly as she felt painful pressure against her chest. "I just need to think." She sat down shakily and took out Greer's phone as she pressed her hand to her chest.

"Rafe, you're being so stubborn!" Letty yelled in frustration.

"I'm not stubborn, Letty!" Rafe snapped angrily. "I'm realistic!" She closed her eyes and took a deep breath trying to calm herself again. After a while, she looked at Letty. "I'll stay at the hotel tonight. Eden can go to the house when they release her in the morning. I'll go on my trip with Greer in the morning, and by the time I get back, Eden should have found a place."

Abby walked in with Bronte and heard what Rafe had said. "Are you going to Greer?" she asked with worry. Rafe just looked at her. "Don't do it, Rafe. This is exactly what Eden told us she was worried you would do."

"What are you talking about, Abby?" Rafe said feeling physically weak and like she had nothing left inside her.

"She said, when you were out of it, you told her you were still in love with Greer," Abby told her nervously.

"Rafe! Did you?" demanded Letty as she took Bronte from Abby.

"I," Rafe hesitated and shook her head slowly, "I don't know."

"She's worried you'll go back to her, Rafe," Abby relayed. "Are you just running away because you think things will be easier with Greer?"

"I thought you were on my side, Abby!" said Rafe frowning.

"I don't know whose side to be on anymore!" Abby said frantically. "This whole thing is so screwed up! She loves you!"

"Abby," Rafe sighed as she rubbed her temples and then looked at the phone in her hand.

"You have things you want to ask and don't, she has things she wants to say but doesn't," Abby said hysterically. "You're both driving me crazy! You both say you don't want to hurt each other, but it's exactly what you're doing!"

"Rafe, you should stay until the adoption court date," said Letty desperately. "Don't let Katheryn file your letter."

"Eden wants this," Abby said knowingly. "She made assurances to all of us."

Letty sat down with Bronte beside Rafe. "Bronte is your daughter, and she needs you both," she said softly.

Abby sat on the other side of Rafe. "Whose phone do you have? Who're you calling?" she asked anxiously and looked at the text message Rafe had typed.

It read: Greer. I need you. I'm coming. I'm ready to go now.

Abby looked up and put her hand on Rafe's. "Rafe, don't. Don't send it," she begged. "Don't leave with her."

19

WEDNESDAY MORNING, THE doctor released Eden Kingsley from the hospital. After all the hospital paperwork was settled Abby drove Eden home while Letty, with Bronte and Jude, followed. It was just before noon when they were helping Eden to her room. She had been ordered to stay in bed and take it easy for the next few days so her body could recover from its pain, stiffness, and bruises, and give her head injury a chance to heal.

"I look like shit," groaned Eden as she saw herself in the bedroom mirror.

"I know," said Abby as she helped Eden to bed. "I didn't want to say anything," she said and shrugged, "but you'll heal."

"You're lucky," Jude said as she watched them from the doorway. "It could have been worse."

"It would have been worse if Flynn hadn't been there," said Eden as she covered up and turned on her side.

"Yeah," agreed Letty as she put Bronte on the bed and took her small shoes off. "I'm glad Katheryn could get him out on bail until the Prosecutor makes up his mind."

"Did you see his face?" asked Abby scandalized. "I can't believe Rafe ripped into him!"

"He's fine," said Jude. "He thinks he deserved it."

"He didn't deserve it," said Eden guiltily.

"Of course, he didn't," Abby scoffed. "Rafe needs to apologize to him."

"Letty," Eden said softly as Bronte crawled into her arms, "is Rafe coming home?"

"No, I'm sorry." Letty sighed in frustration with Rafe.

"Did..." she stammered, "did she go?" she asked sadly.

"Oh, no Eden," Abby assured her. "She didn't leave. Do you want me to call her and let her know you're home?"

"Okay," Eden whispered hoarsely as Bronte wiggled out of her arms and down the bed.

Abby looked at Letty then at Eden and wanted to help. "Letty talked to her for a long time," she told her, "and we all convinced her to stay."

"Eden, I don't think I've seen her so upset and hurting since—" Letty stopped herself and saw Eden looking at her with guilt written on her face. Letty had never told anyone just how hard Rafe took it when Eden left with Bronte. They told everyone Rafe was out of town on business, but really, Rafe was at Letty's house on her pullout bed for over a week. "It was a lot for her to take in," Letty said softly as Bronte crawled back to her, and Letty made sure she didn't tumble off the bed.

"I knew it was too much at once," said Eden as she rested her head in her hands. She knew Letty was being kind to her and was talking about when she left Rafe. Now she had done precisely what she didn't want to do. She had hurt her again.

"Eden," Abby hesitated, "I can't keep this from you anymore. Rafe. She... she was staying with Greer all this time."

"No," Eden said as she burst into tears. "I—" she swallowed, "I've lost her," she cried, her voice raspy, shaking with pain and grief.

"She just needs some time to process everything," said Letty as she tried to comfort her. "She'll come back. She loves you. She won't stay with Greer."

"She loves her," Eden said in misery. "Greer won't let her go."

"She said she would stay until the adoption court date," said Abby as she rubbed her back gently. "We told her about your assurances. Maybe she'll have calmed down by then. She'll realize she was lied to and she shouldn't have gone. She'll know you really love her, and then she'll come back."

Eden turned and lay on her side again, closing her tear-filled eyes. "Maybe," she said as she sobbed.

Letty exchanged a look of concern with Abby. "Why don't we go and let you rest," she said as she picked up Bronte from the bed. "We'll take Bronte to see Rafe and talk to her again."

Abby nodded in agreement. "Get some rest. I'll check in on you later."

Eden wiped the tears from her face and let out a shuddering sigh. "Thank you."

20

THURSDAY AFTERNOON, AT The Kiki Bistro, Rafe Salvaggio was having lunch with Bronte, Greer, and Julia. Greer, with Letty, Abby and Julia's assistance, had convinced Rafe she needed to help take care of Bronte. They kept her overnight and planned to spend the day with her. They didn't have to work too hard to convince Rafe because she missed Bronte very much. The two were inseparable at the table, and Rafe indulged Bronte when she insisted on sitting in Rafe's lap and sharing her chocolate shake.

Letty walked up to the table and was glad Rafe looked better today. She tickled Bronte. "What does Mama have planned for you today?" Letty asked the giggling toddler.

"We're going to the park after lunch then back to the hotel for a nap," said Rafe as she held Bronte in her lap and wiped the chocolate from her face. "When she wakes up, we're going to terrorize everyone in the hotel," she continued as she smiled at Bronte. "I'll have her back around six so you can take her to Eden."

"I'll pick some things up from the market after work and fix dinner," said Julia as she stood up and gathered her things. "It's nice to cook for someone again." She looked at Rafe and Greer. "I'll see both of you at seven over at my place," she said and left for work to put in a half-day.

"Rafe," said Letty looking at her cautiously, "why don't you take Bronte to Eden?"

"No," said Rafe as she shook her head and took a sip of her iced tea then gave a sip to Bronte. "I don't think it would be a good idea right now."

"Don't you even care about how she's doing?" asked Letty annoyed.

"Yes," Rafe said as she looked down at the table. "How is she?" she asked softly.

"She's going to be okay, but she's in a lot of pain," Letty answered. "She has to take it easy for the next few days."

"Oh," Rafe said with little emotion. "Well, I'm glad she's okay," she said and took a bite of her food.

"You have to talk to her sometime," said Letty exasperated.

"You should talk to her, Rafe," said Greer who had been watching the exchange.

"I know." Rafe shrugged indifferently as she chewed. "Sometime." She swallowed her food. "Later." She turned her attention to Bronte and the dessert menu.

21

ABBY VAN FALKOV WAS with Eden helping her prepare dinner while waiting for Bronte to come home. Bronte had ended up spending the night with Rafe. After spending the day with her mama, Letty and Ephraim were bringing her home in time for dinner. Eden had taken her pain medication and was sitting at the kitchen island with a glass of water watching Abby and glad she was such a good friend.

There was a knock on the door, and Abby wiped her hands on a towel. "I'll get it," said Abby. "Maybe Letty's early." She went to the door and opened it. "Julia?" she said in surprise.

"Hi, I need to talk to Eden," said Julia urgently.

"Oh, okay," said Abby flustered. "She's in the kitchen." They walked toward the kitchen. "Eden!" Abby called out. "Julia's here. She needs to talk to you."

Eden stood up as they came into the kitchen and saw she had a grave expression on her face. "What's wrong? What happened? Are Rafe and Bronte okay?" she asked quickly in her raspy voice, frightened that Jake or the Stewards had done something to them.

"They're fine," said Julia calmly. "Let's go sit down," she suggested, and they went to the living room. "I don't have very much time because I'm supposed to meet Greer and Rafe for drinks with Daddy at the hotel before he has to catch his flight home."

"Julia, just tell us what's going on," said Abby impatiently.

"Okay," Julia sighed as she looked at Eden. She never understood what Rafe saw in her, but she would rather Rafe stay in town with Eden than leave town for good with Greer. "Eden, I hope you're not waiting for Rafe to come back and tell you everything is okay," she said, sad in her own way that things had come to this end.

"I—" she stumbled nervously. "She—"

"What do you know, Julia?" Abby demanded.

"This is what I know," said Julia firmly as she looked at Eden. "Whenever I ask her about you, if she responds at all, she tells me she's tired of fighting for a broken dream, and she's not going to waste your time or hers anymore."

"Waste our time..." said Eden stunned.

"She's been making one of her lists," said Julia sympathetically.

"What—" Eden swallowed anxiously. "What's the list for?"

"It's a long list of all the reasons she shouldn't be with you, and you shouldn't be with her," Julia told her uneasily. "She's carrying it around, and I think she's still adding to it."

"Oh," said Eden not knowing what else to say or do.

"I thought she would come around, but I don't think it's going to happen," said Julia doubtfully. "I think she really is still planning to go on her trip after the court date."

"She's going with Greer?" asked Eden hoarsely trying to hold back her tears.

"She hasn't said exactly, but I think so," Julia affirmed. "I'm not really sure what else she's been doing, but last night, when we were having drinks before dinner, and Rafe was off with Daddy, Greer told me Rafe suddenly seemed to be calm and..." she hesitated, "content. "

"Content," repeated Eden numbly.

"Calm?" asked Abby doubtfully. "I don't think Rafe has ever been calm in her life."

"Greer said when Rafe first came to stay at the hotel, she was always pacing like a caged animal, and Rafe would barely come out of her room," said Julia as she looked at Eden who was trembling. "It just about drove Greer mad because she didn't know what was happening. She's not sure if Rafe even slept or ate at times. She did finally come out but then pretended as if nothing was wrong. Now she's just, stopped," she said at a loss. "She's stopped being mad and stopped talking about everything. Greer seems concerned about it and," she paused, "I think Rafe's made up her mind to leave." She put her hand on Eden's knee. "And I don't mean to come back home."

"What are you talking about, Julia?" Abby demanded. "She has to come back! She loves Eden!"

"Abby, she may love Eden, but it doesn't mean she's coming back," said Julia decisively.

"Well, what the hell *do* you mean?" asked Abby in frustration.

Julia looked at Eden who was staring at her hands unable to speak. "Eden, it means if you want her," she said firmly, "you're the one who's going to have to do the fighting. If you love her, you better start coming up with a list of reasons for her to stay. I really don't think she's going to fight for you again."

"This is so fucked!" Abby squealed.

"I have to go," Julia said as she stood. "They'll be expecting me." She gently put her hand on Eden's shoulder. "I wouldn't wait too long if I were you," she advised then showed herself out.

"Abby," Eden said as she put her head in her hands, "what am I going to do?"

Abby looked at Eden seriously. "Eden, do you want her? Do you really love her, I mean like forever love her?" Eden looked up at her and nodded. "If you do, I'll help you because I know," she hesitated, "I know it's how she really feels about you. But if you don't," she shook her head hoping she did love Rafe.

"I do, Abby," Eden cried. "I told you, I told her." She sobbed. "I do love her! I don't want to be without her."

"Okay," said Abby resolutely. "This is Rafe Salvaggio we're dealing with. She's very stubborn, and once she makes up her mind, it's hard to change it. We have to make a plan, and it has to be flawless."

"A plan?" said Eden doubtfully. "I don't think we can gang up on her. It'll just make things worse."

"Well, what are you going to do?" asked Abby frustrated.

"I—" Eden stammered, "I don't know." She sighed and wiped her tears.

22

EDEN KINGSLEY HAD been worrying all evening about the news Julia brought her. After Letty and Ephraim brought Bronte home, they had dinner, and then Abby played with her until bedtime. It was late when Abby went home, and though Eden was tired and in discomfort because of her injuries, she couldn't sleep. She couldn't stop worrying about Rafe. She knew Rafe would be angry about everything, but she thought Rafe would know she loved her and that Eden had just been trying to keep them together. She was sure Rafe would at least want to talk to her about everything. She never expected her to just—stop. On top of everything, Greer was with her, and Rafe loved Greer.

She had to talk to Rafe.

She had to figure out a plan like Abby said. She had to tell her to stay and let her know their dream was not a waste of time. Eden got out her laptop and took it into her room. She got into bed, got as comfortable as possible, and turned on her laptop so she could compose an email.

TO: RSalvaggio@EroinaCD.com
FROM: E_Kingsley@AscesisStudios.com
RE: Apology
Rafe,

I hope you're doing well, and I hope you'll take the time to read this letter. I'm sending it here because I know you still check this account all the time. I never thought we'd have to communicate this way. I always thought we could just talk to each other, but I can see now that I was wrong. The night you fell in the shower, you told me we should email each other more. I thought it was silly at the time, but now I see it might be the only way to reach you right now.

First, I'm sorry, Rafe. I'm sorry I didn't tell you about Jake right away. I see now it was a mistake, but at the time, I was afraid you would doubt me again, and I wanted us to become a family, even if it was just as co-parents and nothing more. But things changed, as I was able to work through everything with Dr. Cathcart, and then you and I began to spend time together again. I realized I love you deeply. I love you so much I couldn't stop no matter how hard I tried and how angry I was at myself for having feelings for you. Then I saw we really are a family so full of love, and I wanted us to stay together. Our dream is not a waste of time, and we shouldn't give it up.

Letty asked me why I couldn't have said one nice thing about you while we were apart, and I told her I had said good things. Now I realize I never told you the good things I said about you. We talked about all the bad things in the article but not about the good things that were left out. I want to tell them to you now, and I hope it's not too late for you to hear them.

These are the things I told people when they asked about you. Your loyalty is absolute and makes you the best friend anyone can have. You have confidence I've never seen in another, and it spills out into everything you do. You have remarkableg courage. You are generous to your friends and others with your time and energy, which seems boundless at times to me. You were always on my side and came to my defense whenever you thought I might need it, and sometimes when I didn't even realize I needed it. Your presence transcends your overwhelming beauty, making you irresistible to almost everyone. You have a loving and sensitive heart, and when you share it with someone, they can't help but love you.

Rafe, you've never wavered in your loyalty to me, even when I made what I know now was a mistake in leaving you. You surprise me every time I see you with how much you've changed while we were apart. When you said you wanted to be with me again, my world started to become complete again. When you told me you loved me, I could feel it physically when you entered the room. It lingered when you left so I could never forget it. I can't get enough of your smile, the one you give just to me. I miss it, and I miss you. You told me my eyes fascinate you, but I've never told you what your eyes do to me. I get lost in your beautiful gray-blue eyes because they really are the portal to your soul. No matter how hard you try to hide your emotions, I know you can't keep them from shining in your eyes. When you're angry, they spark, when you're in love, they are so bright, and when you tell me you love me, they smolder and make my heart beat faster.

I don't want to lose you, Rafe. I don't want it to be too late. Please, don't leave me, Rafe. Don't give up on us. I'd like to talk to you in person. There is a lot more we need to say to each other. I hope you'll give me this chance.

I love you,

Eden

23

SINCE SHE WOKE up Friday morning, Eden Kingsley had checked her email at least a dozen times to see if Rafe had replied. So far, she had not. Lydia came to pick up Bronte early for day school and so Eden could continue to rest. She wanted to keep everything for Bronte as normal as possible and Bronte loved going to school and playing with the other kids. Abby called and said she would be by later and bring breakfast. Eden took a warm shower to help ease her sore body and sat in the steam thinking about Rafe, her list, and Greer.

She felt so helpless.

She never thought things would come to this. She never had to fight for Rafe, because she had always been there. Even when she left her, Rafe was there. She was closed off and had all kinds of rules, but she was there. No matter where she went, or even when they were both with someone else, she could count on one thing—Rafe was there. Now it was all about to change, and Eden didn't know what to do about it. She didn't know where to start. How did she fight against all the things happening, the things leading Rafe away? Rafe was leaving, and Eden didn't know if she was just going to go for a little while or forever, or if she was just leaving her. Any scenario of life without Rafe was unimaginable.

Content.

Content was the word Julia used. How does she fight against Rafe becoming 'content and calm' since she has been spending time with Greer?

Eden got out of the shower and put her clothes on carefully, then decided to compose another email.

TO: RSalvaggio@EroinaCD.com
FROM: E_Kingsley@AscesisStudios.com
RE: Our Connection

Rafe,

I'm counting on the connection we both feel. I'm relying on it to bring us back to a place where we can be there for each other again. The place where we both feel complete, the place where nothing can touch us, but the love we feel for each other. I know you still feel it. We can both feel it. It's not something ever going away no matter how much you think you want it to.

It's a connection we feel with no one but each other. I know it's true because it's what happened to me. It's what brought us together almost seven years ago. It's what keeps bringing us back together—even after all the things we faced over the past two years. I'm counting on our connection to bring us back together again now.

Rafe, I didn't leave you again. I know you left because you thought it was what I wanted, but you were tricked just like I was. I don't want you to leave me. Please, don't let everything we've been fighting against continue to cause us pain. I don't want either of us to hurt anymore. We belong together. It's the reason it was so hard to keep us apart. Don't let it happen. Don't let them win when we have so much more to give to each other. I genuinely believe our love is unbreakable.

Do you still love me? Do you? You asked me the same question, and my answer is—yes, I still love you. I'll never stop loving you. I told you I wanted to fix my mistakes, and I do. I want to correct our mistakes so we can be a family again. I don't want either of us to lose our dream, Rafe. Together we can fix this. I know it will take time, and I just want you to tell me you'll give us the time we need. Don't leave, Rafe. Stay and give us the chance to work through all of this.

Please reply, Rafe. Don't fight our connection. I think it's the only thing holding you here right now. I don't want to lose it. We need to talk about everything. I'll meet you wherever you want.

I love you,
Eden

24

ASLEEP WITH HER laptop close by, Eden Kingsley was awakened by someone knocking on her front door and ringing the bell. She got up groggily and moved her laptop to the nightstand. Making her way out of her room and to the front of the house, she turned off the alarm. When she opened the door, she found Abby holding up a paper bag and cardboard drinks tray.

"I have breakfast and coffee," said Abby happily.

"Thank you," said Eden as she yawned and let her inside. They made their way to the kitchen where Abby doled out their breakfast sandwiches and coffee onto the table.

"How are you feeling?" asked Abby and then blew on her coffee.

"Okay," she said as she unwrapped her sandwich. "I'm a little stiff. I took some pain medicine, so I'm not in a lot of pain right now. I have to make sure I don't move wrong, and I go slowly. I just wish there was a way to get rid of these bruises faster."

"It's only been three days," said Abby and took a bite of her sandwich.

"I know," groaned Eden, "but I hate them. I hate looking at them." She put her hand on her face and throat. "The doctor said it may take over two weeks for them to totally go away."

"Well, at least your throat isn't as bad as they thought. Eat your breakfast," said Abby and watched as Eden began to eat.

"I talked to Rafe earlier this morning," she said casually. She didn't mention the chilly welcome she got from Rafe for showing up so early. But she had her reasons. Abby wanted to be sure Rafe was still there and not leaving again without a word.

Eden looked up in surprise. "You did?"

"And, I mean 'I' talked," Abby said as she pointed to herself. "She didn't say much of anything."

"Do you know if she got my emails? She hasn't been drinking or anything was she?" Eden asked, obviously worried.

"She got them," said Abby. "She's not drinking as far as I know. At the hotel morning she was on her computer and said she had a photography project she was going to work on at Topanga Beach today while Greer worked remotely."

"Did she say anything about me, about the emails?" Eden asked desperately.

"She said," Abby hesitated, "she said she wasn't going to respond to your begging again."

"Abby," Eden put down her coffee and burst into tears, "I don't know what else to do."

"You have to find another way," said Abby as she rubbed Eden's back gently, avoiding her bruises.

25

DRIVING DOWN THE beach highway, Eden Kingsley had made the thirty-minute drive to Topanga Beach. She pulled off into the parking area and looked for Rafe's car. As soon as Abby left, she got dressed, covered her bruised face with makeup, and headed out. She went to the hotel and called the room, but there was no answer. She checked the parking garage of the hotel and Rafe's car wasn't there so she knew Rafe must be out taking pictures like Abby had told her.

After talking with Abby, it was clear she had to find another way to talk to Rafe. The only thing she could think of was to find her and make her listen. She tried to think about all the things Rafe had done for her when she was fighting for her, but she was sure none of those things would work on Rafe. This problem was beyond flowers, gifts, grand gestures of love, or outright seduction. Though, she was prepared to use them all if it was what it would take. Eden never had to do any of those things before. She knew this was going to be a hard uphill fight and she was feeling ill-prepared. She was going into this situation blind, but she knew in her heart she had to do it. She had to get her back. She had to make her see they still belonged together. She had to convince her to stay.

Eden finally spotted Rafe's car and pulled into the space next to it. She got out of her car and started looking around for Rafe. She walked down to the beach, and after a while, she saw her by the ocean focusing her camera on something in the distance. She made her way over and stopped a few feet away.

"Rafe!" Eden called and watched Rafe turn and look at her in surprise. "I need to talk to you."

"There's nothing to talk about." Rafe started to walk away.

"Rafe, stop!" Eden shouted. "There's a lot to talk about," she said and followed Rafe. "I'm sorry. I'm sorry all of this happened. I'm sorry I didn't tell you about Jake."

"I know," said Rafe still walking away. "I read your emails."

"Why didn't you reply?" asked Eden frustrated. "I wasn't begging. I was telling you the truth," she said as she caught up to Rafe and put her hand on her shoulder to stop her. "Please, stop!"

"Don't touch me!" Rafe snapped as she pulled away from her.

"I'm sorry," said Eden startled by her animosity. "I was just," she watched Rafe start walking away again. "Rafe stop! I'm trying to talk to you!" She followed Rafe. "I'm sorry about everything. I'm sorry about not telling you about Jake. I was just trying to protect you!"

Rafe stopped and turned angrily. "It's not your job to protect me!"

Eden stood her ground. "Well, whose job is it?"

"It's no one's job!" Rafe yelled. "I don't need to be protected!"

"Well, what is it you need then?" Eden yelled back. "What do you need to stay with me?"

"I don't know, Eden," said Rafe acidly. "Maybe you can start by telling me the truth for a change!"

"I have been telling you the truth," insisted Eden.

"Right." Rafe laughed scathingly. "The truth with really important things left out." She took a deep breath to calm herself. "It's you who doesn't need me anyway. I think you'd be better off without me around."

"You're wrong!" insisted Eden.

"Eden," said Rafe very calmly, "even your fucking therapist is telling you I'm the reason for your fears or whatever. Maybe he's been trying to tell you to stay away from me."

"That's stupid, Rafe!" said Eden angrily. "He's not saying you're the reason for my fears at all! Since when do you listen to what therapists say anyway?"

"Since Greer," said Rafe and crossed her arms.

"So that's why you're with her?" asked Eden as she tried not to cry. "For therapy? She wants more than just being your therapist, you know!"

"Yes, I know," confirmed Rafe with a nod. "She tells me things. She doesn't keep things from me."

"Really?" Jealous, Eden laughed. "Did she tell you she slapped me across the face and told me you had talked to Jake when she was here?"

"What?" said Rafe confused.

"You heard right," said Eden shakily. "I guess she thought I needed some shock therapy! She slapped me, told me about Jake, and said if you went back to her, I wouldn't get you back. So I guess she doesn't tell you everything!"

"She did?" asked Rafe and smiled.

"Why are you smiling?" Eden asked angrily.

"Because she did tell me," said Rafe thoughtfully, "not exactly like you did, but she told me she was fighting for me in her own way."

"Great!" said Eden furiously. "So she's fucking perfect! Just like you, right? You two are going to be so fucking perfect together! The blind and the deaf! Are you fucking her?"

"I'm not talking to you about this anymore," said Rafe with a frown then turned and started to walk away.

"Rafe, I'm sorry," said Eden frustrated at herself for cursing and insulting them in anger, and because she knew that she was screwing up. "I know you love her. I just don't understand why you can listen to her but hated every minute we were in therapy."

Rafe turned and stared Eden down. "Do you really want to know why I hated the fucking therapy shit?" Rafe asked intently and watched as Eden nodded. "Because, Eden, all it did was make me doubt and question myself even though I knew what I wanted."

"Your doubts were already there. The therapy didn't cause them!" Eden argued.

"It did! I wasn't the one who didn't want to have sex," said Rafe sadly and evenly. "I wasn't the one who wanted to make sure we were solid. Therapy was for you. You're the one who has always had the doubts. And by forcing me to go, you made me start doubting everything."

"Bull crap, Rafe!" Eden disagreed. "You had no idea what was going on with me. You were just pushing—pushing to get what you wanted!"

"I seem to recall we discussed everything and you agreed," Rafe said softly then sighed and shrugged. "It wasn't just what I wanted. You're the one who insisted having a baby was what you wanted because you were ready."

"I was ready!" insisted Eden. "If you hadn't fought so hard against the therapy, maybe it would have helped us more!"

"Those therapy sessions made me question everything from my abilities to my feelings for you," said Rafe softly as she shook her head. "Now I know the therapy sessions were more for you and your feelings than for me anyway. At least when I talk to Greer, she helps me find answers and doesn't just throw a bunch of new questions at me that I didn't even know I was supposed to be asking."

Eden sat down in the sand feeling exhausted and put her head in her hands because Rafe was right about the therapy. She was afraid to tell Rafe about her feelings for men while they were having problems getting pregnant. "She helps you find answers?" she asked shakily as she looked up at Rafe. "What answers?"

"Answers about you," Rafe divulged with a slight shrug.

"Me?" said Eden sadly.

"Yes," said Rafe evenly. "For your information, she's sent me back to you twice."

"She did?" asked Eden in misery.

"Yeah, I guess she has a 'three strikes you're out' policy," said Rafe frankly as she looked down at Eden. "You should just go back home," she said and walked away.

Eden pushed herself up as fast as she could without causing herself too much pain and followed Rafe. "Rafe, wait," she called out. "Won't you just listen to why I thought I had to do the things I did?"

"You already told me," said Rafe calmly as she stopped and waited for her. "You wanted to protect me, and you didn't want me to doubt you."

Eden looked at Rafe, surprised she hadn't yelled or become angry again. Her calmness was unnerving. "It's true," said Eden shakily. "I didn't know he was still talking to you. If I knew, I would have told you. I could see you were hurting and under a lot of stress because you weren't sure of me, and because of the injunction. I didn't want to cause you anymore heartache," she insisted. "I thought telling you about him would cause you more pain. I wanted to protect you from more pain."

"Stop lying!" screamed Rafe suddenly angry. "You weren't protecting me from anything! I don't need you to protect me! I don't need a mother! I need a partner! I need a lover! I can handle stress, heartache, and pain," she said hotly, "but not the lies and secrets causing it all!"

"I wasn't lying!" Eden yelled back at her indignant. "You do need to be protected! Look at what you did when everything was happening! You just shut down, you were drinking all the time, and you got stoned! I think you do need a mother! I think not having a mother is one of your big problems!" She saw Rafe glare at her in anger then turn and walk away. She knew she hit a sore spot by bringing up her mother. She went after her almost relieved she was getting a familiar reaction now. "I'm sorry! I didn't mean it like it sounded," she swore. "I just meant sometimes you do need someone to look out for you. Rafe, please, stop!"

"Get the fuck away from me!" Rafe yelled and kept walking incensed Eden would stoop to bringing up her mother. Eden knew nothing about Rafe's mother or what the loss meant to her.

"No!" she yelled and kept following her. "I thought I was protecting you! Tell me why you don't think I was!"

Rafe turned and looked at Eden with a scowl. "I don't think you even know what it means to protect someone!" she seethed. "Life isn't one of your happily-ever-after scripts! Real life has real consequences!"

"Tell me what it means to you then," said Eden out of breath. She had not missing Rafe's insinuation that she had not considered the consequences. But she thought she had. All she ever thought about was Rafe and what might happen to them if she had made different decisions. She was sure things would have been worse.

"It's not just to me, Eden!" Rafe said hotly. "It's to everyone," she said throwing her hands up, "everyone except you, I guess. You're not protecting someone by keeping important things a secret! You kept it a secret you and Bronte were in danger! You were definitely not protecting me! Your secret about the danger the two of you were in hurts me more than telling me about Jake ever could have hurt me! Keeping dangerous secrets about someone kidnapping your child makes me doubt you much more than I would have if you had told me about Jake!"

"I'm sorry," cried Eden, and she couldn't keep the tears from her eyes. "I made a mistake, Rafe, a big mistake. But you have to understand, at the time, I felt like it was the right decision. How could I have known all of this was going to happen?"

Rafe closed her eyes and fought to control herself. She took several breaths and became very calm again. "Eden, you just keep proving you don't need me," she said sadly. "You've become this new person, and you've just..." she looked up then back at Eden, "outgrown me. It's like you want to do all of this on your own and there's nothing I can do about it. So, if you want to do it on your own, it's okay. Just don't lie to me, and don't lie to yourself."

"I don't know what you're talking about, Rafe," Eden sobbed. "I do need you. I don't want to do everything on my own! I want to be with you! I want to do everything with you! I love you! It's the truth!"

"Eden," said Rafe softly and shook her head, "it's not just those things. This isn't the first time you've done something like this to me."

"When did I do something else like this to you?" asked Eden in disbelief. "Please, don't walk away. I need to rest," she said exhausted then sat in the sand again. "Sit down and tell me, Rafe. I need to know."

Rafe watched Eden for a moment and took in the bruises on her face, which she had tried to hide with makeup. By her slumped shoulders, Rafe could see Eden was tired. She wanted to leave but couldn't bring herself to just leave her stranded on the sand. She sat across from her in the sand with her camera in her lap and sighed. "Eden, you started doing this before you even got pregnant. I've been thinking about this a lot, and it was all right in front of me. I just didn't see it then. I guess I didn't want to see it."

"What? What was I doing?" she asked trying to hide the pain returning to her body.

"You always wanted to check if we were solid, you weren't interested in sex with me, and you kept secret when you were ovulating, for starters."

"We were doing a big thing, Rafe. I wanted to be sure we were good," said Eden as she looked sadly at Rafe.

"I was sure I was ready before you insisted we go to therapy," said Rafe sullenly. "Then after Bronte was born, I thought we were doing better until you started not wanting to have sex again.

"You're the one who always said sex wasn't everything in a relationship," Eden reminded her.

"I did say those words, but I didn't mean I didn't ever want to have sex again. I just said it so you'd feel better and so you didn't feel..." she paused, "pressured. And it is something you do when the person you love suddenly wants to be..." she sighed, "to be with—" she shook her head.

"Men?" Eden finished for her.

"Yes." Rafe nodded and looked down at the camera in her lap. "And now I find out your feelings for men started way before you told me about them, and your nightly chats on the computer were for online sex," she took a breath and shook her head.

"Well, I told you..." said Eden upset, "it was only one time, and it was a mistake, and I can't stop having feelings!"

"Obviously, you can stop," said Rafe calmly. "You stopped having them for me."

"I don't think I did, I know I didn't," said Eden honestly. "Rafe, I want to be with you. Please, believe me," she said wanting to change the subject. "Well," she cleared her throat because her voice was going again, "I didn't tell you about the ovulating once because," she bit her lip, "because I was mad. I was going to tell you."

"See," Rafe sighed, "even back then you weren't happy, and you were always pissed at me—probably for all the same reasons published in the article. I should just leave you alone. You'd be happier," she assured her.

"Don't say I'd be happier! It's not true!" Eden said frustrated. "Just because you piss me off sometimes doesn't mean I don't love you," she said hoarsely. "I know I piss you off all the time, and you still love me. I told you the article twisted everything!"

"Chalk up another lie, right?" asked Rafe calmly as Eden's head snapped up and she looked at her not understanding. "You told me you couldn't remember who you said those things to, and now I find out you told them to your man Jake," she said cynically.

"Stop it, Rafe!" said Eden harshly in misery. "I couldn't tell you! You were drinking yourself blind!"

"Well, if you were about to lose everything, and you couldn't do a thing about it, you would probably do the same thing." Rafe looked at her with a frown. "Did you ever think by telling me it could have all stopped?"

"It wouldn't have stopped," said Eden shaking her head. "They would have found another way, and I was afraid of what else they could come up with to hurt you."

"So you put yourself and Bronte in danger?" Rafe laughed at the absurdity. "You're just making no sense to me, Eden."

"It did make sense, at the time," insisted Eden. "I wanted to stay with you. I wanted you to be happy. I wanted us to be happy."

"What makes you so sure you'll be happy with me now?" asked Rafe skeptically.

"I'm sure because I love you, and I've always loved you, and now I see the changes in you, and I love you even more," said Eden emphatically.

"I know I've changed, but I haven't changed as much as you think," Rafe said doubtfully.

"I've changed too, and I haven't outgrown you," Eden insisted. "I just," she hesitated, "I just got lost for a while, but now I have no doubts and realize I was lost because I wasn't with you. You do make me happy, Rafe. You do still love me, don't you?"

"I don't know," Rafe said calmly. "I don't know if it matters anymore."

"It matters," Eden said softly. "I've been happy with you. We were happy before," she swallowed, "before you left. I love you, Rafe."

"You think we were happy?" Rafe asked curiously. "I'm not so sure. I was fighting a lie, Eden. I was desperate and afraid and in pain. The worst part of everything is now I know I was fighting two lies..." she paused. "Yours and Jake's. I wouldn't have had to fight either one if you had just told me what was going on. I don't think I can be with someone whose lies I have to fight. Someone who thinks they have to keep secrets from me to protect me. Like I said, this isn't the first time this has happened, and I don't think I can take it happening again."

"It won't happen again," said Eden desperately. "I promise. I'll always tell you everything." She leaned over and put her face in her hands to rub her forehead then looked up at Rafe again. "When did it happen before? I haven't done this before."

"You did it with the insemination," Rafe smiled sadly.

"Rafe," Eden shook her head, "I just wanted to be sure before I told you. When the first one didn't take, you were so disappointed. Then we did the second, and it didn't work. I could see your disappointment growing. She looked up at her. "When we thought the third one had worked, and it turned out to be a false positive, I thought you were going to kill the doctor and everyone at the sperm bank because you thought maybe the sperm wasn't any good."

"I know," she said wryly, "you wanted to protect me. But you didn't protect me, Eden. You took something away from me that I can't ever get back."

"No, we have Bronte," said Eden positively. "She's our daughter."

"But," Rafe said as she ran her hand over her face in frustration and tried to remain calm, "I wasn't there, Eden. I wasn't part of everything. You pushed me away thinking you were protecting me. I didn't get to make love to you and help create her. I didn't get to be with you during your morning sickness. You kept your pregnancy a secret from me for four months. Gabri is my childhood friend, and you didn't even consider what it meant to me. I missed out on almost everything."

"I'm so sorry," Eden said regretfully as she wiped her tears on her sleeve. "I never thought about those things," she whispered. "At the time, I was having doubts about him. I told you, it was different when I met the donor rather than just picking from a list of names and stats. Then I thought about meeting him the night of your birthday party, and the way you two talked and how you both looked like these beautiful angels together, and I was overwhelmed. When I got home from New York, I was thinking about everything, and suddenly, I just knew I loved you and my unsure feelings were just my anxiety. I knew I wanted to start our family and make you happy."

Rafe's head was spinning with all of this new information, and none of it helped her understand why some of the things had happened to bring them to this place.

"I'm still not sure of the reason you kept your pregnancy a secret. Was it because you wanted to punish me, or you were afraid of me or was it you just thought I was a monster because I fucked up?" asked Rafe sadly. "I had to find out about it from a stranger. I wasn't even sure if you had used our sperm or if you went out and fucked some random guy. From the moment you finally came and told me it was ours, I've lived in fear of not being part of Bronte's life. Because, again, you've proven you don't need me."

"I do need you," said Eden as she looked warily at Rafe.

"I don't think you do anymore, Eden," Rafe said as she stood up and brushed sand off herself. "You should go home now," she sighed and held out her hand to help Eden up.

Eden took Rafe's hand and got up slowly and carefully. "I really do need you, I love you," she said keeping hold of Rafe's hand. "Will you come home?"

"No," said Rafe as she pulled her hand away and shook her head.

"Why? We need to talk more," Eden implored her. "We can work this out. We can learn from this and fix things. We can be happy."

"Your car is up there." Rafe pointed then turned and walked in the opposite direction.

"Rafe, stop!" called Eden and watched as Rafe turned and looked at her. "Why won't you even try?"

"Because," Rafe looked at her sadly, "I have no idea how many more secrets you have. I don't know if I can take hearing them."

"I—" started Eden as she closed her eyes and looked down to find her courage, "I only have two more things I haven't told you."

"Will it kill me not to know them?" asked Rafe as she crossed her arms. "Will it put your life, or Bronte's, in danger? If others find out about it, will it destroy another part of my life or what's left of my career?"

"I don't know," she said as she looked up at her annoyed. "It's not dangerous. Do you want me to tell you?"

"Sure, why not?" Rafe sighed and threw her hands up.

"I..." Eden breathed and ran her hand over her head. "The first time I moved out before I found out I was pregnant, I went out with a writer I met, and I slept with her." She looked up, and Rafe had looked away. "I also had sex with a director at the studio. His name was Michael. I thought he was going to work out after Jake. Then I found out," she sighed, "I found out he was married." She looked up at Rafe sadly. "I found out the day I talked to you about Lauren at the beach. I couldn't believe what I had done." She shook her head. "I wasn't even smart enough to ask him if he was married." She burst into tears and sat down in the sand again. "What's wrong with me?"

"Oh, Eden," said Rafe not really knowing how to answer her question. "You really don't need me. I don't know what you want me to say." She sighed. "It's your life. We weren't together so I can't say much. Besides, I did have sex with a lot of other women."

"I know," Eden sobbed and let out a small laugh at the same time, "a lot of other women. "

"Well," said Rafe as her lips twitched into a quick smile, "I was feeling a bit deprived for a while, and Julia was very convincing."

"I do need you," insisted Eden as she looked up at Rafe in fear. "You didn't—" she hesitated. "Not with Julia!"

"No! No, way!" Rafe laughed softly. "She's been my friend for a long time, and I think 'just friends' is the way it should be with us."

"I think it would be hard to see her knowing." Eden stopped. "I'm glad you didn't," she said softly. "Michael was just—" she started.

Rafe frowned. "I don't need to know the details."

"You said you didn't want me to have any secrets," Eden reminded her.

Rafe ran her hand over her head and looked out at the ocean then back at Eden. "Eden, we haven't..." she hesitated, "Greer and me. We haven't."

"Thank you," said Eden as she looked at Rafe with sad relief. "Thank you for telling me."

"How'd you find me anyway?" asked Rafe curiously.

"Abby told me she talked to you this morning and you had told her you'd be on this beach," she said frankly. "I just drove around until I found your car."

"She can't keep her mouth shut!" Rafe said irritated. "She knew about Jake, you know. I'm not sure how. She did manage to keep that one secret, though. I guess she's getting a little better."

"No," said Eden trying not to laugh, "she's not."

"What do you mean?" asked Rafe suspiciously.

"She really didn't know about Jake," Eden said rolling her eyes.

"Yes she did," said Rafe annoyed. "She told me she saw and she found out."

"She wasn't talking about the same thing you were," said Eden as she looked down trying not to laugh and cause herself more pain in her back and ribs.

"Well, then what was she talking about?" demanded Rafe.

"I can't tell you right now," said Eden shaking her head.

"Why not?" asked Rafe getting mad.

"We have other things we need to talk about," said Eden and took a painful deep breath to pull herself together.

"Are you protecting me again?" Rafe asked crossly.

"No," Eden reassured her.

"No? Just keeping a secret?" said Rafe tersely.

"Fine! I'll tell you!" said Eden annoyed as she stood up. "My god, you piss me off sometimes!" She dusted the sand off herself. "She thought I was comparing you to Jake."

"Yeah," Rafe agreed, "I thought you were too."

"No, I mean really comparing you to him." Eden sighed and rolled her eyes as she spoke very quickly. "She thought I was forcing you to use a strap-on."

"What?" Rafe said taken aback.

Eden groaned because she had to repeat herself. "She thought I was forcing you to use a strap-on!" she said clearly and watched as Rafe turned and put her face in her hands and began to shake. "Rafe?"

"Is—" Rafe said as she turned around and began laughing hard. "She was talking about—" She still could not control her laughing. "I was kind of confused when she said..." she took a gasping breath, "she said comparing, but I just thought it was the only word she could come up with!"

"Why do you even have one?" she asked, loving the sight of Rafe laughing. "Never mind," she said regretting asking the question. She really didn't want to know what Rafe was doing with it or who she used it on.

Rafe grimaced and shook her head. She didn't want to confess she had considered using it to try and get Eden back. "An impulse buy." She chuckled then shrugged slightly. She could see Eden was trying to hide her discomfort about what she might have done with it. "I didn't use it."

Rafe's words came as a relief to Eden. "Abby was so mad when I told her I thought you were messing with her." She laughed with Rafe trying not to cause herself pain.

"I'll bet she was!" Rafe scoffed.

"Why is she so fixated on you and strap-ons?" asked Eden curiously. "Did you?"

"No! It's probably why—" said Rafe and continued to laugh. "Sometimes it's not what you do, but what you don't do." Rafe winked. "I gave her a line about Picasso and masterpieces."

"You are really bad," Eden said as she laughed. "You know? Poor Abby!"

"Poor Abby? What about me?" Rafe demanded annoyed. "Who knows how many people she's told her crazy story! I wonder what newspaper it'll show up in!"

"Rafe," Eden suddenly stopped laughing, "I don't feel very good. I need to go home." She looked at Rafe with a grimace as her body began to throb painfully. "We need to talk some more," she gasped in pain, "maybe tomorrow."

"Maybe," said Rafe uncommitted. She watched Eden turn and start walking back down the beach and saw she wasn't doing well. She caught up with her and took her arm. "You're probably not even supposed to be driving yet. I'll drive you home."

Rafe walked with Eden back down the beach to their cars. Eden let Rafe hold her arm and help her through the sand as they walked in relative silence with Rafe asking if she was okay and Eden answering when she could. Eden thought it had to be one of the most peaceful times they'd had together in a long time and wished it could last longer, but she was getting tired, and her pain medicine had worn off. When they finally made it up the stairs and to the cars, she was more than a little relieved. Rafe opened the passenger door of her car and helped Eden in then got in herself.

"What about my car?" Eden asked as Rafe started the car.

"We'll figure it out later," Rafe answered and pulled out of the parking space and drove around the parking area to the exit and headed down the coast highway. She saw Eden pulling out some papers lying on the seat she had sat on. "Just put it in the glove box."

"What is it?" asked Eden as she pulled it out.

"Nothing," said Rafe irritably. "Just put it in the glove box."

"It's one of your lists," said Eden as she looked over the papers.

"Just—" Rafe tried to grab the papers, "put it away."

"No," said Eden as she moved, ignoring her pain, so Rafe couldn't get the papers, "it's a list of reasons we shouldn't be together. I should look at it, so I'll know why you aren't coming home."

"I already told you a lot of the things on it," Rafe said annoyed.

"This is a long list," said Eden as she flipped to another page, and Rafe just looked straight ahead frowning. "Maybe I should keep this copy."

"Will you just put it away?" Rafe sighed.

Eden folded the list in half. "No," she said and started tearing it up.

"What!" Rafe yelled as she saw her tear up her list. "What are you doing!" she retorted as she tried to grab the list.

"Watch the road!" Eden shouted, and she kept the papers out of her reach and tore them in half again.

"What are you doing?" demanded Rafe and she watched her tear up her list.

"It's no good," said Eden as she tore it into smaller and smaller pieces.

"What!" Rafe yelled in frustration.

"The list—" Eden said as she tore. "It's no good."

"How can a list be no good?" yelled Rafe annoyed.

"Well, the way I see it, the most important thing is not on the list," she said and tore it again, "so it's no good." She tore the list one more time then threw the torn pieces out of the car.

Rafe turned her head and saw all the pieces fly out of the car and swirl away behind them. "Eden!" Rafe roared. "We could get a fucking ticket for littering! You—" she looked at her in disbelief, "you threw out my list!"

"I'm sure you have a half a dozen more copies at the hotel," Eden said calmly.

"Damn it, Eden!" Rafe yelled in frustration and anger.

"Like I said, it was no good anyway," said Eden and tried to stay calm because she was now paying for her actions with excruciating pain.

"It was fine!" raged Rafe.

"No, it didn't say you stopped loving me," said Eden trying not to grit her teeth. "So, it was no good."

"Well, maybe I'll add it!" seethed Rafe.

"No, you won't!" Eden yelled heatedly and feeling sick. "You won't! It also didn't say I stopped loving you, and you can't add it either because it isn't true! I do love you!" She looked at Rafe who had the steering wheel in a very tight white-knuckle grip looking straight ahead barely controlling her anger. Eden watched Rafe for a while in silence then laid her head back and closed her eyes. She couldn't help noticing Rafe was more upset about her list than anything they talked about, and she was not exactly sure how to take it.

26

AFTER PULLING INTO the driveway, Rafe Salvaggio was still not over her irritation of Eden throwing out her list. She got out and went around the car to help Eden. Seeing Eden was shaking, and in so much pain it was hard for her to move, Rafe let go of her irritation. Gently she helped Eden into the house and into her room. Eden went directly into the bathroom to get her pain pills and some water. She picked up the pill bottle and tried to open it but couldn't. She sat down on the toilet and started to cry in pain and frustration from more than just her injuries.

Rafe heard Eden crying and looked inside the bathroom. "What is it?" Rafe asked with concern. "What's wrong?"

"I—" she sobbed, "I'm sorry. My hands are too weak," she said and showed Rafe the pill bottle. "Can you help me open this?"

"Sure." Rafe sighed then walked in and took the bottle. "These child-proof caps are always hard to open." She opened the bottle and handed a pill and a glass of water to Eden.

"Thanks," said Eden shakily and took the pill. She sighed and started to take her top off so she could change back into her pajamas.

"Eden," said Rafe. She hesitated for a moment as she saw Eden struggling and in pain. "Do you want me to help you?"

"Would you?" said Eden as she looked up at Rafe sorrowfully.

Okay," she said as she nodded sadly. She gently helped Eden take her shirt off and was shocked when she saw the large angry bruises on her neck, shoulders, chest, and side, and the image locked in her mind. "Shit, Eden!"

"I know," said Eden, tears still falling. "They hurt." She was shaking. "My whole body hurts."

"I'm sorry," whispered Rafe. She picked up the pajama top and hesitantly helped her put it on noting more bruising across her back. "Eden," she said as she slipped the pajama shirt around her, "these are my pajamas."

"I know." Eden sniffed and wiped the tears from her bruised face. "Help me get these jeans off." She stood up and let Rafe take off her pants.

Rafe noticed more injuries and bruising on Eden's knees, thighs, and hips from Jake slamming her to the ground and against the car. A wave of angry heat ran through her as she helped Eden put the pajama bottoms on.

"They're very comfortable pajamas," said Eden weakly, "and they smell like you." She could see that Rafe's face had darkened. Rafe's body had tensed and Eden could feel the heat rolling off Rafe from anger.

"You can have them," said Rafe fighting to control the burning rage inside her at Jake, and at Eden. "Do you need anything else?"

"No," Eden whispered not wanting Rafe to say she could have the pajama's. Tears fell from Eden's eyes again for more than just the pain in her body.

"Eden," said Rafe choking back her anger as she saw Eden's tears. "I really am sorry this happened," she said and leaned in and kissed Eden's forehead gently.

"Me too," she sobbed, shaking with fatigue. "Rafe?"

"Yeah?" Rafe sighed looking away from her.

"I..." Eden hesitated, "I do need something," she said cautiously and reached for her.

"What?" asked Rafe concerned as she helped her stand.

"I was so scared," said Eden as she held on to Rafe as she helped her to the bed. "I..." she gritted her teeth against the pain, "I need you to hold me," she said softly, "please."

Rafe's whole body stiffened, and her mind reeled with suspicion and doubt. She could see Eden was in pain, but she didn't want to give her any false hope. She looked at Eden's pleading eyes and her weak and shaking body and then relented.

"Okay," she agreed, "for a little while." She helped Eden into the bed and under the covers. Then she lay on the bed next to Eden, keeping her shoes on. Eden pulled the covers off herself and rolled on to her side and put her arm and leg over Rafe and her head on her chest.

"When the pain goes away," she whispered, "I can lie on my back. Just hold me until then."

"Okay," said Rafe and gently stroked Eden's dark golden hair.

"Rafe," said Eden with a shaky breath, "you have to talk to me again," she sighed, "tomorrow. If you don't, I'll find you again," she promised through her tears, "and I'll kick your ass."

She felt Rafe kiss the top of her head and stroke her hair as she cried herself to sleep holding tightly to Rafe.

27

AFTER RAFE SALVAGGIO was certain that Eden had finally fallen asleep, she worked herself gently out from under her so Eden could continue to lie on her side. She was not sure if the pills had made all of Eden's pain go away or not and did not want her to wake up in pain from moving onto her back. She went into the bathroom and picked Eden's clothes up off the floor then searched her jeans pockets and found her car keys. She put the keys in her pocket and headed out of the house.

Outside, Abby pulled into Jude's driveway and spotted Rafe as she was walking to her car. "Rafe! Rafe, I'm so glad you're here!" called Abby as she jumped from her car and ran up to her. "We don't know where Eden went! She's not supposed to be driving around, and she didn't take her cell phone. You have to help us find her!"

"Calm down, Abby," snapped Rafe irritably. "She's in the house asleep."

"What?" Abby said in confusion. "She is? How?"

"This is all your fault, Abby!" Rafe snapped angrily. "You shouldn't have told her where I was! I had to drive her home! If you had kept your mouth shut, she would have stayed home! Why'd you tell her? What if she was in an accident?"

"I'm sorry," said Abby weakly. "I didn't know she'd do this. Where's her car?"

"It doesn't matter," said Rafe reining her anger in and calming herself. "I'm taking her car keys, so even if she tells you where it is, she can't drive it. I have to go."

"You can't take her keys!" argued Abby. "What if she needs her car?"

"She's not supposed to be driving," Rafe pointed out. "I'll give you her keys Sunday. Bring someone with you so one of you can drive her car home."

"Rafe," Abby said cautiously, "are you really leaving after the court date?" Rafe just glared at her. "You can't! You just," she stomped her foot, "can't!"

"I can do anything I want," said Rafe annoyed.

"But you two love each other!" insisted Abby. "Did you even think about what I told you this morning?"

Rafe laughed dryly. "She said she forever loves me?"

"Yes! Right," nodded Abby.

"I thought about it," said Rafe putting her hands in her pockets as she leaned on her car.

"So why are you doing this?" Abby asked desperately.

"Because I still think she would be better off without me," said Rafe frankly. "She'll be happier."

"Rafe! You're so stubborn!" screeched Abby.

"I know," said Rafe sadly. "People keep telling me I am. But I think I'm just being realistic."

"Why do you always hurt people?" Abby demanded angrily. "You hurt everyone, Rafe!"

Rafe looked at Abby searchingly, hurt by her words. "Maybe it's why I'm leaving," she said thoughtfully.

"Rafe! No! I'm sorry," Abby apologized as she saw the look on Rafe's face. "It's just—" she complained, "you can't do this to Eden."

"What? Let her have some happiness?" Rafe asked and shook her head as she opened her car door.

"She won't be happy, Rafe!" said Abby gravely.

"Abby," Rafe sighed, "it's really none of your business, anyway."

"You're both my friends," Abby pointed out, "so it is my business! You two belong together!"

"Did you see her?" Rafe snapped angrily. "Did you see her body and what he did to her?"

"Yes," said Abby sadly, "I saw it, Rafe. She's going to be okay."

"This time!" said Rafe in a fury. "This time, she'll be okay! What about the next time she does this? The next time she tries to protect me or not make me angry, stressed or whatever! The next time she keeps a secret and puts herself in a bad situation! Will she be okay then too?" she demanded. "Her lies and secrets just keep getting bigger and more dangerous! I just can't take it Abby! I just can't—" She looked at Abby in a rage. "I can't face it again!" Rafe got into her car and slammed the car door, and then she started the engine and sped away, her anger burning away the tears before they had a chance to fall.

28

STOMPING NEXT DOOR after Rafe sped off, Abby Van Falkov convinced Jude and Flynn to go with her back to Rafe's house. They were all sitting on the patio by the pool waiting for Eden to wake up. They were discussing Rafe, and Abby was telling them about her latest frustrating encounter with her.

"She said what?" said Jude surprised. "She can't face it again?"

"Yeah," confirmed Abby.

"Well, what do you think she meant," asked Jude with worry.

Abby shrugged. "I think she thinks Eden has a death wish or something."

"It's just not true!" said Flynn emphatically.

"Well, it doesn't mean Rafe doesn't think she does," said Abby then sipped her beer.

"How did this situation get so fucked up?" asked Jude, sad for her friends.

"I don't know," answered Abby frustrated. "I don't even know which one of them to be pissed off at anymore. I guess I'll just be pissed off at both of them."

"Maybe I should talk to Rafe," suggested Jude.

"Jude, I've seen you 'talking' to Rafe," Abby scoffed.

"So," said Jude with a smirk.

"So, you just sit there and drink beer and say one word every once in a while."

"So," said Jude with a shrug.

"So! So what?" Abby said frustrated with Jude's one-word comments.

"So... maybe she just needs to be calm," Jude supposed, knowing it was useless to try to drag things out of Rafe.

"Jude!" Abby uttered in disbelief. "Julia said she was content and calm! I don't think she needs to be any calmer on top of what she is now!"

"Content?" asked Flynn not understanding why it was a bad thing.

"Happy content?" asked Jude trying to clarify.

"I don't know." Abby sighed. "More like, she's made up her mind content."

"Shit," said Jude softly.

"Hey," said Eden hoarsely as she walked out still in her pajamas and Flynn gave her his chair. "Thanks."

"No problem," said Flynn and went to drag another chair over.

Eden smiled sadly at Flynn with his bruised face and broken arm as she sat down carefully. "Are you doing okay?" she asked with concern,

"I'm good," said Flynn shrugging off her concern.

"Is Rafe still here?" asked Eden looking at Abby hopefully.

"No," said Abby dejected, "she left a while ago."

"Oh," said Eden as she smiled weakly. "We had a good talk," she said trying to be positive. "We're going to talk again tomorrow."

"She said she'd come back?" asked Abby suspiciously.

Eden frowned. "Not exactly. But I told her if she didn't talk to me tomorrow, I'd come looking for her again," she said ardently.

"Eden, she took your car keys," Abby informed her.

"Oh, well maybe she's going to bring my car back," she said trustingly.

"No," Abby said shaking her head. "She told me to bring someone over Sunday to pick up the car and the keys."

"What? What if I need the car?" demanded Eden upset.

"She pointed out you're not supposed to be driving," Abby said softly.

"Dang it!" said Eden angrily and started to cry. "She did this so I can't look for her!"

"Well, she was worried you'd get into an accident or something," Jude explained.

"She's not coming back to talk," Eden cried, and her body shook with sorrow.

"Do you want me to talk to her?" asked Jude sympathetically.

"I don't know if it'll help," said Eden as she looked at her in misery. She looked down at her pajamas, and more tears fell.

"She might come back," Abby said as she tried to reassure her.

"No," said Eden as she looked at Abby sadly. "These are her pajamas," she sobbed. "She told me I could keep them." She leaned forward into Abby.

"Well, that's good, Eden," said Abby as she held her. "She wants you to be comfortable."

"No," said Eden as she sat up and shook her head. "We always argued about me taking her pajamas. I'd wear them, and she would always make me promise to give them back," she sobbed. "I'd tease her about them, and she would always act mad, but I knew she was playing. Today she just calmly said I could keep them," she said in misery, "like she doesn't need them or want them anymore," she sobbed, "like she won't be back for them."

"Eden, maybe you're reading too much into this," Abby said sensitively.

"Yeah," said Flynn trying to be supportive, "maybe she just wanted to let you know she didn't mind."

"No," Eden wiping her tears. "She's leaving with Greer. I—" she sobbed, "I saw the list. It was three pages long!"

"The list?" asked Jude confused.

"Three pages?" asked Abby in disbelief. "What the hell was on it?"

"I didn't read the whole list," said Eden and looked up determinedly. "I tore it up and threw it out the car window."

"You didn't!" squeaked Abby.

"I did," confirmed Eden.

"What'd she do?" asked Jude alarmed.

"Nothing," said Eden sadly.

"Nothing? I don't believe it! Was she mad?" demanded Abby.

"Of course, she was mad!" cried Eden. "It was her list!"

"I don't know if tearing up her list helped your cause, Eden," said Jude concerned.

"I told her it was no good because it didn't say she stopped loving me and I haven't stopped loving her," said Eden defiantly.

"Jesus, Eden, you're really pushing her," said Abby worried. "Do you think it was a good idea?"

"I don't know what else to do," Eden confessed. "I have to make her talk to me. I have to point out the flaws in her logic. The thing is," she took a shaky breath, "it's extremely difficult to do with her. She's made up her mind I don't need her and—" she sobbed, "she loves Greer."

"I know this sounds crazy, Eden, but..." Abby said timidly, "maybe we should call Greer and talk to her. Maybe she can talk to Rafe and help you."

"What?" Eden asked offended. "Why would I want to tell her anything? I know she wants Rafe to move to Baltimore with her, and Rafe will do it because she listens to her, and she says Greer helps her find answers. Greer is probably telling her I'm not the answer!" she said barely holding in her panic.

"I don't think Greer's the type of person who'd say those things," Abby tried to assure her.

"Why," asked Eden angrily, "because she sent Rafe back to me twice? What makes you so sure she'll do it again! Greer told me if Rafe came to her again, I'd never get her back. I'm not telling her anything!"

"She sent her back to you," Jude iterated, "twice?"

"It's what Rafe told me," said Eden as she nodded feeling her anxiety building from talking about Greer. "She thinks Greer has a 'three strikes you're out' policy. This will be my third strike!" she said in anguish then got up and stormed back into the house.

"They need help," said Abby at a loss about what to do. "We've got to figure out how to help them."

"Abby, we can talk to them, but it's up to them how this turns out," Jude said firmly. "I'll go talk to Rafe."

"Try to say more than one word an hour to her," said Abby wryly.

29

WAITING IN THE lobby of the Wilshire Hotel, Jude Atwood watched the elevator for Rafe Salvaggio to come down from her room. As Jude waited, she also kept an eye on all the women who walked by her. There weren't many who didn't look back to give her an admiring smile. She thought about her business and checking into the possibility of offering massage services at the hotel. Rafe came out of the elevator, and Jude gave her a small wave.

"Hey," said Jude. "Thanks for coming down."

"It's good to see you," said Rafe.

"Come on. Let's get out of here," said Jude and headed toward the door. "Want me to take you somewhere?" Jude asked as they walked out of the hotel and Rafe laughed softly. "What?"

"Nothing." Rafe smiled, but she didn't reveal those were the same words Rafe used to say to women when she picked them up in her father's car. She knew Jude came to see her because she understood her dilemma. Jude had gone through something similar with Chloe and ended up having to let her go. Rafe thought she would have to do the same with Eden. Rafe knew Jude understood the situation.

"Get in," said Jude as she opened her car door.

Rafe got in, and they made their way in silence down the street to the museum park. After parking the car, they got out and started walking through the park.

Jude was holding a package under her arm. "I brought the beer," she said and indicated the package under her arm. They sat on a bench, and Jude opened the package she had been carrying and pulled out two cold beers. Handing one to Rafe, she offered, "Beer?" She knew it was risky to be drinking in public, but she figured it was worth the risk.

"Sound's nice, thanks," said Rafe as she took a beer and twisted the cap. They both sat for a while in silence taking a drink occasionally.

"Things are fucked," Jude said finally. She watched Rafe as she sat in silence wondering if she forgot she had a beer in her hand.

"Yeah," Rafe finally answered then took another sip of beer.

After a while, Jude saw Rafe's beer bottle was empty and handed her another. "She loves you," said Jude softly.

Rafe took the beer offered and looked at Jude then looked in the distance for a while. "Don't," she told her softly. Jude should know leaving was the best thing to do.

Jude nodded as she finished her second beer and then placed the empty in the sack. "Scared?" she asked and took out a third beer.

Rafe slowly peeled the label off her bottle and dropped the shreds on the ground. "No," she answered.

After a while, Jude took Rafe's empty bottle and handed her the last beer. "What then?" she asked and took a drink of her own.

Rafe took a long draw of her beer then looked out across the park and sighed. "Sad," she answered and squeezed the glass bottle tight feeling its coldness in her hands.

Jude took a drink of her beer then looked down at the bottle. "Love sucks," she said.

Rafe closed her eyes and sighed. "Like a vampire," she said and took a swig.

Jude finished her beer and waited for Rafe to finish hers. She put the empties in the sack and stood up. "Let's go. I have a hot date with a possible vampire in a while," she said with a wink.

They rode in silence back to the hotel where Rafe went inside, and Jude headed out into the night.

30

ABBY VAN FALKOV refilled Eden Kingsley's wine glass and handed it to her. She knew Eden was probably not supposed to be drinking while on her pain medication, but she didn't think a little would hurt. It was only her second glass, but combined with the medication, it was enough to help her relax and make her more talkative. Abby figured Eden needed to relax after what happened today with Rafe. Flynn had watched over her most of the day and now Jude was out somewhere sitting in silence with Rafe so Abby figured it was her turn to stay with Eden. Since Eden hadn't been doing well all day, they called Letty and arranged for Bronte to stay the night with her.

Sitting down in her chair, Abby looked at Eden, who was lying back on the couch holding her wine glass. Over the years, Eden had confided a lot in Abby, and now she knew quite a bit about her life. So much so, sometimes Abby had a hard time remembering she had known Rafe longer and she was her friend first. She guessed it was why she always felt protective of Eden—besides the fact that she was so much younger than Rafe and the youngest of their group when Rafe first brought her around. Now Flynn, Erica, and Stacey were the youngest in their group.

Rafe hardly ever confided in her, but being a confidant was not what made Abby her friend. She had dated Rafe for about three months. After Rafe broke up with her, Abby had no intention of remaining friends. But Rafe answered all her calls and met her to talk when she was heartbroken and upset. She also helped her with interviews for her job at the time. Rafe always made it clear they were friends. Eventually, Abby accepted their new relationship. She wondered if Eden would have to do the same now.

Rafe had done all kinds of things for Eden after she had left that Abby didn't understand. Things like sending her herbs from the garden, inviting her to the house to swim, including her in the invitations to all the parties they had. She even went to the birthday party that Eden and Jake wanted to have in Canada. Maybe everything Rafe was doing for Eden was the same thing Rafe had done for her. Maybe Rafe was trying to save something of their relationship, save the friendship part. Abby had no idea if Rafe and Eden were ever really just friends.

She looked up at the sound of Eden's voice. It seemed like Eden couldn't stop talking about Rafe and went from anger to sadness to hopefulness. "What were you saying," asked Abby. "Sorry, I was off in my own world there."

"It's okay," said Eden with a small, sad smile. "I was just saying Rafe held me today. It felt good to feel her arms around me again."

"It's great she seems to be coming around," said Abby as she nodded, trying to be positive.

"It's another thing I love about her," said Eden softly.

"What, her holding you?" asked Abby wondering if Eden was going to start another list of things she loved about Rafe. Apparently, she thought that saying good things about Rafe would make everyone forget about all the bad things listed in the paper.

"Yeah, her arms around me." Eden nodded and sipped her wine. "She has incredible hands too." She gave a small laugh. "But you know about those, don't you." She got quiet again, and a tear left her eye. "Greer and the others do, too."

"Don't think about those girls," said Abby seeing her swing back into sadness. "She told you she hasn't slept with Greer."

"I know," said Eden and wiped her eyes then took another sip of wine. "I need her back," she said and looked at Abby. "I keep thinking about what my life was like without her and," she sniffed, "I can't live without her again."

"She'll come back," Abby assured her, "just give her time." She knew Rafe couldn't stay away forever. She loved Bronte and Eden so she would be around in some capacity.

Eden sat up slowly and downed the last of her wine. She stood up and unsteadily walked out of the living room.

"Where are you going?" asked Abby and followed her since she was clearly unsteady from the wine and medication mixture.

"In here," she said as she walked down the hallway and opened the door to Rafe's room. She went inside and looked around the room. It was just like she remembered it. "She doesn't make love to me in here anymore," she slurred softly.

"What?" Abby said not catching her words. "We probably shouldn't be in here."

Eden walked to Rafe's closet, opening it and then went inside. "Look at all the room in here." She laughed as she opened empty drawers. "When I first moved in, she downsized her wardrobe so I could have half the closet. I guess she never went shopping to fill it back up."

"Or maybe she thought you'd need the space again," said Abby uncomfortable being in Rafe's room.

"Do you really think so?" asked Eden her face filled with hope again. She touched Rafe's clothes and picked up one of her t-shirts. "I wish she were here," she said and smelled the shirt. It smelled just like Rafe.

"Come on, Eden," said Abby coaxingly. "We shouldn't be in here."

Eden followed Abby out of the closet still holding Rafe's t-shirt but wasn't ready to leave. She sat down on the bed remembering when she used to sleep in the comfortable bed with Rafe every night. She looked at the photo on the nightstand. It was the picture Rafe took of her and Bronte in the park. She picked it up and looked at it. "Look at this," she said to Abby. "She has our picture. She's really good at photography." She sat the photo down and eased herself carefully onto the bed. She smelled Rafe's t-shirt again. "You know, you still haven't told me all the stuff about Rafe you keep hinting about. Her wildling ways," she said in a mysterious voice then laughed softly, wishing Rafe was running her hands over her and kissing her.

"Yeah, I don't know if this is the time," said Abby. She knew Rafe didn't want her to tell Eden her opinions about how Rafe was before Eden came along.

Oh, man," Eden groaned with disappointment then smiled. "I'll tell you something about her, and then you can tell me something." Before Abby could speak, she continued. "She likes it when I tell her I want her to fuck me," she confessed and grinned. "She really likes it when I say I want to fuck her." She laughed and brought the t-shirt to her face inhaling Rafe's scent. She pushed the shirt down her body wishing it was Rafe. "She thinks she's corrupting me, but I kind of like saying those things to her." She raised her eyebrows as she looked at Abby. "Now it's your turn."

Abby wasn't sure what to say since she knew Eden wasn't one hundred percent in her right mind because of the meds and wine. It was surprising to hear Eden say 'fuck' because she so rarely cussed, but not surprising Rafe and Eden talked dirty to each other. People do all kinds of things behind closed doors. What Abby was sure about was Rafe would not like her personal business discussed. She and Eden talked about a lot of things, but not about what happened in Eden and Rafe's bedroom.

"Uhmm," Abby started as she tried to buy herself more time to think. "Rafe just seemed to have a lot of fun back then," said Abby. She knew it sounded lame.

"Oh, yeah?" Eden smiled as her eyes shone from the meds and alcohol high she was on. "Did you know she can fuck me and keep me wet all night long? No one else I know could come close to what she can do," she revealed and laughed softly. "Not even the men I slept with could make me come like Rafe can." She looked up at Abby and smiled. "Where's the strap-on you found?" she asked and tried to sit up. "I'll compare it to Jake like you thought I was doing." She laughed at the thought. "But I've got to tell you," she giggled, "Rafe's hands are better than what he has between his legs." She couldn't help laughing at her own words. "Honestly, if Rafe had a dick, I would probably be dead because my brain would explode!" She laughed again and felt a tingle run through her at the thought of what Rafe could do to her. "Hers would probably be double jointed like her hands," she said and grinned. "Has she shown you how flexible her hands are? She can bend her fingers all the way back." Eden tried to bend her own back to show Abby.

"Uh..." was all Abby could get out as she tried to think of a way out of the situation, and the conversation.

"She can twist her fingers," she said trying to twist her own together, "kind of like this, I think, but she can still bend hers. I think she can because they're so long. Oh, my god, it feels good, especially when she has them deep inside me." She breathed in Rafe's scent again and smiled. "Did she do it to you?"

"Uhm, no," said Abby and swallowed nervously.

"Magical, flexible fingers," Eden said in a singsong voice then laughed.

"I think we should probably go back into the other room," she suggested and tried to help Eden gently off the bed.

"But you haven't told me anything yet," Eden complained as Abby pulled her to her feet. "Whoa," she said and leaned heavily on Abby as the room spun in her vision. Her body began to shake, and tears sprang from her eyes. "Will you call Rafe and tell her I need her to come home?" she asked as her head rested on Abby's shoulder. "I love her," she sobbed. She lifted her head and looked at Abby with red-rimmed eyes. "I know what you're thinking. But I'm not saying it because of the sex," she insisted. "I really, really love her, and I think I might die if she goes with Greer," Eden cried as Abby held her up and pain coursed through Eden's heart and body.

"Oh, Eden." Abby sighed sympathetically. "Come on. Let's get you to your room." She led a tearful Eden out of Rafe's room and into her own room. Carefully, she helped Eden sit on the bed on her side. "Just try to get some sleep now."

Eden caught Abby's arm and looked up at her. "Please," she whispered shakily, "help me. I hurt so much. I think I'm going to die."

"You'll be fine," said Abby softly pulling her arm from Eden's wet tear-covered hand and running her other hand gently over Eden's head. She knew it wasn't Eden's injuries causing her pain right now because she was well medicated, probably over medicated.

"I need Rafe," Eden croaked out her voice strained because of the injury to her neck. "Tell her I need her to come home," she begged. "I love her," she said as tears flooded her eyes. "I know everything is my fault because I was so stupid. I'm sorry, I'm sorry. I'll do anything," she said and looked at Abby with desperation. "Tell her not to leave me, please! Tell her not to go with her," she pleaded. "I can't," she gasped for air, "I can't breathe." Eden struggled to take in air.

"Shit, Eden!" Abby cried out and sat her up as Eden gasped. "Calm down. It's okay," she said frantically. "Look at me," she said. Eden looked at her with wide eyes as she struggled to take a breath. "Fuck," she hissed and pulled open Eden's nightstand drawer and dug through it quickly until she found an inhaler. "I hope this has something in it," she said as she shook it then put it to Eden's lips.

Eden wheezed in a shot of the medication and coughed when she finally let out her breath. She trembled weakly and sobbed.

"Jesus Christ, Eden! You scared the shit out of me," Abby said trying to calm herself.

"I'm sorry," Eden whimpered and lay back down trying to breathe deeper.

"You need to calm down and stop thinking about those things, or it will give you another anxiety attack," Abby said with frustration listening to her wheeze. "You can't take any more medication right now!"

Eden burst into tears again because of Abby's angry outburst toward her. It felt like more pain piled on top of all the other bad things happening to her. "I can't help it," she sobbed and wheezed painfully. "I can't stop thinking about her. I love her, and she'll hardly even talk to me now."

Abby took a calming breath and looked at the ceiling then back down at Eden. "Okay," she said softly, "I know. I'm sorry I yelled at you." She sat down on the bed next to her to try to comfort her. "I'll help you, okay?" She watched as Eden nodded. "Just try to rest."

"I need her to hold me again," Eden whispered. "I can't be without her." She looked at Abby and took her hand. "I love her. I've always loved her." She sobbed. "I was just lost for a while."

Abby leaned down and hugged her. "I know," she said hoping she really could help her, and help Rafe too.

31

LATE SATURDAY MORNING, Eden Kingsley was awake but showing signs of the tormented night. One she had spent thinking and dreaming about Rafe. She was feeling awful last night, and Abby had stayed late keeping her company. As she lay in bed, she put her hand to her head remembering the things she said to Abby after drinking her wine. Groaning, she felt embarrassed and dreaded facing Abby when she came back over. Eden was glad Letty agreed to keep Bronte so she could sleep in and rest, but rest would not come. Too many thoughts were filling her head. She couldn't relax, and the pain from her injuries had come back.

She got out of bed and made her way to the bathroom to take her meds. After taking them, she climbed back into bed and tried to go back to sleep. Thinking about Rafe, the things she said, the things she did, were making her angry, scared, and hopeless. The worst part was she did not even know if anything she said had any influence on Rafe.

Fighting for someone's love, for Rafe's love, for their love, was so hard when it was the first battle she ever had to fight. All the times she came back to Rafe, it seemed like she only had to ask. This time, she was being told no, and her world was falling apart again. Her mind was frantic. Her anxiety was boiling over inside her, and her tremors of worry and grief on top of her physical pain were making it hard to even move.

Sleep was not coming so she slowly sat up in bed and propped the pillows so she could sit against the headboard. She took her phone from the nightstand with the thought she would call or text Rafe, or maybe send another email even though she knew it might be useless. She scrolled through the phone and saw Rafe's Messenger was active. She tapped on her name, and the message screen opened.

EK: Rafe, Come over, please.

RS: No, I'm busy now.

EK: Are you with Greer?

RS: No, why?

EK: We need to talk.

RS: We did.

EK: There's more to say.

RS: Don't do this.

EK: Come over.

RS: No.

EK: I need you.

RS: No.

EK: RAFE!

EK: We still have things to talk about.

RS: No.

EK: Bring my car back.

RS: No, you shouldn't be driving.

EK: I won't. Bring it back.

RS: No, I'm busy.

EK: I'm coming to you.

RS: I have your keys and your car.

EK: I'll call a cab.

RS: I won't be there.

EK: Where are you?

RS: Out.

EK: Tell me where you are!

RS: No, go rest.

EK: I don't want to rest. I want to talk to you.

RS: No.

"Rafe! Gad blast it!" Eden yelled at the phone, frustrated. "You better come over!"

The doorbell rang. Eden made her way to the door slowly. "Hi," she said as she peeked out.

"Hi, I have a delivery for Rafe Salvaggio. Can you sign?" asked the deliveryman.

"Sure," said Eden as she opened the door further. "What is it?"

"Sign here," said the deliveryman as he handed Eden the electronic clipboard and stylus. He looked at the box label. "It looks like its photography stuff," he said helpfully.

"Can you set it inside?" Eden asked after she signed and handed the clipboard back to him.

"Sure." The deliveryman smiled and put the box inside the door. "Have a nice day," he said as he made his way down the stairs.

"Thank you," said Eden and closed the door. She looked at the box label then sat on the floor in front of the door and began typing on her phone to Rafe again.

EK: Studio Express. 1 box.

RS: What?

EK: Studio Express Photography Supplies

RS: My equip.

EK: I guess.

RS: Leave it by the door.

EK: Are you coming to get it?

RS: Later maybe.

EK: No. You have to come and get it now.

RS: I'll get it later.

"You're coming over here today, dang it!" Eden argued out loud determinedly. She typed into her phone again.

EK: If you're not here in 30 min., I'm throwing the box in the pool!

RS: What? Are you crazy!

EK: It's going in the pool!

RS: It's expensive equip!

EK: The pool!

RS: Damn it, Eden! What the hell is wrong with you?

EK: 29 Min. POOL!

RS: Don't do it!

EK: I'm doing it. I want you over here now!

RS: FUCK! FUCK! FUCK! You're pissing me off!

EK: Good! I'm already pissed! Get over here! 28 min!

RS: HAS LOGGED OFF

"You better be on your way," Eden croaked with a frown. She looked at her phone and dialed again. "Flynn? Can you come over for a sec? Thanks."

Eden had moved into the living room when Flynn showed up at the front door. "Come in," she told him. "It's unlocked."

"Are you okay?" asked Flynn worried when he found her.

"Yes," Eden confirmed. "Can you take the box by the door to your house?" she asked as tried to stand.

"Sure, I guess," Flynn agreed, confused. "What is it?"

"It's something for Rafe," Eden replied shortly. "I'll send her over to get it after we've talked. Hurry, she should be here soon."

"Okay," Flynn shrugged. "Why can't she just pick it up here?"

"Because," she looked at him intently, "I'm holding it hostage." She looked at the clock on her phone. "She has 25 minutes."

32

BY FOCUSING ON making lunch, Eden Kingsley was able to manage her anxiety while waiting for Rafe. After Flynn took the box, Eden went back into her bedroom to get dressed and ready to confront the anger she knew she had caused in Rafe. Hoping it would help, she made salads with all the things she knew Rafe liked in them. Just in case Rafe wouldn't eat, Eden made a pitcher of iced tea and a pot of coffee too she hoped would entice Rafe to stay so they could talk. Then she set the table on the patio, making sure everything was perfect, and then turned on some soft music. She would do everything in her power to make Rafe stay and talk. Even though she had to move slowly, everything was finally ready, and she looked at the time on her phone. Rafe had five more minutes.

Eden sat down to rest and try to calm the anxiety and the desperation she was feeling. She knew from their conversation yesterday Rafe was not going to make it easy for her. She heard a car door slam and went to the door to confirm it was Rafe. She wiped her nervous hands on her hips as the door swung open and Rafe walked inside.

Rafe stopped just inside the door and glared at Eden. "Where's my stuff?" she demanded brusquely.

"I'll tell you after we talk," said Eden trying to hide her shaking hands.

"We talked, Eden," Rafe reminded her, "and I don't think there's anything more to say."

"Rafe, you have to talk to me," argued Eden anxiously. "I've made us lunch. Go out and sit down," she instructed firmly and walked into the kitchen to get the salad and drinks.

Rafe immediately started going to every room and closet looking for her box of photography supplies but couldn't find the box. "Fuck!" she cursed in frustration and followed Eden to the patio. "I don't want lunch. I just want to get my stuff and go."

"Well, too bad!" she retorted angrily as she sat the salads on the table. "I told you we need to talk, and if you want your precious box, you'll sit down, have lunch, and talk to me," she threatened her.

Rafe took a deep breath and glared at Eden, "Fine!" she relented and sat down then picked up her fork and angrily stabbed her salad.

Eden sat down relieved Rafe had stayed. Now she just hoped she would talk. She started eating her salad and decided to wait until Rafe calmed down. They ate in silence for a while then Eden decided it was time for her to fight for Rafe again.

"Rafe," she started hesitantly. "I'm sorry. I thought I was doing the right thing. I'm sorry for everything. I love you, and I need you to come home," she implored shakily.

Rafe looked up at Eden and her bruised face. "Eden, are you going to tell me anything new, anything I haven't already talked to you about, anything you haven't already said?" she asked calmly. "Or are you just going to repeat yourself?"

"I keep repeating myself because I don't think you're really hearing me," Eden retorted angrily. "I think you're cutting me off again and only hearing what you want to hear."

"I've heard everything you've said and every excuse you gave. I heard all your lies and all your faulty logic. I've heard about every fault you think I have," she said evenly, "the entire fucking state of California has heard about them." She looked at Eden, holding in her anger. "Based on everything you said, I think," she paused, "no, I *know* you would be better off without me," she declared and took a drink of her iced tea to cool herself.

"Rafe, I'm not better off without you! The only time I get anything right is with you," Eden insisted. "I love you."

Rafe shook her head as she chewed her food and swallowed. "No, like I said, you've outgrown me," she reminded her. "You don't need me for anything anymore. I don't think you even really want me. Don't lie to yourself. You just need to go have feelings for someone else."

Eden looked at Rafe stricken, and her hands began to shake with anxiety again, "What about Bronte?" she asked softly.

"I'll do whatever you want me to do," said Rafe with a shrug.

"What does that mean?" asked Eden frustrated Rafe still didn't believe she wanted the adoption.

"Eden," sighed Rafe, "I'm just taking whatever crumbs you'll give me right now."

"She's your daughter too!" Eden reminded her. "You can't just walk away from her."

"I'd never just walk away, Eden," she asserted as she shook her head then looked at her hard. "But I can be pushed away."

"I'm not pushing you away!" Eden insisted. "I told you I want you!"

"Don't worry. I'll make sure you have the security you want for Bronte," she promised calmly.

"Rafe!" Eden fought her anger. "I want you to be Bronte's parent! I always wanted it! That was Jake's lie!"

"I see," said Rafe and took a sip of her tea. "It was all his idea I miss almost the entire first year of her life. You had nothing to do with any of those decisions. Maybe he twisted your arm."

"I'm sorry," she said fighting back her tears. "I know it was a mistake. Bronte loves you so much, and I want you to stay in her life."

"Like I said, I'm not convinced you really do want me in your life, so it's up to you."

"You still believe the things he said!" she cried as tears sprang from her eyes, and she quickly wiped them away.

"Only the things you confirmed," said Rafe sadly.

"But he twisted everything!"

"He twisted everything you said about how your fears were caused by my infidelity?" scoffed Rafe. "He twisted they were the reason you left me? Is all his twisting why you fucked him in my room?"

"You're still not over that?" she snapped in frustration.

"You're still not over Lauren?" Rafe threw back at her and raised her eyebrow waiting for her answer.

Eden took a breath to calm herself. "Okay, I deserved that," she said weakly. "I'm sorry. I just want you to believe me when I tell you I love you."

"I'm not sure if you really know who you love. I have no fucking idea when you will leave me again or even who you might leave me for."

"Rafe, please, I'm not going to leave you for—" she forced her tears back, "for anyone."

"You can't know for sure," said Rafe sadly. "Next week, you may have some feelings for some random stranger, and I don't want to go through this again."

"I'm not going to have feelings for random strangers, Rafe!" Eden maintained angrily. "I know now if I have feelings or anxieties I can't handle, I need to talk to someone. And I know I only want to have feelings for you!"

Rafe shook her head and looked at her sadly. "If you hadn't got the information on Jake you'd probably still be with him, and I know for sure, if you were, the adoption wouldn't go through."

Eden looked at Rafe stunned. "No," she choked out, "No, Rafe. It's not true. I was already having doubts about him, and I already tried to break off the engagement once before I got the information. He was pressuring me to move away and to stop the adoption, and it wasn't what I wanted. I wanted you to be Bronte's parent no matter what our relationship was."

Rafe just looked at her sadly. "Well, you shouldn't want to have a relationship with me. You accused me of pressuring you all the time too."

"It's not the same, Rafe! I only want to be with you," she professed desperately. "I only have feelings for you. I only love you!"

"You can barely know what you feel for anyone," Rafe sighed. "For all I know, your latent feelings for men will... what was it you said, overwhelm you? Yeah, that was it. They will overwhelm you again and, like you said, you just can't help having feelings."

"What are you talking about, Rafe? Latent feelings? I was under pressure and trying to manage everything without you. You were gone, and I was alone! You swept in and out while I dealt with your anger when the inseminations didn't work, and on top of you being gone, I was trying to deal with my own failure to conceive and everything else."

"Oh, right. It was entirely my fault you made the choices you made," Rafe agreed calmly. "I guess I just forgot there for a second. But thank you for reminding me," she said and took another bite of her salad.

"Dang it, Rafe! That's not what I said! Stop twisting my words!"

"Eden," Rafe laughed cynically, "I don't have to twist your words," she said calmly. "There's no reason to twist them. You had feelings for men, and you got your cyber fuck. Which I guess you don't consider cheating because I never got an apology for your fuck up! Then you put yourself and Bronte in danger by leaving my house in the dark of night with a man you barely knew. Then you kept information from me, and it almost cost you your life. Did I twist anything yet?"

"Rafe, I am sorry, I'm sorry for everything! There are so many things I've done to you!" She cried because the conversation and her emotions were spiraling out of control. "You remember everything. Why did you even let me come back and move into your house again?"

"I don't know." Rafe and leaned back in her chair wanting to leave.

"You do know! I know you do!"

"I thought I could make it work," said Rafe forcing herself to sound indifferent, "but I was wrong."

Eden looked at Rafe and knew she was getting nowhere. "We have to stop making each other angry," she said softly.

Rafe threw her napkin on the table and took the last sip of her tea. "I'm finished now."

"Rafe, please," Eden pleaded.

"I've talked, I've eaten, so now tell me where my box is so I can go," she said flatly.

"No, I'm not finished talking," she insisted. She couldn't let her leave yet. "Help me take everything inside," she requested then started cleaning dishes off the table. "Come on."

Rafe glared at her as she walked away. It was clear she was in pain as she walked. "Fine!" she growled and started helping her move everything from the table inside.

"Do you want coffee or anything while we talk?" asked Eden.

"How about scotch," Rafe quipped sullenly.

"No," she said as shook her head. "No scotch. Coffee or tea. I want you sober."

"Believe me I won't be drunk," Rafe scoffed. "I want to be able to drive away. I'll get myself a scotch."

Eden fought to hold in her anger. "I'll get the coffee."

Rafe poured herself a scotch then sat on the couch. She recognized the soft tune *Late at Night* from Kristie Lee coming from the speakers but ignored the sultry love song. "I hope you don't have too much more," she called out and took a sip of her calming drink.

"I have a lot more to say," Eden stressed as she brought out the pot of coffee and two cups. She sat down and poured herself a coffee.

"Well, I have to admit it's a big change," chided Rafe sarcastically. "Last week, you couldn't tell me anything, and now you won't shut up."

"You're trying to make me angry, aren't you?" Eden asked upset as she sat her cup down on the saucer.

"No, just telling the truth."

"Let's talk about truth," suggested Eden.

"Are you sure you're ready?" Rafe scowled as she took another drink.

"Are you?" Eden asked angrily.

Rafe laughed harshly. "It's what I've been asking you for."

Eden closed her eyes and took a calming breath. She had to fight for her, not against her, she reminded herself. "Rafe," she sighed, "I want to thank you for holding me yesterday. I really needed it, your touch. I've missed it. It made me feel so much better."

Rafe wasn't sure what to say at the sudden subject change, so she just looked down at her drink as Eden continued.

"I always feel better when you're holding me," she said quietly as she touched Rafe's arm. "I think it's the connection we have, the connection we both feel," she said softly as she reached out and played with a lock of Rafe's dark hair. "Will you hold me now?"

Rafe took a drink but didn't answer her.

Eden took Rafe's drink from her and sat it on the table as Rafe frowned at her. She pulled Rafe's hand to herself and kissed it then looked into Rafe's eyes. "Please hold me," she requested softly and put her head on Rafe's shoulder, nuzzling her neck as she held her hand and laced their fingers together. She stroked Rafe's palm and caressed her fingers. "I love this, being close to you." She sighed and brought Rafe's hand to her lips to kiss her fingers then rubbed Rafe's hand against her face. "I love your touch."

"Eden, what are you doing," Rafe groaned as Eden touched her softly and moved closer.

Eden climbed up on the couch and straddled Rafe. She took her face in her hands and kissed her forehead then looked into her eyes. "I love you," she whispered.

Rafe closed her eyes, thinking Eden really had gone crazy. She didn't respond to her kisses as Eden was now moving down her face with them. She could smell the scent her soft perfume and her shampoo as her kisses made their way to her lips. She forced herself to stay calm and not respond to what Eden was doing to her, and a tear escaped her eye. *Why did she have to do this*, she thought. *Why did she have to feel so good against me and smell so good?*

"I missed you," whispered Eden as she kissed Rafe's tear away then kissed the corners of her mouth and ran her hands down her arms. She forced all of the intent in her body toward Rafe to make her see she loved her with everything inside her heart and soul. She knew Rafe was fighting, but she was fighting too. She had to show her they belonged together. "I'm the one who really loves you," she breathed, using Rafe's words, and kissed her on her lips gently. *"Sei la mia anima gemella[1]*," she whispered. They were the same words Rafe had told her so many times in the past.

Hearing Eden say those familiar words, and feeling their lips touch, caused the searing desire Rafe had for Eden to shoot through her. She fought her body's attempt to chase after her kiss and taste her. She tried to turn her head, but Eden took her face in her hands and kissed her again gently forcing her tongue into her mouth so she could taste her. She had to have more of her. Her resolve broke, and she opened her mouth and met Eden's kisses with her own.

The thrill of triumph flashed through Eden as she felt Rafe give into her and return her kisses. Hope filled her, and her heart beat faster. "We can do this," she breathed into Rafe's mouth as they kissed. "We belong together." She ran her hands over Rafe feeling her strong arms and shoulders and then her breasts under her hands. "I want to take care of you. You have to stay with me," she said and pulled Rafe's hands up and put them around herself. "Will you touch me now?"

Rafe's senses were reeling as Eden's lips, breath and hands moved against her. Eden was the person she had always needed, and her body was defying her doubtful mind. She felt Eden pull her hands up to wrap them around her waist. Feeling Eden's body was breaking her again. She opened her eyes, looked into Eden's face, and saw the openness of her emotions.

---

[1] You are my soul mate.

"Tell me you love me," breathed Eden, repeating Rafe's words again. "I love your touch," she said as she moved against Rafe feeling her body heat with desire.

Rafe saw the determined invitation Eden was offering her, and her desire pushed the waring thoughts in her mind away. She brought her hands up from Eden's hips and gripped her shirt. She looked intently into her eyes as she dragged it up her body and over her head then tossed it aside. She ran her hand over her body feeling the familiar tingle of her silky skin against her palm.

She heard Eden gasp unexpectedly and then felt her body as it flinched in pain. Rafe's mind immediately shut down the building desire. She automatically pulled away from Eden as her mind suddenly cleared. She could see Eden without the cloud of passion created by her, and a searing pain went through Rafe's head as she looked at Eden.

"It's okay, babe," said Eden as she saw the shock and wide-eyed look of concern on Rafe's face. She kissed Rafe again.

Rafe just looked at her and took in Eden's body and the bruises covering her. She reached out and ran the tips of her fingers over the bruises on her shoulder and neck.

This is what's real, she thought. *This is the truth*, she realized as she felt a firm pressure against her chest. She pushed Eden back gently and pulled herself away. "I can't do this," she said shakily.

"We can do this," Eden assured her as she tried to kiss her, but Rafe pulled away again. "Please, Rafe, please don't tear us apart," she whispered. "We can fix this."

"No," she said and gently pushed her back. She looked into Eden's eyes and could feel the pain flair in her head almost blinding her for a moment. "You have to stop. This isn't right. You have to understand," Rafe breathed out in a panic as the pain in her head increased, and she felt a stabbing pain press into her chest.

"No, I don't understand," said Eden desperate to get back to the place they were, the place where Rafe wanted her and needed her. "I want you, and I can see and feel how much you want and need me," she said and pushed forward to kiss Rafe again.

"Eden. Stop! Your dignity and self-respect mean more to me than photography equipment," said Rafe as panic ran through her and the pressure on her chest increased. She took Eden by her arms then lifted her gently and moved her off her legs and onto the couch. Once she was out from under Eden, Rafe stood up to give herself more distance. She took in the sight of Eden's damaged body again then quickly looked away.

"We can't do this!"

"Why?" Eden asked hurt Rafe was rejecting her again.

Rafe just looked at her again, placed her hand on her head and started walking to the door.

"Rafe!" Eden called and rushed after her. "Where are you going?" she demanded. "Are you going back to Greer?" She burst into tears at the thought.

Rafe turned and looked at Eden and could see she was talking, but she couldn't hear anything she was saying. "I can't," she said shakily wondering if she might be having a heart attack because her chest hurt so badly. She looked into Eden's eyes as they suddenly came into sharp focus. She licked her lips because they had gone dry. "Goodbye, you need to find someone else," she said softly—at least it seemed soft because she could barely hear her own words—and then walked out of the house.

"Rafe!" screamed Eden as she slipped her shirt back on and followed her out the door. "Rafe, stop!" she shouted through her tears. "Please! Come back, I'm sorry!" she cried and gasped in pain as she moved wrong. She made her way painfully down the porch and saw Rafe was already getting into her car. "Rafe!" she yelled as she stumbled toward Rafe's car. "No! Rafe! Come back!" she screamed as Rafe pulled out of the driveway and sped away. Eden fell to the ground in misery and pain calling and crying for Rafe.

Hearing Eden's screams, Jude came running out of the house and saw Eden on the ground crying for Rafe as Rafe's car sped down the street.

"Oh, shit." She sighed and rushed over to her.

Jude helped Eden back into the house and got her settled back into her bedroom. She called Abby to let her know Rafe had been there to see Eden and things had not gone well. Eden wouldn't talk about it, and she wasn't sure where Rafe had gone. After hanging up with Abby, she went to the kitchen and grabbed a beer then sat in the living room to wait for her to show up. She wished she knew how to use all the remotes Rafe had for her television and sound system so she could go upstairs and watch TV.

33

AFTER DRIVING AWAY and leaving Eden Kingsley behind, Rafe Salvaggio was able to calm her mind, and the pain in her chest began to ease. She had made her way to the private garage where she kept her father's car. *My car now*, she remembered. When it was brought down, she got in and took her father's old driving cap out of the glove compartment. She had brought it back with her from New York and liked to wear it for him now whenever she drove his car. She put the cap on then pulled out of the garage and headed down to the coast highway. Her head hurt, and she had to think. Sometimes, taking out the Maserati and opening it up helped.

Rafe handled the Maserati with the ease of familiarity and experience as she made her way down the highway. She took the last curve a little too fast but recovered and opened up along the straightaway picking up her speed.

Her mind wandered back to Eden in the hospital. Seeing her torn hands along with her bruised and blackened face and body, all wrapped in bandages, and being so, so still.

Rafe was still unsure if Eden had more secrets or if she was telling lies to get what she wanted—or until she found something better. Those possibilities and everything else she found out Eden had been doing made her furious and question everything. She couldn't see how she could trust her now or how they could ever reconcile after all the damage done to their relationship.

Rafe couldn't get the things Jake said about Eden out of her mind. She knew he was dead wrong about everything else he had talked about, but what if he was right about Eden. He lived with her for almost a year, and Eden had told him all those things she could never say to her.

Rafe shifted gears to take another sharp turn. Her mind brought her back to when she found out Jake was there, in the same hospital as Eden, and on the same floor.

Rafe had made her way into room 224, Jakes room. She was met by the sight and sound of the machines, tubes, and wires coming from the prone body lying motionless. She stood over him and waited until his eyes slowly opened.

"You're lucky to be alive," Rafe had said as Jake just looked at her. "If you go near my family again, the outcome won't be so lucky."

"Threats," croaked Jake with an easy smile for her. The meds they gave him took away the pain his injuries caused him. His throat was dry, and he was light-headed a bit, but not enough to cause him problems.

"Promise," said Rafe menacingly. "I know all about your group and your lies now. I know you were lying about Eden, and you were the one behind everything,"

Jake gave a slight laugh. "Rafe, I didn't have to lie much. Most of the things I told you she had said, and the things she told me, we put in the article."

"Just twisted," she said calmly.

"No." Jake sighed and cleared his dry throat. "I think everything was fairly verbatim. Eden really opened up to me.

She needed me, and I was there for her emotionally and physically when you couldn't be bothered. I was her confidant and secret keeper. She said she was never able to talk to you like she did with me."

Rafe clenched her fists but gave no other outward sign his words about Eden confiding her secrets added to the fury she already felt. However, it did add proof Eden didn't trust her or even need her anymore.

Sensing Rafe wasn't going to be easily goaded, Jake continued his efforts. "She should have never left me," he said softly. "But I suppose she'll eventually find another man."

Rafe saw the smug look on his face and wanted to reach out and punch it off him. "She doesn't need a man," she seethed.

"You dyke women are all the same." He wheezed as he tried to laugh. "You think you're better because you don't need a man, but then suddenly, you start having feelings just like every other woman. Then you like to say, 'well, she wasn't really gay' or 'she must be bi-sexual' or some other excuse when one of you goes back to men." He shook his head and tried to moisten his dry mouth. "Sometimes you even hate them and ostracize them so they can't go back into the fold, or at least, make them feel like they can't."

"What the fuck are you talking about? No one ostracized or did anything similar to Eden," Rafe said with a low growl.

"Are you kidding me?" He barked out a laugh. "Oh, right, you just abandoned her. It was your friends who did the rest, especially your nut job friend, Abby. I can't count how many times I found Eden at home crying and miserable because of the things the spiteful woman said to her." He worked to moisten his throat then continued. "She would work up the nerve to invite them over, and they would just blow her off. You dykes do more to leave women helpless and vulnerable than men do," he said shaking his head in sincere sadness.

"I don't know where you get your information, but it's unequivocally wrong," said Rafe tersely. "I did not abandon Eden. She knew right where I was. As for Abby and the others, it seems to me they've worked through their issues." She leaned over him slightly. "Just because your organization has made a study of creating victims out of gay women does not mean you have defined them as a whole. The obviously insufficient and bias information you seem to think you have about us proves the complete disregard for—"

"No," interrupted Jake shaking his head at her attempt to argue, "Rafe, I know a lot more than you think. You live a very sheltered life inside the bubble of your small community. Did you know there are large groups of gay women out there who get worked up about something and isolate themselves then end up abandoning other women at the same time?" He looked at Rafe's beautiful face showing her doubt of his words. "It's true. All the while they think they're making a statement, or are going to better their situation, but they're wrong. They call themselves separatists, but really, they're of the same mentality as preppers. They just want to save themselves and fuck everyone else," he said wanting to impress upon her he knew the truth of what was really happening in the world. "They're delusional and a tool of evil in the world."

"What?" Rafe laughed at the ridiculousness. "So, preppers and lesbian separatists are evil. There's a new one," she scoffed. This was beyond crazy to her.

"Absolutely," said Jake confidently. "They're both defying God. One in their choice of sexuality and in abandoning their own sex based on their carnal needs. The others, preppers, by attempting to defy God in his last days of judgment and thinking it is His will they survive in a world He has chosen to destroy. But at least the preppers have the possibility, when there's an earthly war, God will want someone to survive. Those women are just basing things on how they think they feel." He looked up at Rafe with a smirk. "It's why we must make sure righteous men are in charge because women have too many feelings and emotions. They have to face the fact they need righteous men to guide them. And righteous men need righteous women to obey them and raise children in the proper righteous environment. It's the way God intended things."

It was unbelievable to him Rafe couldn't see the Lord's truth. But she was part of the darkness destroying this nation and the world, so he had to try to make her see the truth. It was part of his new Mission to bring others to the light. If he recruited her, it would be a coup. She had a lot of money and influence. Then he could work with her and not against her. If she worked with him, then maybe she would see they could belong together, or at least, he could help turn her to the Light and to a proper union.

Rafe looked at him and was taken aback by his words and his views. "Fuck you." Rafe laughed at his absurdity. "You have no idea what you're talking about."

"Really?" Jake chuckled condescendingly. "I've been doing this for years Rafe, years, and it's always the same. One woman has feelings for men, and the relationship crumbles. The one who leaves for men always ends up staying in the hetero world, the world God intended in the end," he paused, "even if they go back to women for a while. This is why it's been so easy for us to complete our Missions."

"Well," said Rafe controlling herself, "I guess it didn't work out this time."

"Yeah." Jake shook his head slightly. "And just think about why. Eden got some information on me from someone. Do you really think if she hadn't received the information about me, she would be back with you? She's just with you because she couldn't find another convenient man who could keep her in the comfort she is used to, so she went back to a familiar life with you. You think that's love?"

"She does love me and wants to be with me," said Rafe but she remembered her time with Greer in Baltimore. Greer's words about going back to familiar situations to get through trauma ran through her mind. She couldn't help but wonder if security, convenience, and having a familiar standard of living was all it was for Eden. The sound of the machine dispensing more pain medication to Jake brought her back to the present. "You're just trying to make me doubt her again. It won't work."

"I don't have to make you doubt her. From my understanding, your relationship was over almost three years ago," he said wondering how she could be so stubborn. "It's why she was with me, remember?"

"She was only with you because you tricked her when she was vulnerable," said Rafe barely controlling herself. "I doubt you were ever really anything to her, just like she was nothing to you. She came back to me, and she's made assurances she won't stop the adoption."

"Of course, she wants you to be Bronte's other parent. Why wouldn't she?" he asked with a short laugh. "You think she's really capable of raising a baby on her own? You know she can't with her anxiety and naivety. She needs security for her daughter, and you can give it to her. You're her best and most convenient solution. But still, it's not love. Next month, next year, who knows when, she'll have those feelings again, and you'll be in the same situation. I've seen it too many times to count. You both would be better off if you stayed away from her, Rafe."

"She won't change her mind," Rafe said stubbornly.

"It's not a matter of her changing her mind," said Jake with a rattling sigh. "It's a matter of predisposed emotions and latent memories."

"What the hell are you talking about?"

"She remembers sex with men, and she can't help wanting and needing the emotional connection she can get with them again," he explained sympathetically.

"Jake, you're full of so much bullshit. Lots of lesbians experiment with men when they are trying to figure themselves out. Once they realize who they're innately drawn to, they don't go out looking for men again."

"Those women," Jake chuckled, "are what we call 'jumpers.' They started out having sex with both men and women when they're emotional development was at its height. So they have a fifty-fifty chance their development will jump them toward women. If it does, then it's what they know and is programmed in for them."

"Your theory makes no sense. What about women who come out of long-term heterosexual relationships."

"We don't worry about them. They're usually older and have raised their children in the proper environment. As long as they don't adopt or have more children out of holy wedlock with a man, they've done their duty to God."

"Oh," Rafe scoffed, "you mean like Ruth and Naomi. There are gay people who have read the bible too. Why do people like you cherry pick everything and give it your own spin instead of doing actual critical thinking and take into consideration the time the books were written and the fact the bible was voted into existence because of politics?"

"Ruth and Naomi," he laughed, "wasn't a lesbian story. It was a survival story."

"Whatever," said Rafe and shook her head. She was not going to argue about a theology she didn't even care about with an obviously brainwashed person. "So, you cherry pick the women you go after too? You're even sicker than I imagined."

"Cherry pick," he chuckled softly. "No, we're very strategic." He looked up at her with sympathy because he felt she just needed to be educated, like most women. "Most women who believe they're gay are women who aren't feeling an emotional connection they need anymore with men. Probably because of rejection from men or some other trauma, so they turn to the more intense connection they get with women. Sometimes it lasts, sometimes not. The hardest ones to crack are the ones like you."

"Like me?" asked Rafe not sure what he was talking about. She was afraid to ask his opinions about gay men at this point. She was sure his opinions would be just as crazy.

"Yes," Jake affirmed as he nodded, "we call you 'lifers.' Women who, at the time of emotional and sexual development, were only with women so were programmed for their deviancy in error." He stopped and let out a long sigh. "It seems like there are more and more like you lately. It's why our Mission is so important. But, don't get me wrong, we've brought some of them back to the light too."

"You mean you've tricked them and taken advantage of them when they were vulnerable," she corrected him.

"Of course not. They came willingly and are very happy now," he insisted.

"I don't know how Eden could be with you," Rafe said scathingly as she could see he was an extreme fanatic who was buried so deep in his flawed ideology that he would probably never allow himself to be dug out. "She couldn't have known you were this crazy."

Jake chuckled and flexed his hand to ease the discomfort from his I.V. "She was coming along slowly. I admit her anxieties made her a bit more... challenging to re-educate. But I think for most things, she was already there. Her parents did a good job with her." He looked up at Rafe and licked his dry lips. "Eden was never meant to be with someone like you. She was raised differently. Just think about it, Rafe. You've been exclusive with women your entire life. Eden has only been with one woman, you, for four years and some change. It's a big difference between you."

Rafe looked at him silently as she remembered her conversation with Eden by the pool when she said those exact words. "I see what you're doing," Rafe said smoothly. "You're repeating the conversation you heard to try to convince me you're right."

"Rafe, those aren't her words." Jake chuckled enjoying her discomfort because it proved the Lord was working through him. "They are words she heard from me and has repeated. Repeated because they are in her mind now, and it's how she really feels. When you were forming emotional bonds for women, she was forming them for men. It's why she has all her feelings for men."

"Had," Rafe reminded him.

"Has," he rebuked. "They aren't going away. They'll always be there and be part of her."

"So, you're telling me I'm screwed up because of a cosmic error and Eden is confused?" Rafe laughed mockingly. "You really have been brainwashed. You try to make it sound so logical and scientific, but it doesn't explain love. The genuine love I have for Eden."

"Well, I'm sure you do love her," said Jake honestly. "I can't say the same for her. But, if you really love her, you would let her live the life that would make her happiest."

"Make her happiest?" asked Rafe as she shook her head, unsure where he was going and not sure she wanted to know.

Jake sighed because Rafe was just not getting the picture. "Your relationship is over. It's now just based on how you feel, not how she feels. Now it's all about the physical and not the emotional. Is it enough for both of you? Will you be able to love her enough to let her go once more when she tells you she's having feelings for men again?"

Rafe clenched her fists in anger and slowly relaxed enough to speak. "She loves me. Her feelings won't change again, and she won't go back to men."

"Oh, Rafe," he sighed in exasperation. "She will need a man, eventually. How many women, besides you, do you think will put up with her and her anxiety? You do a great job, but it won't be long before she feels like a man might be able to do better." He looked up at her with a mocking smile. "Maybe you could keep her if you told her about all your money."

"What?" Rafe scowled.

"Sure," Jake chuckled, "we have excellent investigators who looked into you. We know all about the obscene amount of money you have. I was amazed when you didn't go after Eden with your high priced lawyer." He looked at her for a moment. "I was so sure you would use your money to take the kid off to

Italy or somewhere and try to hide out when you pulled your stunt in Canada. I just wish I knew what you said to her to make her start to let you see the kid more after scaring her like you did."

Rafe stared at Jake angrily as she thought about how close she came to doing what he was suggesting. She couldn't bring herself to do it, though, knowing it would hurt Eden and Bronte. "Maybe I should have," she said flatly. "Then I wouldn't have had to deal with either of you."

"Oh, we would have still kept our Mission to find and rescue the child from you and your lifestyle," Jake assured her. "I wanted you to do it. It would have helped bind Eden to us, and we could have brought her home where she belongs. Then we could have had her blessing to take the child from you no matter where you ran. She would have come to understand she and the child belonged with us, and in a proper family."

"Well, I'm glad you didn't get what you wanted from me," said Rafe angry people like Jake existed.

"You have so much money," he said softly and shook his head in wonder. "You didn't even use it to try to get her back. I just don't understand why you wouldn't have used it to your advantage. I might have been open to a donation to the cause in exchange for Eden," he laughed, "a big one."

"You really are disgusting," Rafe said evenly. She would never insult Eden by trying to buy her love, and she would never allow her or her father's money to be used for taking children from their families, especially not from Eden.

Jake chuckled and wheezed a bit. "See, there it is, faulty emotional thinking. It's why you're in this situation, and our Missions are so successful. This is why a man will do a better job with Eden, and with Bronte," he said frankly. "She wouldn't have been with me for so long if it weren't true."

Rafe could see Jake apparently had no remorse for what he had done to Eden. It pissed her off he was acting like he was concerned about her. "You don't care about her," she said evenly barely holding in her anger.

"You're wrong," he insisted. "I care about her and her daughter's eternal soul. Freeing them from you and saving them from the world you're mired in is my calling from God."

"So, your god told you to beat her in a parking lot? You and you're group are fucked up."

Jake closed his eyes and shook his head. "No, I was angry. I felt God had abandoned me, and I lashed out at who I thought was the cause of my loss. But now I know God still wants me here. I survived this for a reason." He smiled at the thought of his new Mission and looked down at the pin Mason had attached to his hospital gown representing his new rank in the Stewards.

"I guess the reason includes prison," said Rafe as she rolled her eyes at him. "At least there won't be innocent women in there for you to victimize. I'm sure women everywhere will be happy about one less crazy man on the streets."

Jake ignored her remark because he knew God had a plan for him, and he was ready to serve again—however he was called. Right now, he knew God wanted him to continue to do what he could with this Mission.

"I suggest you break things off sooner rather than later for their sake, so Eden can start looking for someone. Not many men are interested in dating women like her with all her issues and a child, and the fact they may have to deal with you. If you truly care about them, you should stop the adoption. This way Bronte can have a father in her future."

Glaring at him with fury, Rafe growled out her words, "Eden doesn't need to start looking for anyone, and Bronte has a donor father, and I am her parent."

Jake looked up at Rafe and yawned. "It's not the same. I'm tired. Good luck, Rafe. Nothing is ever a hundred percent accurate, but I think I'm right when it comes to Eden. You should be with someone more like yourself, a lifer," he said and closed his eyes. "Oh, and you shouldn't bring any more children into your dark unrighteous life," he said and touched the cross that was pinned to his gown.

"Don't forget my promise," said Rafe with cool anger realizing talking to him was a lost cause. His theology and perception of family and women, especially gay women, was warped beyond reasoning. Rafe was glad the FBI was taking this group down. "Don't come near them again," she said, her threat to him clear, and then she turned and walked out the door so angry about the conversation she could barely control her urge to punch something.

34

THE MASERATI HUMMED down the highway, and Rafe Salvaggio's emotions stormed through her as she remembered everything Katheryn had told her at the hospital. She couldn't understand why Eden kept all of those things she found out about Jake from her. She said it was to protect her, but she still didn't understand what Eden thought she was protecting her from. It just made no sense. Eden said she loved her, but she couldn't talk to her.

But she could talk to Jake.

Maybe there was a kernel of truth in what Jake said about Eden. The thought pissed her off, and she stepped on the gas as she pushed the car faster, making the engine sing with speed.

But Jake didn't know everything.

Eden had been with another woman. Rafe didn't know if it meant anything or not because Eden had admitted to being with other men too. It just seemed clear Eden wanted anyone else but her, and she had no idea who she would have feelings for from one day to the next. All those feelings Eden couldn't help having led her into a situation where she was an inch from being shot. An inch from being killed. It looked to Rafe like Eden would run into the arms of death to get away from her.

Anger sped through her veins as she thought about everything Jake had said along with what Eden had caused by keeping secrets. She pushed the Maserati speed to over a hundred twenty miles per hour on the straightaway.

Rafe felt like she had to get away from everything. She was sure she was at her breaking point. She felt like everything happening was proof that, no matter how she felt, Eden was better off without her. She just had to bide her time and accept whatever bone was thrown to her by Eden, and then she was going with Greer—if Greer would have her.

If not, she would go back to Italy and stay there. She would see Gabri again and meet his new wife. Gabri had been disappointed she hadn't made it to the wedding, but she couldn't leave at the time. Now, since things were over with Eden, she could make it up to him. She would do her best to explain about Bronte. She could only hope he wouldn't feel she had betrayed him and would understand she did everything she could. If she were lucky, Eden would let her stay in contact with Bronte and maybe let her come to Italy for a visit someday.

Rafe could feel the pressure against her head again and against her chest. She didn't think she was in danger of having a heart attack anymore. She thought she finally understood what it meant and why the pain was happening so often. It was a warning to stay away. The sound of the racing engine seemed to agree 'awaaaayyy' was where she needed to be.

The memory of Abby's words rang in her ears. *You hurt everyone, Rafe!* All her friends seemed to have turned against her. Now everyone was so quick to take Eden's side in everything. Everyone thought they were right and they knew the truth. All she saw were layers of lies and secrets.

Secrets and death.

Rafe could feel the wave of dread wash over her, and she let off the gas, letting her speed decline. Her body shook as she thought about all the people she had lost to death. She didn't know if she could take any more of the kind of pain that another death would bring.

Eden was an inch from death.

The memory of Eden gasping in pain shot through her mind, and the images of her torn and bruised body filled her vision. Maybe if Eden could have talked to her, none of this would have happened. A tear ran down Rafe's face. She could see now Greer and Jake were right—this was all just temporary for Eden. Whether it was because of trauma or for temporary security, Rafe didn't know. All she knew was she had caused Eden too much pain for her to love her anymore. No, she couldn't cause Eden more pain, and she knew she couldn't take the pain of Eden leaving her again. The thought of Eden being an inch—*an inch*—from death made it very clear Eden was better off with anyone but her.

And what about Geer? What if she started to do these things? No, Rafe shook her head at the thought. It wasn't going to happen again. She would make sure of it.

Rafe knew the solution was to make sure she didn't hurt anyone again. She had already hurt too many people in her life. She didn't want to put them in harm's way again. She couldn't face it.

To keep them safe, she needed to let them go.

Let them both go, Eden and Greer.

She looked up and realized she had driven all the way to Chase Palm Park. She looked at the time then turned the car around to head back to Los Angeles. As she got closer to L. A., she could feel the pain in her head begin to build and the pressure on her chest increase. She thought she knew why. She felt she finally knew what it meant.

35

EDEN KINGSLEY WAS in her bed, angry with Rafe for rejecting her, and mad at herself for pushing Rafe too far. She was convinced Rafe didn't want her because she was going to be with Greer. She didn't know what else to do now. She went into the bathroom and took another pill for her pain, wishing it would take the sting out of her heart too. She knew Rafe was convinced she didn't need her or want her, and Eden couldn't break through to make her see it wasn't true. She climbed into bed and tried to sleep, but her anxiety was building inside her. As she lay crying in torment and her body shook, her mind was reeling with scenarios of what Rafe was doing with Greer.

Eden opened her eyes as she heard a knock at the door and then heard Jude answer it. She heard Abby's voice, so she got out of bed to go talk with her. As she walked into the living room, she saw Greer at the door.

Her body froze in place.

Anxiety rushed through Eden as her heart pounded in her chest painfully. She felt like it was being crushed from the inside. Her lungs and throat burned and contracted so she couldn't breathe. Her head filled with a shrill buzzing cutting all other sounds from her ears. Her vision tunneled, and she was surrounded by darkness as her world shrank to a small pinpoint of light.

Then blackness.

Jude and Flynn ran to Eden as she fell, barely breaking her fall. They carried her to the couch where Abby and Julia were trying to bring her back to consciousness. Greer and Beth stood back out of the way of Eden's vision, so they didn't cause another anxiety attack.

"Eden," said Abby softly as she gently shook her, "Eden, wake up." She looked worriedly up at Julia. "I've never seen her do this before."

"Well, she's never been in this situation before," said Julia with concern.

"Yeah, she was already upset about Rafe. Why didn't you tell me you were bringing Greer so I could have warned her," said Jude upset.

"I didn't know she would pass out!" said Abby defensively. "I just thought... well, Eden had said Greer told her if Rafe came to 'her,' not if she came to Rafe. So I thought I should go talk to her and see if she could help."

"I think she's coming around," said Julia as she watched Eden's eyes flutter.

"Eden, are you okay?" asked Abby.

"What," croaked Eden feeling pain rush through her, "what happened?"

"You had a fainting spell," Julia informed her.

"Yeah, you almost got another head injury," said Abby worriedly. "Can you sit up?"

"I..." she grimaced in pain, "I think so," she whispered unsteadily, and she began to sit up.

"Here's some water," said Julia as she handed her the glass.

"Eden," said Abby hesitantly as Eden gave the glass back to Julia, "just so you know... Greer is here."

"Why?" Eden asked as she shook with pain and sadness while clinging to Abby. "Why is she here? Tell her Rafe's not here. I don't know where she is."

"She's not here for Rafe," said Abby reassuringly. "She's here to talk to you. I told her what's been going on with Jake and everything. Will you be okay?"

"I..." Eden started worried, "I don't' know. I don't think so," she said. She was shaking as fear ran through her and pain ran over her skin like pins and needles. Her last memory of Greer was being hit in the face, and she couldn't take more pain. "Don't leave me," she said in a panic and tightening her grip when Abby tried to pull her arm away.

"I'm not leaving," Abby assured her and grimaced from the pain of Eden's grip. "It's okay. She's just here to talk. I told you I was going to help you. I think talking to her might help." Abby looked up at Greer and Beth and then motioned them over. "Come and sit down," she told them.

Greer and Beth sat down across from Eden. It was the first time they had seen her since they had been back. As Greer took in Eden's frailness and the bruises on her body, she was struck for the first time at just how young Eden was. Greer realized she was old enough to be Eden's mother. When Abby approached her about helping Eden, she had doubted she could be impartial enough to be of any use because of her feelings for Rafe. Feelings she had to resolve one way or another before going home and possibly taking Rafe with her. But now, seeing the young woman's vulnerability and the desperation she knew came from heartache, she felt compelled to set her own feelings aside—for the moment, at least.

"Eden, this is my interpreter, Beth," Greer voiced gently. "You can listen to her voice and look at me. When you talk, you can talk to me. I can read your lips, and she will sign what you're saying so I can be sure I get everything. Okay?"

"Okay," was all Eden could force out, terrified of what Greer was going to tell her or might do to her.

"I brought this puzzle for us to work on while we talk," she said and placed the puzzle on the table between them and then opened the box. "I know a little about your anxiety from talking to Rafe," she said gently. "I know we've had our problems, but I promise you I'm here to help if I can." She saw Eden look at her doubtfully and didn't blame her at all. "I know how much you love Rafe and how much she loves you too." She put the box she was holding on the table. "This puzzle will help you keep your hands and mind busy while we talk and help everyone relax." Greer poured the puzzle out on the table.

"It's all white!" Abby complained.

36

COLLECTIVELY, THE GROUP had been working on the puzzle Greer Noble brought as a relaxation tool and talking about small things for over an hour. Eden was hesitant to engage with Greer, but with the help of her friends around her, she was finally able to open up. She was surprised how relaxed Greer had made her feel in such a short time, and how she had actually laughed with the group as they talked about themselves and about Rafe. She was sure it was only because her friends were near and making her feel safer.

Finally, with encouragement from others, Eden worked up the nerve to talk about what was happening with her and Rafe. Greer listened and didn't ask a lot of hard or uncomfortable questions. She just let Eden go at her own pace. They talked about her conversations with Rafe and how they made her feel and how she desperately wanted Rafe to believe her. She spoke about how Rafe rejected her and how she felt about it, too.

"I just don't know why she's doing these things," said Eden. "Did I make too big of a mistake? I told her I was trying to protect her and I was sorry that I made a mistake. I didn't know how to get through to her, especially when she said she couldn't be with me. She kept telling me I've outgrown her, and I'd be happier without her. It's not true!" she said as tears escaped her eyes. "I love her," she said softly. "I need her with us."

"People are like puzzles," signed Greer and Beth voiced for her. "We look at them and try to figure them out and put them together in our minds. Some people have a few pieces, and others have too many to count."

"I'm a simple puzzle," said Jude thoughtfully.

"Really?" voiced Greer with a smile. "I think you have a lot more pieces than you admit."

"I think I'm about twenty-five hundred pieces," said Abby.

"How many pieces do you think you would be, Eden?" asked Greer gently.

"I think I'd be like Abby," she guessed hesitantly, "somewhere in the middle."

"What about Rafe," Greer asked with a smile.

"Lord!" Abby screeched. "She's at least a ten-thousand piece puzzle!"

Greer laughed. "I don't know, maybe she's five thousand. What do you think Eden?"

"Yeah," she nodded, "probably five thousand."

"You know, the thing about puzzles," Greer said softly, "if you don't have all the pieces, you'll never see the picture like you're supposed to see it."

"Unless it's white," said Jude. "This is frustrating."

"The white doesn't fill our minds with a picture," explained Greer through Beth. "It lets our minds see what it wants to, to see what is just in front of it, without distraction. But, when you don't have all the pieces, even the white puzzle isn't complete. When I was younger, my brother would hide the pieces so he would always be able to put in the last piece."

"I did it too!" Abby laughed.

"You would," Jude said perturbed. "It sounds just... so mean!"

"It was a way to control everything," Greer revealed.

"Are we talking about Rafe again?" asked Abby suspiciously.

"Well, I think she hides some pieces, don't you?" asked Greer and looked at Eden.

"Yes," agreed Eden, "she does."

"But, you don't, Eden. It seems like you leave all the pieces out. It's very refreshing. I think it's something Rafe loves about you and one of the reasons why she found it hard to be away from you."

Julia wanted to help, but Rafe had told her so many things in confidence that she didn't know what she could reveal without feeling like she had betrayed her. She thought Rafe would be okay with a simple truth. She cleared her throat. "Eden, I think I can verify what Greer is saying is fairly close to the truth of the matter. Rafe did mention to me that when she first met you, she felt like she knew you very well almost immediately because you were so willing to share everything about yourself. I think she found it endearing, and it may have made her believe you thought she was special to you. It may have been one of the main reasons she pursued you like she did." She looked at Abby then back at Eden. "It could even be why she treated you differently than other people in her life."

Abby looked at Julia confused. "So, that's it?" she said bewildered. "Eden being amicable is why she treated her different? Eden's friendly with everyone."

"Rafe is very complex," said Julia with a shrug knowing there was more to it as Abby rolled her eyes.

Greer watched as Beth interpreted their conversation and redirected to Eden. "You could say you and Rafe were opposite. You were very open, and she was hiding pieces. I also think people can become even more complex puzzles. Like children are five hundred, teenagers a thousand, and then adults two to three thousand—and some people, like Rafe, five thousand and even more. You say you're twenty-five hundred, Eden, but I think now you're a three thousand, and Rafe may be having a problem with your changes right now."

"Why?" Eden asked sadly.

"Well, I believe before you started having problems, she thought she had you all put together perfectly," said Greer, "and she didn't have to worry about you because she knew you so well and you were so open. She didn't have to look close anymore."

Eden looked at the white puzzle and the piece she held in her hand. "So it may be why she hated the therapy we tried so much."

"She may not have seen all your discontent and unhappiness. She didn't see you were becoming less open, but she could probably feel it, even if it's something she won't admit to herself. She wasn't unhappy, so why should you be, she may have thought," Beth interpreted.

"Maybe," said Eden wondering just how much Rafe had told this woman about their problems. How did she know that when she had started hiding things from Rafe, everything seemed to start going wrong? "She said therapy just gave her doubts about herself."

"So she started doubting herself, and maybe other things," Beth paused waiting for Greer to sign, "then you two broke up twice, and the second time you went to Jake, and you were apart for about a year, maybe more." Greer shrugged not knowing how long Eden was with Jake. "When you and Rafe got back together, you were a different puzzle. Maybe not completely different, but you suddenly had more pieces she was trying to figure out again. She wanted to have the puzzle done overnight, but sometimes it can't happen the way she wants."

"You guys were going really fast," Abby agreed.

"Rafe probably wasn't looking at it closely a lot, or often, while you were apart," voiced Beth for Greer. "So, when she did look again, and it wasn't how she left it, it was... unsettling. Because she couldn't figure out things, or know them, without you being open to tell her, and you weren't ready to share them with her. She also knew things weren't the same with her. That's why she warned you about herself and how she had changed."

"You mean she went back to being her crazed wildling self," Abby guessed.

"Abby," Jude groaned.

"She was out of control," screeched Abby and looked hard at Julia. "Ms. Let's Make a Wager over there was no help at all!"

"She's a big girl," said Julia without remorse. "Believe me she could have done worse."

"Well, thank god for Greer!" huffed Abby. "Sorry Eden, but really."

Greer watched as Eden's face flushed red at the way they talked about Rafe and knew it made her uncomfortable. "Rafe is a very passionate woman," said Greer and looked at Eden with kindness. "But the person she gave to those lovers, even to me, wasn't the person she gave to you." She took a breath, pushing away the pain in her heart remembering the love Rafe showed her and how hard it was not to take it and keep it for herself. "Even if she only let you see a fraction of her puzzle, it is infinitely more than she's shown anyone else."

Eden looked at Greer and knew this woman was still trying to let Rafe go, and it was very hard for her. She understood the difficulty because she couldn't do it herself. "Thank you," she said graciously.

Greer smiled and nodded to Eden then looked at Abby. "What I meant was Rafe had changed in other ways," said Greer. "I'm not saying you're wrong about a little bit of wildling coming out," she voiced and released a short laugh, "but like Julia said, Rafe is very complex."

"Yeah," agreed Eden nodding her head, "it was more than a simple change. She seemed to be more," she paused, "more under control, especially where Bronte was concerned."

Eden wrung her hands thinking about how she and Jake had treated Rafe when they were together. How they always found an excuse not to give her time with Bronte and didn't include her in the milestones of her first year.

She looked up at Greer. "When I see her now with Bronte, I can't believe I kept her from seeing her or even thought about not going through with the adoption. Sometimes I think she's a better mother than I am. She does things with her I couldn't even imagine doing. But lately, when we were all together, we've had so much fun. Bronte seems to just flourish and make huge strides when she spends time with Rafe."

"I think she's very good with her too," said Greer letting Eden take them down another train of thought for a moment. "I think another problem you're facing is you're both concentrating so hard on being parents that you end up parenting each other. Neither one of you needs to parent the other. It has to come to a point where you remain good parents but are equally good partners. Neither of you has been really working on being a good partner."

Eden nodded as she thought about Greer's words. "I think she tries extra hard because of all the time she lost because of me," she said quietly. "We've been so busy fighting and worrying about Jake and the injunction and everything. Truly concentrating on us has been hard."

Greer smiled. She was happy Eden knew there was more to Rafe's changes than what Abby suggested. "Rafe had a lot of things change in her life, and she's now holding on to a lot of new pieces of her own," Greer continued, turning the conversation to another topic. "It's hard to deal with all your own new pieces, and at the same time, trying to figure out someone else's pieces. So, instead of working with you, she was trying to see if she could do it on her own. Look at this puzzle. If there weren't six of us here working on it, do you think we would be this far along? Probably not." Greer smiled. "Did you notice how we started putting the puzzle together?"

"What do you mean?" asked Jude.

"Well, we laid out all the edges and put it together first," said Greer.

"It's just how you do it." Abby shrugged. "Then you can go from the outside in."

"Yeah," agreed Jude, "you'll never get to the middle if you don't do the edges first. I mean, you could do it, but it'd be hard."

"It's one way puzzles are definitely not like people," said Greer. "Most people build their edges so others can't get into the middle. To figure out people, you have to get through the edge somehow. They have to let you in. Some don't ever open up. When they do, it's usually because of friendship or love. Most people open up a little and others a lot. Some open up right away, and you know everything about them the first time you meet them. Others you might be around all your life but never really know them.

"Well, I know there are a lot of things I don't know about Rafe," said Abby as she rolled her eyes. "I mean, I just found out she has a doctorate, and I've known her for years!"

"She has two," said Eden quietly.

"And two Masters," added Julia.

"Of course she does," said Abby sarcastically.

"With people, sometimes you have to look at the pieces they have shown you, not the entire picture they're trying to show you. Each piece is a part of what's going on, and it can be formed into any picture you could imagine. Life is like a puzzle you're trying to put together without any reference to anything else."

"So, what does this have to do with control?" asked Abby. "What's the point?"

"The point is, when everything happened, and broke her and Eden's relationship apart, she lost her control. When Eden came back and added all of her new puzzle pieces, she couldn't get things back to when she felt they were happy and things were perfect," answered Greer. "She couldn't go back, and she couldn't figure out how to fit all Eden's new pieces into the puzzle she thought was complete."

"So, what can I do? I need her to come home," said Eden in misery. "I love her. But I can't go back in time."

"We have to keep talking to her," said Greer then signed for Beth again. "A lot of pieces of this new puzzle are floating around, and it's hard to find out how they fit together. She has pieces in her mind that don't even belong in the puzzle because of Jake. It's like someone dropped in pieces from another puzzle into the box and she's trying to make them fit."

Tears fell again from Eden's eyes. She had nothing left inside her to help her hold in her emotions. "I just need her to forgive me for making so many mistakes," she said as Abby hugged her gently and Julia shook her head.

"Abby, I know you think we shouldn't tell Rafe I was here," said Greer, "but don't you think enough things have been kept from her? I know I don't want to lose her trust."

"You should tell her," Eden agreed as she wiped her tears, then they continued to put the puzzle together and talk.

37

LETTY CARVER WAS home for a while resting before she had to go work at The Kiki Bistro to help close for the night. Her husband, Ephraim Holden, was home too and was in the kitchen making cookies with Bronte. It was one of their favorite things to do together. They were watching the baby tonight until it was time for Lydia to come and take her to Eden. There was a knock on the door, and when Letty opened it, she was surprised to see a hurt and haunted Rafe standing in the waning evening light.

"Rafe, come in," said Letty surprised at how sick Rafe looked again with dark circles around her eyes and running down her drawn face looking pale in contrast. She thought she was doing better after everything at the hospital, but she looked like she might be worse. "What's wrong?"

"Letty, I—" Rafe started then looked into the apartment as she caught the baby's laughter, "Bronte's here?"

"Yeah, she and Ephraim are making cookies," she said and stepped back so Rafe could come inside.

"Oh, well..." said Rafe as she looked down at her hands and then backed away. "I'll go then."

"Rafe, come in," said Letty worried because she had seen the hurt and haunted look on Rafe's face before, and it wasn't a good sign. "Tell me what's going on, Cugina."

Rafe shook her head. "I don't want to do this with Bronte here," she said and began to walk away.

"Hang on," said Letty as she caught Rafe's arm. "I'll come out. Just let me get my shoes on. I was getting ready to go to the bistro anyway."

Rafe paced in the hallway while she waited for Letty as the darkness of the night crept around her. When Letty finally came out, they went to the dimly lit parking lot, and Rafe got into Letty's car with her.

"Okay, Cugina," Letty sighed, "tell me what's going on."

Rafe looked at Letty. She was then enveloped in the realness of what she had to do. "Letty, I can't go home," she divulged in a shaky voice. "Can you help Eden find a new place?"

"You're really going to make her move out?" queried Letty worried and shocked.

"I think it would be best. She..." Rafe hesitated, "she needs to find someone else. I told her today."

"You did what?" Letty yelled. "Why, Rafe?"

"Letty," Rafe sighed as she looked at her with glassy eyes, "life is just too short."

"What?"

"It—" She swallowed and fought the panic inside herself. "It seems like death just gets closer and closer to me."

"What the hell are you talking about?" demanded Letty as she looked at Rafe in confusion.

"Remember when Papa was sick?" asked Rafe changing gears in her mind.

"Yes?" she said her head spinning.

"I tried to help him," Rafe revealed shakily and rubbed her temples. "I tried to help him feel better and relax."

"I remember, Rafe," said Letty as she reached out to try to calm Rafe as she trembled. "You went to see him in New York, and you called me."

"Yes." She nodded and closed her eyes. "I couldn't stop thinking about my mamma," she muttered changing directions again, "all the things we missed about her."

"I know. It was a hard time for you." Letty remembered having to take care of Rafe as she dealt with her grief for her father. She had talked about her mother a lot because of all the things Rafe found belonging to her after her father's death.

"Yes, he was going so fast, Letty, but I didn't know," she said switching her thoughts back to her father as tears started falling from her eyes. "I should have spent more time with him. I should have stayed with him. I should have been there when he died. He was all alone."

"Rafe," said Letty at a loss.

"Remember, I skipped school to go to the stupid festival in the neighborhood with Gabri and Brettito?" She sat silently for a moment thinking about Brettito. "It was the day he died," she said and shivered not realizing she was revealing her thoughts out loud. "He was just..." she choked sadly, "just shot in the street. Gabri and I..." she swallowed as tears ran down her face. "We saw, we saw..." she whispered but couldn't say the words to describe the bloody scene she still saw in her mind.

Shaking her head, Letty wasn't sure what to say because she knew very little about Rafe's life in Italy. "I remember your father talking to my parents about it," said Letty. She looked into Rafe's haunted eyes, unsure why she was suddenly talking about her childhood friend.

"His..." she paused, "his blood is still on me," she mumbled as she looked at her hands and her vision clouded with the color of blood.

"Rafe, no," said Letty as she watched Rafe's eyes shift quickly from side to side. "It wasn't your fault."

"I'm..." she took a breath, "feeling so guilty... about them all," she said wiping away her hot tears and trying to clear her vision.

"Rafe, there was nothing you could have done," she assured her and held her ice-cold hand thinking how rare it was to see Rafe's tears. She had only seen Rafe cry for her father and for Eden.

"No, not about then," she whispered and pulled her hand away.

"What then?"

"We were in your apartment," she said quickly. "I had to stay with you because," she hesitated, "Eden."

"I know," said Letty remembering the mess Rafe was when she came home after taking care of everything in New York, and then the loss of Eden. Rafe came over grieving and confessed she had cheated on Eden. Eden had left her sometime in the night without a word. She was so upset because she didn't know where Eden had gone and no one would tell her. Guilt ran through Letty because even she didn't tell her when she found out. At the time, she thought it would be worse for Rafe if she knew and tried to see Eden. It seemed like more rejection from Eden would drive Rafe into a deeper depression, and Letty couldn't let that happen to her.

"I never got to say goodbye," she revealed and took a shuddering breath.

"Yes, and I told you your papa loved you," Letty reminded her trying to keep up with another sudden subject change, "and he knew you loved him." She remembered consoling her and not understanding Rafe's relationship with Ettore and how she could love him as she did.

"Letty," Rafe said as her eyes burned feverishly. "Letty. I was talking about Eden," she confessed. "I should have been talking about Papa, but I wasn't."

"Oh, Rafe," said Letty as she rubbed Rafe's shoulder. She felt the heat radiating from her and wondered if she had a fever. "You know, your papa would have understood."

"I shouldn't have gone on those business trips," she railed with desperate regret. "I should have been there for Papa and Eden."

"You couldn't have known," Letty assured her wondering why she was talking this way. "You were working. You had to do your job and run the businesses for both of them," she reminded her.

"It just didn't feel right when I was there," Rafe told her as she held her head. "I couldn't find peace, I felt…" she paused, "alone. It's why I had to sell the businesses, Letty. So I could be here for them."

"Rafe, don't do this to yourself," insisted Letty wondering who she was talking about now.

"Then, there is Mamma," Rafe fretted sadly.

"You feel guilty about your mom?" she asked as her head spun from subject to subject.

"I should have been better," she confessed in distress. "I should have just ridden my bike to school," she hesitated, "by myself." She looked at Letty with red-rimmed eyes. "She would still be alive if I hadn't planned on skipping school, and if I hadn't," she stopped not able to say more about her part in her mother's death. "I can still see her, Letty. She was just so… so still on the street." She remembered the day vividly in her mind and pushed away the old feeling of panic. "Papa," she said shakily, "I could see him slipping away but I—" she stopped suddenly. She sat staring straight ahead at the blood-tinted visions flashing in front of her eyes.

"Rafe, your mamma was in an accident," Letty said sorrowfully, trying to keep up with what she was talking about. "The driver ran a light, and your papa had cancer, so there was nothing you could have done."

Rafe pulled out of her visions and looked back at Letty in misery. "I should have been thinking about him. I should have gotten him out of the hospital. I think it would have been better for him," she said hoarsely. "I should have had him with me like he took care of me."

"Rafe, I know you're a force to be reckoned with now, but you're not the cure for cancer!"

"I know but," she paused, "he was dying, and I was thinking about Eden again."

"What are you saying, Rafe?" Dread was beginning to unfold the more she listened to Rafe talk.

"It's getting closer." Rafe looked at Letty with fear in her eyes. "Death."

"It's not getting closer, Rafe," she insisted anxiously.

"Letty." Rafe put her hand on her aching head. "Eden was an inch—an *inch* from death," she whispered.

"Don't do this to yourself," begged Letty as she tried to comfort Rafe. "It wasn't your fault. She's going to be okay."

"I can feel it, death," Rafe revealed. "It keeps pressing into me."

"No, please." Letty shook her head nervously. "Don't say those things."

"I think," she said shakily. "I think it's Flynn's gun."

"Flynn's gun?" Letty said in confusion.

"Death," she said, "it's pressing into me. My head," she whispered, "my heart."

"I don't understand," she said hoping Rafe would explain herself.

"I can feel it pressing under my chin, it's so cold," she whispered.

"Please, Rafe, tell me what you're talking about."

"She never gave me the chance to say goodbye."

"Cugina, I'm so sorry you're feeling so bad about your mamma," said Letty thinking Rafe was going back to talking about her mother.

"I just didn't think things would go as fast as they did," she said through tear-stained eyes.

"Oh, Cugina." Letty sighed as she was trying to keep up with all of Rafe's changes in subject. "Your papa was sick for a long time," she said thinking she was now talking about her father again.

"I go to Milano for ten days, and she becomes a stranger," said Rafe as she held her head willing the pain to go away. "I think she's still a stranger because, while I was away selling my business, she... she just left. I came home to an empty house, and the only thing around me was... death."

"No, Cugina, don't think those thoughts. Eden came back to you," said Letty trying to be positive. She remembered when Rafe came home and found Eden gone. She had to bring her home where she and Ephraim could watch over her because she was such a mess again that she could barely function. They ended up telling everyone she was out of town. Only Jude knew she was at the apartment because Letty had asked her to help take care of Rafe's house.

Rafe looked at Letty feverishly. "I made her say goodbye to me. I didn't want to leave her with the empty feeling she left me with."

"Eden?" asked Letty, unsure if she understood who Rafe was talking about this time.

"Yes, I didn't want to go without letting her say it," she said as she swallowed, "like she didn't let me."

"Rafe, Eden isn't going to die," she reassured her.

"She's okay this time," Rafe agreed then looked up at Letty with panic in her eyes. "If I go back," she held her head again, "what if she does it again? She was so close. I don't even know if she realizes how close."

"Rafe, going back to her won't make her die," she said wondering why Rafe would think such a thing.

"I'm not so sure," she shook her head against the pain starting to overpower her. "They say you can't escape death, and it keeps getting closer."

"Rafe, this is crazy! You can't think this way. Not you," she said.

"You know what they all have in common?"

"What?"

"Secrets," Rafe whispered. "They all kept a secret because they wanted to protect me."

"Secrets? Rafe, what are you talking about?"

"Mamma, Brettito, Papa," she hesitated because she knew she skipped a name—one not said aloud since she was very young. "Eden," she added and looked up at Letty. "You see how it's getting closer?"

"Rafe," Letty shook her head not knowing what to think. "This is... I just don't know what you're saying."

"I know," Rafe gave a short laugh, "it sounds really self-centered, doesn't it? But with all of those people, I was out just thinking about myself," she confessed feverishly.

"You said you were thinking about Eden when your dad died," she said in confusion.

"Yeah, thinking about how I could get her back for myself!" She laughed manically. "You see, not really for her," she whispered, "for me."

"But," Letty sputtered and shook her head, "you love her."

"Do I?" Rafe looked at her with uncertainty. "Maybe I just love myself. Maybe I'm all those things Eden said I was because I can't love anyone but myself."

"Rafe, no! What about Greer?"

"No." Rafe shook her head. "I couldn't put her through this too. I can't go with her."

"What are you saying?"

"I think I should leave and be on my own," Rafe declared zealously. "I have to make myself let them go. I don't think I should be with anyone. Abby was right." She nodded with fevered eyes.

"Abby?"

"Yes, and Jude."

"Jude?"

"Yes," Rafe confirmed with a nod. "Abby said I always hurt everyone, and Jude could see I was scared of losing someone else. I can't face it again, Letty," Rafe said as she held her shaking hand to her chest. "You understand?"

"No, no I don't," said Letty at a loss. "Are you drunk or high?"

"No," she said softly and sat silently for a while. "Letty, can you tell them?" she asked suddenly. "Tell them I can't be with either of them?"

"I—" started Letty, uncertain what she was supposed to be telling them. "Rafe, I don't know—" she tried to say but was cut off.

"Maybe I should let Eden stay," said Rafe not paying attention to anything Letty was saying.

"She wants to stay with you."

"No. She can stay in the house. I'll sell it to her," she paused, "give it to her."

"What? Rafe, where will you go?"

"I think maybe Canada."

"Canada?"

"Yeah, or Italy," Rafe said as she looked out the car window into the dark. "Maybe I'll ask Jude if she wants to go too."

"Jude?"

"Yes, she knows about giving up who you want so they'll be happier," she looked back at Letty, "and won't get hurt. She understands what I have to do."

"Eden's going to hurt if you leave," Letty tried to reason with her.

"But she won't die."

"Rafe, you have to stay," Letty commanded firmly hoping to snap Rafe out of her strange behavior.

"Maybe I can't be with Eden for me. Maybe I'm not what's best for her."

"What's best for her? What do you mean, Rafe?"

"It's why her feelings changed. It's why she had to leave me," she said as if she finally understood the truth of the matter. "She's not supposed to be with me anymore. She has to be here for Bronte."

"Rafe, what about you? You have to stay for Bronte too."

"I know," said Rafe tormented. "But I'm not sure how I can be and still go. I have to figure it all out." She thought for a moment. "Maybe email."

"You have to be here! In her life!" insisted Letty. "Stop this, Rafe. Stop thinking like this!"

"I guess I'll have to think some more. I don't want to fail her too, but—" she stopped and held her hand to her head again.

"You'll only fail if you leave, Rafe," she said as she watched Rafe shake in distress.

"I have to think," said Rafe shakily. "My head hurts, I hurt," she said as she held her head. "I can't talk about this anymore. I have to go," she said and grabbed the door handle.

"Rafe, what are you doing?" Letty took hold of Rafe's arm to keep her in the car.

"Can I stay with you?" Rafe asked suddenly changing the subject again. "After Greer leaves?"

"I think you should. I think it would be best."

"Okay. Here's a list and a timeline I made." Rafe handed Letty a large package. "It shows everything."

"What the hell?" exclaimed Letty as she took the package.

"You should show it to them. It'll help explain everything." Rafe got out of the car. "Maybe, I'll come back later, okay?"

"Okay," said Letty at a loss because Rafe had changed her mind about when she would come back to stay at the apartment. Her head was spinning from all the contradictions and subject changes Rafe was making. "I'll tell Ephraim to pull out the sofa bed."

"Great, thanks for understanding," said Rafe. She closed the car door then walked away.

"What the hell is she driving?" Letty asked softly as she watched Rafe get into an unfamiliar car and race away with her tires squealing. "My god, I think she's lost her mind."

38

THE SCENT OF the midnight ocean carried on a cool breeze flowed over Rafe Salvaggio as she sat in her father's car with the top down. The only sound was the surf as the water pushed and pulled against the beach then curled and crashed into itself. It was so relaxing, so hypnotizing, so freeing. It blocked out everything and filled her mind with a steady rhythm that lulled her into sleep.

Her sleeping mind was slowly awakening to a soft noise disrupting the rhythm of the ocean. Her mind raced through all of her sound memories trying to identify the offending noise, and as all the possibilities flowed past, it became suddenly clear it was footsteps. Footsteps in the sand—to be exact. Someone was coming. Her mind struggled against her bodies desire to sleep. Her mind sent out the call for her eyes to open, but they did not. They were locked closed, and her mind raged against her body's unwillingness to comply with its demands.

Her ears went back to listening, and a new sound had added its tone to the night. It was a searching voice calling her name.

"Rafe. Rafe," it called.

Her mind wanted to see who was calling, but her eyes still wouldn't open. The catalog was opened again to identify the voice only by its sound. She had heard the voice before. It was familiar. It was Eden.

Eden.

Eden had found her again. How could she? Suddenly, the mind did not need the eyes anymore. It could see Eden clearly walking under the moon along the beach.

Eden approached the car and leaned against the door. "Rafe, what are you doing out here?"

Couldn't she see? Rafe thought. It was so obvious, but maybe she couldn't see well, even though it was a full moon tonight. "I'm sleeping. You should go home and sleep, too."

Eden smiled and shook her head. "I don't want to go home. I want to stay with you. Come on. Get out of the car and sit on the sand with me."

Rafe's body felt like lead as she tried to move, and she slowly opened the door, got out of the car, and sat next to Eden. "You shouldn't be here." *Here, at night, next to me, on a blanket*, she thought. "Where did the blanket come from?"

Eden pushed Rafe back and ran her agile fingers over her face. "I brought it with me."

Rafe thought about her explanation for a moment and realized it must be true. "You always think of everything. How'd you know I'd be here?"

Eden's soft laugh filled Rafe's ears, and she whispered, "Abby told me."

Rafe frowned, unhappy with Abby, as Eden continued to run her fingers tenderly over Rafe's face. She looked up at Eden and watched as she lowered herself, granting her a soft kiss, and then she gently glided her tongue over Rafe's lips. The sensation burned through Rafe, and she whispered breathlessly, "Eden, we can't."

Ignoring Rafe's words, Eden continued to run her tongue over Rafe's mouth, moving to her chin and neck and ears, then back to her lips where she used it to pry open Rafe's mouth and delved inside to explore and taste. Eden sucked Rafe's tongue into her mouth and wrapped hers around it then let go, sucking gently on Rafe's lower lip.

"We belong together."

Rafe's mind was overcome with Eden's seduction. A spinning sensation ran through her mind and through her body as she felt Eden unbutton her shirt and then move her hands deftly over her body.

"Eden, I can't, please."

Eden smiled down at Rafe and kissed her nose as she pushed off Rafe's shirt and opened her bra.

"We can do this."

She moved down Rafe and took her aroused breast into her mouth and circled the nipple with her tongue then sucked and pulled up until only her lips were around the hardened nipple. She released it, and the cool air mixed with the moisture Eden left created tiny goose bumps.

"I want to take care of you," Eden declared huskily. She moved down and skillfully released the button and lowered the zipper on Rafe's pants, pulling them off along with the undergarments. She stood up and looked down on Rafe hungrily, "You have to stay with me."

Rafe watched as Eden removed her own clothes leisurely and sensuously, and then lowered herself and crawled stealthily up Rafe's body, raking her tongue over her skin and leaving a trail of kisses as she made her way back to her lips. The taste and smell of Eden filled Rafe's senses, and as Eden moved her body against her, agonizing waves of desire shot through her core and her heart raced. "I'm so addicted to you," Rafe thought, or maybe she whispered—she just didn't know.

Eden released a throaty laugh. "In a good way, I hope."

Rafe looked sadly into her eyes remembering her conversation with Jake. "No, I don't think it's a good addiction," she said, amazed Eden could hear her thoughts. "I don't think it's good for you."

Eden shook her head and offered a sultry smile, her smoldering golden brown eyes with molten flecks of gold were filled with desire. "Let me feed your addiction." She navigated Rafe's body expertly, locating every erogenous zone, and driving every thought out of Rafe's mind except for thoughts of Eden.

Did she know she was the only one who had ever been able to find those so easily, Rafe thought. No, Eden had never heard those words spoken out loud. From the first time that they had made love, she had been able to find, and sometimes even create, sensitive areas on her body and cause her to lose all control. How did she do it? She was a savant of ecstasy, a seductress—this must be the answer. Maybe it was because she was so naïve and could see and find what others couldn't because she looked with innocent, untainted eyes. Maybe it was because she could somehow read her mind and body like no other lover.

The sound of Eden's voice brought her back from the edge of pleasure. "Don't cry, babe. It's okay."

Rafe felt the tears she couldn't stop as they were running down the sides of her face and into her ears. "We have to stop, Eden. Don't you understand?"

Eden looked at Rafe curiously. "No, I don't understand. I want you, and I can see and feel how much you want and need me."

Rafe could feel Eden lick up her tears. "Eden, don't. Don't drink those."

"Why not?" Eden whispered with a heart-melting pout.

Rafe closed her eyes and tried to make her tears stop, to stay in control. "Because those tears are full of fear and sadness. I don't want them in you."

Eden kissed the last of the tears off Rafe's face. "It's okay. I want all of you in me. *Sei la mia anima gemella.*"

Eden's words reverberated through Rafe's mind. She had said those words to Eden many times. Hearing them come from Eden's lips made her want to kiss her and pull her close. Rafe frowned as she tried to reach for Eden, but her arms wouldn't answer her call, reminding her she couldn't follow those desires anymore.

Rafe's arms were stretched out from her body and they felt like lead. She couldn't lift them. It was as if something was holding them down. She watched Eden as she lowered herself again and began moving down her body. Rafe felt Eden's tongue and lips caressing and sucking on her body. This caused tingling sensations to shoot through her body, arousing every nerve. She felt Eden's hands begin their sensual journey over her face and through her hair then down her neck and chest. They reached her breasts, and she could feel Eden's gentle touch as she circled them then embraced and kneaded them, increasing the pressure of her touch and using her thumb and forefinger to grasp the erect and firm nipple causing Rafe to take a deep shuddering breath. Eden's hair brushed against Rafe, making her ache, and she felt Eden take her breast into her mouth again, nipping and sucking as she moved her hand further down Rafe's body.

Fighting her body's growing need for Eden, Rafe struggled to find her voice. "Eden, please. Can't."

Eden ignored her and continued down Rafe's writhing body as Rafe struggled to move her arms and sit up, but she found she was still being held down by some invisible force.

She heard Eden moan and whisper, "I can't wait to taste you."

Rafe threw her head back and cried out as Eden spread her legs and ran her tongue down her thigh, "Stop. Don't! Stop! Please!"

Eden's tongue touched Rafe's swollen and sensitive nerves, sending electric shocks through her body, numbing her mind as her hands flexed into fists gripping the sand tightly, the pressure forcing it through her fingers. Eden didn't stop. She circled Rafe with her tongue and sucked her into her mouth repeatedly until Rafe was sweating and begging Eden through her tears to release her. Finally, Rafe felt Eden move her tongue inside her as she begged Eden to stop, but only in her screaming mind because her voice refused to leave. Rafe was unable to utter coherent words as her body shook with its need for the detonation of the building pressure filling her core and overloading her senses.

Unexpectedly a new sensation lit her fuse as Eden's fingers entered her, stroking and beckoning as the fuse burned and the pressure built. Every stroke, every thrust was fanning the flame of rapture. Rafe was helpless, and sweat covered her body, her voice gone. Her eyes rolled back in her head as she gasped for each breath. Eden relentlessly plunged herself into Rafe and took her nerves into her mouth again and sucked them and pressed against them as Rafe emitted only incoherent sounds.

Closer and closer, the fuse burned down as Eden's thrusts went deeper into her until the excruciating pressure in Rafe's body exploded around Eden, releasing the warm essence within Rafe as her body shook and trembled with the aftershocks preventing her from breathing deeply.

When her trembling subsided, and she could catch her breath again, Rafe felt Eden pull her fingers away and crawl up Rafe's sweat-covered body.

Rafe looked up at Eden, still unable to speak and saw her blond locks stuck to her flushed face and the gold in her eyes making its presence known when she was feeling desire.

"I love you, Rafe." Rafe could only swallow and lick her lips as Eden kissed her again tenderly. "Tell me you love me."

Rafe felt the sharp cut of fear run through her, and she tried to lift her arms again, but still, they were held down. She looked to see what was holding her down and saw Abby was sitting on one arm and Jude on the other.

Abby looked at her seriously, "We can't let you push her away."

Jude nodded. "Yeah, you're just scared."

Rafe struggled but couldn't free herself as she felt Eden brush back the dark wet curls from her face.

"Rafe, tell me you love me."

Rafe looked into her eyes and opened her mouth to speak but couldn't say the words Eden wanted to hear. "I... I can't," she said shakily.

"You have to tell her!" Abby shouted shrilly. They all agreed and looked at Rafe with confusion and anger.

"You just don't understand. I can't tell her," Rafe pleaded with hoarsely formed words. Eden began to cry, and Rafe could feel heaviness building in her chest. It caused a sharp, heavy pain and felt like it was boring into her. She looked away from Eden and down at her chest. She saw Flynn. He was forcing his gun against her chest creating a painful pressure. Her heart rate increased. "Flynn! Flynn, what are you doing?" she asked in a panic.

Flynn looked sadly at her. "You have to tell her." He pressed the gun forcefully into Rafe's chest. "I'll use this on you to protect her if you don't."

Rafe looked at Flynn and then the gun in pain and terror. "You don't understand. I can't say it anymore! If I do, he'll come!"

Eden put her face close to Rafe's. "You have to tell me you love me. We belong together!"

Abby pulled Rafe's head back by her hair making Rafe grimace in pain. "Tell her or Flynn will do it!"

Jude shook her head in sorrow. "Rafe, you can't get away. She loves you."

Eden and the others began to shout and plead with her as Flynn re-gripped his gun, pressing it into her chest. Fear and pain filled Rafe's body, and her mind throbbed in torment. She had no choice but to give in to them. "Ede! Eden, I do! I love you," she cried out in her panic.

Eden rewarded Rafe with another tender kiss. "There, see? It's okay, babe."

The deafening sound of the earth snapping apart filled the air, and the ground trembled and separated under them. Rafe could hear the screams of her friends and captors.

"Earthquake! Oh, my god!"

Flynn, Abby, and Jude were thrown off Rafe, and she was able to stand and run from the edge of the opening in the ground as it grew. As she ran, a wave of blood rose up, washing over her naked body, and then trickled back down into the darkness.

A black form rose up from the depths with a thick rasping laugh as red streaks of blood flowed over it. The dark form oozed out and made a straight line for Rafe. It took hold of her, keeping her close to the edge of the rift. It surrounded her and covered her naked, bloodstained body entirely in its darkness. Tearing through her painfully, its thick voice resonated through her. "Now, you're mine! You escaped me twice. I intend to take my due!"

Rafe was frozen in fear and pain as she felt the blood drip from her dark hair onto her shoulders and down her back. She watched as the others turned and looked back in astonishment at the gaping fissure in the ground. They didn't see the shadow surrounding Rafe. Only she knew it was there, and she cried out in despair. "You should all go! You should all just go! Run! Move on! I can't go with you!"

They all looked at her, showing their anger, and Eden made her way back toward Rafe. "It's okay, Rafe. Come with me." She smiled and held out her arms. "I love your touch. Will you touch me now?"

Rafe took in Eden's glistening naked body, her golden hair, and gold-flecked eyes. Desire filled her, and the thick voice of the shadow whispered excitedly in her ear. "Touch her. Do it. Go on. Do it." She saw the need in Eden's eyes and reached out to touch her. She gently placed the tips of her fingers on Eden's collarbone and glided them over her shoulder. Slowly, a dark shape took form on Eden's body where Rafe's fingers had brushed her, and a trail of angry reds, purples, and blacks followed Rafe's hand.

Rafe jerked her hand away from Eden. "No! I'm sorry! I'm so sorry, Eden!"

Eden smiled and reached for Rafe. "It's okay. I'll be fine. Touch me, Rafe. I want you."

Rafe looked down at her bloody hands in horror then back up at Eden and the bruises her fingers had caused. "I can't. I can't touch you!"

The dark shadow solidified beside Rafe, and she heard the clicking and smelled the gun oil before she felt the gun press against her temple.

"Touch her," the shadow growled.

The movement to her side caught Rafe's attention, and she saw Abby leading a group of women toward her. "Touch her, Rafe! What are you waiting for?" Abby screamed. "Why are you treating her differently than all of us?"

A line of faces and bodies was illuminated, all with bruises and crying for Rafe to touch them. Rafe recognized Greer as she moved forward and spoke with Beth's voice, "You've bruised all of our hearts."

Rafe saw movement from the corner of her eye, and Brettito ran toward her. Pain ran through her body as he called out to her. "*Ti ho dato il mio sangue per la magia zingara. Si deve amare me!*"[2]

"*Mi spiace!*"[3] Rafe cried in pain at the sight of his young face. "*Sono molto dispiaciuto!*"[4]

Abby nodded her head in agreement with Greer and pointed accusingly at Rafe. "You're a wildling savage! You hurt everyone you touch!"

Tears flowed heavily down Rafe's face, and her voice cracked, "*Mi spiace.* I'm sorry." Her vision cleared and another face came into view. Rafe's heart ached because the girl was so beautiful with dark hair, dark skin, and dark eyes.

"*Cosa ci fai qui ancora una volta, Rafe?*"[5] she asked with concern. "*Te avevo detto di non venire in questo modo.*"[6]

"*Non lo so,*"[7] cried Rafe. "*Non so dove sono!*"[8]

"*Te dimentica sempre,*"[9] she said sadly. "*Seguimi se è possibile,*"[10] she instructed then turned and disappeared.

---

[2] I gave my blood for the magic Gypsy. You must love me!

[3] I'm sorry!

[4] I'm very sorry!

[5] What are you doing here again, Rafe?

[6] I told you not to come this way.

[7] I don't know,

[8] I don't know where I am!

[9] You always forget,

[10] Follow me if you can

"Wait!" shouted Rafe reaching out to the girl just as Eden called her name.

"Rafe, please touch me," she restated her desire. "I love your touch."

The shadow raked painfully over Rafe and pulled her close. It pushed the gun into her temple cutting into her skin. "Touch her!"

Rafe shook and clasped her hands together to defy the command. "No! No! I won't!" Rafe said defiantly as she fell to her knees taking the shadow down with her.

Rafe looked up and watched Jake take form next to Eden. "I'll touch you, Eden." He grinned as he reached for her.

Eden looked at Rafe with pleading eyes. "Rafe, I'm having these feelings I don't know what to do with. Help me, Rafe."

Shaking with anger, "Don't touch her!" Rafe screamed. "I told you I'd kill you if you touch her again!"

Jake laughed and shook his head then put his arms around Eden. "I'm who she needs. She won't ever stop having feelings for men. I told you, it's programmed into her latent memory. I will always be part of her. My touch will never leave her." He kissed Eden and ran his hands down her back leaving his mark on her as she moaned with desire.

Rafe reached out as she cried. "Eden, please, stop! You said you would talk to someone first." She touched Eden's back, and blackness erupted across it. Eden screamed in pain and fell to her knees.

Jake laughed as he slowly disappeared. "She's better off without you. She'll be happier."

Rafe covered her ears to block out the laughter and Eden's screams of pain, but she couldn't block out the voice of the shadow, "I'm so much closer now."

Pounding her fists into the sand, Rafe roared in anguish, "No! No!" She tried to stand and stumbled back, but then lost her balance and fell over the edge of the fissure. She was clinging desperately to the edge, her heart racing, and her lungs burning.

She looked up and saw Eden, with bruises covering her body, looking over the edge. "Hang on, Rafe. I'm coming too. I'll protect you." She climbed over the side and clung to the edge next to Rafe.

"What are you doing? No! Coming in here doesn't protect me!" Rafe screamed. "You have to go back! You can't be with me! I can't be with you! Go back!"

Eden looked at Rafe sadly. "Rafe, why are you doing this?"

Rafe closed her eyes and struggled to hang on as the thick voice of the shadow ripped through her mind again. "Let go, Rafe. Just let go. It's not hard. Just let go."

Rafe fought the voice and shouted angrily, "I won't! I won't do it!"

The shadow laughed thickly, and Rafe looked up at it and saw the gun he held. There was a light from the explosion propelling the bullet to its target. She followed the bullet and watched as it hit the rock next to Eden.

"Oh, I missed by less than an inch," the voice affirmed. "It's okay, I'm getting closer. Let go, Rafe."

Rafe's arms and back were burning as she tried to maintain her grip. "I won't," she whispered. Looking up, she watched as the shadow took aim, and her body began to tremble with fear and torment.

She heard the sound of a bullet being loaded into the chamber as the thick voice calmly declared, "I won't miss this time. I'm just too close to her. You're too close to her."

A deafening report cut through the air, and a flash of light filled the night. Rafe screamed and let go of the edge to reach for Eden. "No!" she shouted as she fell back into darkness and the bullet sped toward Eden.

Hanging out of the open car door, Rafe was startled awake by her nightmare. She had fallen the rest of the way out of the car and into the sand, sweating and trembling.

"No! No!" Rafe gasped as she clawed at her chest and pressed her other hand to her head where she felt the gun in a panic and tried to catch her breath. Her body shook, and she breathed deep trying to force the nightmare from her mind. "It's getting closer," she whispered in pain and panic. "I... I have to let go!"

I have to get far away from here.

39

EDEN KINGSLEY WAS inside Rafe's house, wearing Rafe's pajamas again. She dreamed fitfully as she lay in bed. Sweat covered her body, and she shook in pain as she slept. She woke with a start and ran her hand over her face and through her hair. Tears of agony and anxiety ran down her cheeks.

"Rafe, you have to love me," she cried into the night.

40

WAKING WITH A start early Sunday morning, Letty Carver's first thought was of Rafe. She had worried all night and had fallen asleep waiting for her to come back to the apartment. When she got home from work, she found Rafe had not made it back yet, and it was after midnight. Calling her didn't help because Rafe hadn't answered her phone. She looked through the papers Rafe gave her again and wasn't sure what to make of them, or the strange conversation she'd had with her. She looked at the clock. It was seven o'clock. Not too early to call someone on a Sunday morning, she hoped. She knew Rafe was usually up by now. She picked up the phone and dialed.

"Good morning, yes, could you ring room 506, please? Thank you." She listened to the ringing and let it go on for a while, but there was no answer. She hung up the phone then dialed again. "Yes, room 504, please. Thank you." Again, there was no answer. "They must still be asleep, I hope," she said to herself as she hung up. She redialed the phone, and it was answered on the first ring. "Eden? Sorry to wake you so early," she said into the phone.

"You didn't wake me, Letty," Eden's voice came through.

"Have you heard from Rafe?" asked Letty hopefully.

"No, I was hoping you were her. I saw her yesterday afternoon," she said sadly. "Things didn't go well."

"Oh, okay." She was disappointed Eden didn't know where Rafe was either. "I'm sorry things didn't go well."

"Is something wrong?" asked Eden concerned.

"I'm not sure," Letty answered hesitantly. "I talked to her last night, and she was supposed to come and stay with me. She never showed up."

"Maybe she's still at the hotel," Eden suggested, wondering why Rafe was going to stay with Letty.

"I called, no answer." Letty sighed. "So either they're still asleep or not there."

"Well, Greer might not answer, but if Rafe were there, she would," she said hoping to help. "Maybe she's in the shower, or they're out of their rooms. You should try again."

"You're right," said Letty hoping it was true. "Listen, if you see her will you tell her to call me?"

"Sure. I'm going to the hotel with Abby to get my car keys and see if I can talk to Rafe again. I'm sure she's there. I talked to Greer last night, and she said she was going to talk with Rafe."

"You talked to Greer," asked Letty astonished, "about Rafe?"

"Yes, I know it's strange," admitted Eden softly. "Greer is an amazing person. I want to talk to her again too before she has to leave today."

"I guess I've missed a lot," marveled Letty. "Well, have Rafe call me. Bye," she said and hung up the phone.

41

AFTER FINALLY GETTING everyone loaded into the car, Abby Van Falkov drove Eden Kingsley and Bronte to the Wilshire Hotel. Flynn followed closely in his truck. They were all going so they could see Rafe and Greer, and to get Eden's car keys. They were hoping Greer was able to get Rafe to agree to come home and talk to a therapist so she and Eden could work through things. They walked into the hotel and went into the restaurant where they had agreed to meet for brunch. Spotting Greer and Beth already seated, they walked over to the table.

"Good morning," Greer greeted them with a smile as they joined them.

"Good morning," said Eden returning the smile as she held Bronte. She looked around for Rafe. "Did you talk to Rafe? Where is she?"

"No, I didn't," voiced Greer as she shook her head and motioned to Beth to interpret as everyone began to take their seats. "She left a note saying she was going to stay with her cousin Letty and she took her things. I thought when you got here, we could call Letty and see if we could go to her apartment and talk to Rafe."

"Greer," Eden rasped through her damaged throat. "Letty called this morning," she hesitated, worried as she put Bronte in a highchair, "she said Rafe did show up last night, but she didn't stay. She said she might come back, but she didn't."

"Where else would she have gone?" voiced Greer with concern after Beth interpreted.

"Maybe Julia's," suggested Abby. "I'll call her," she said and called her on her cellular phone. "Hey, it's me. Did Rafe show up at your place last night? Oh, okay. I'll call you back later. If you see Rafe, call me. Bye." She hung up and looked at Eden. "Not there," she shrugged.

"She left! I drove her away," Eden said as she looked at Greer in horror and was barely able to hold her tears back. "I pushed too hard!"

"Calm down, Eden," Beth interpreted for Greer. "Let's call Letty and let her know what's going on. Maybe she knows of another place she could be."

"I'll call her," said Abby and dialed her phone. "Letty? Hey, I'm here at the hotel with Eden and Greer. Rafe isn't here. Do you know where else she might be? What? Oh, okay, we're in the restaurant. We won't go anywhere." She hung up. "She said we're not to move. She's coming to us. She sounded really upset," she said anxiously.

42

TWENTY MINUTES LATER, Letty Carver walked determinedly into Wilshire Hotel and made her way to the restaurant. As she approached the table, the worried group could see she was upset.

"Letty!" Abby signaled to her. "Over here!"

"Hey," said Letty as she sat at the table next to Eden and Bronte and then put the papers Rafe gave her on the table. "I have a terrible feeling."

Seeing Letty so upset worried Eden, and she felt her stomach turn. "What..." she stammered, "what's happening, Letty?"

"I told you I talked to her last night," Letty reminded her. "Well, it was such a strange conversation. Then I watched her get into some sort of racecar or something, and she just gunned it down the road like something was after her."

Eden looked at Letty with a frown. "Was it her father's Maserati? I thought she sold it when she sold her business."

"It was dark, but it might have been," said Letty. "I'm not sure. It's been a while since I've seen it."

"I knew she could never get rid of her sexy car!" said Abby. "But I haven't seen her in it for years. Where does she keep it?"

"I have no idea," Letty admitted as Eden shook her head, bewildered and surprised Rafe still had the car.

"Oh, my god!" exclaimed Abby suddenly. "She said she had a private garage! I wonder where it is."

"I have no idea," Letty repeated shaking her head.

"What did she talk to you about, Letty," asked Greer with concern and wanting to get on topic.

Letty looked at Greer as the memory of last night ran through her mind. "All about her having to leave and feeling guilty," Letty said worriedly. "I just don't understand what's happening to her." She pushed the papers toward Eden. "She gave this to me to show you and Greer. She wanted me to tell you she couldn't be with either of you."

"What?" asked Eden shakily and looked at Greer in agony. "I knew it," she said frantically. "She's just, just leaving!" She picked up the stack of papers. "This is her list," she said as she looked at the papers in astonishment.

"What's this?" asked Abby as she looked at the other stack of papers.

"She said it was a timeline," answered Letty at a loss on how to interpret the information on the paper.

"A timeline," Abby parroted baffled.

"Yeah, she says it explains everything," said Letty. "I don't understand it at all!"

"Whoa!" Abby drew out the word as she looked at the list. "This is way more than three pages!"

"Please, slow down," voiced Greer. "Letty, start from the beginning."

Letty sighed and put her hand to her head. "She came over last night. She wasn't looking very well, and she wouldn't come inside because Bronte was there. I went out with her, and we sat in my car. She started going on about feeling guilty about everything. She was feeling guilty about her mamma and papa and her friend in Italy—and you, Eden. It was like she was putting the blame for everything that happened to everyone on herself. She kept talking about death getting closer.

"Death?" repeated Eden and went pale. "Oh my god," she whispered. "Oh my god, no!" she cried afraid Rafe was going to hurt herself.

"I think she was talking about you, Eden," explained Letty as she put her hand on Eden's arm to calm her. "I think she believes if she comes back, you'll die."

"What?" Abby screeched. "That's crazy!"

"I know. I told her," Letty assured her. "But she kept going on about being able to feel death pressing up against her."

"I can't take this," said Eden as she shook with dread. "Why was she saying those things?"

"I don't know," admitted Letty overwrought. She looked over at Flynn with his bruised face and a broken arm. "Flynn, she said she thought it was your gun."

"My gun?" Flynn asked in surprise.

"You don't have it anywhere she can get it, do you?" asked Letty worried.

"The police still have it," said Flynn as he shook his head.

"Good." Letty sighed with relief. "Good."

"Why would she do this," asked Flynn. "Everything's good now."

"It's her controlling ways," Abby declared. "Look at this." She pointed to the papers. "She's practically turned herself into some kind of monster and oppressor and Eden into some kind of tormented saint or something."

"What are you talking about, Abby?" asked Eden as she looked at the papers.

"Well, the way she sees things," Abby explained as she pointed things out in the papers, "she's causing you to do things and make decisions making you hurt yourself. Eden, it's like she is trying to free you from some kind of hell."

"I..." stammered Eden, "She..." Eden took a deep breath. "Why is this happening? I'm not in any kind of hell," Eden insisted. "I mean some things she did hurt me, and I made some horrible choices," she admitted, "but in the end, like she told me, they were my choices."

"Well, according to her, she's the culprit," said Abby frankly. "I think it's like Greer said, she can't control things like she did before. I think she's doing this to give herself an excuse to not be with you." She looked over the papers again. "You know she may be right. Look at some of this stuff. Eden, were you really this controlled and oppressed?"

"She's not right, Abby!" yelled Eden, her anger was crossed between Abby and Rafe. She looked around and lowered her voice. "She's blown everything out of proportion! I mean when everything is compiled like this, how can it not look bad?"

"We know she's controlling, but she's not controlling to make you feel oppressed, Eden," Beth interpreted for Greer.

"She's just like her father," said Letty upset. "He was always in control. I could never understand their relationship. She worshiped him, and he was very controlling of her and everyone around him."

"Letty, don't," Eden said knowing she complained about Rafe's father a lot, and Rafe didn't like it.

"You just don't know, Eden," she said in frustration. "After her mother had died, he packed her off to a boarding school, and when they came here, he made her go to a private school full of egocentric teachers and bullies."

"You mean like Julia," asked Abby with a snicker.

Letty gave her a disapproving look then turned her attention back to Eden. "Ettore Salvaggio was a tyrant to everyone around him. He traveled and left her in their house alone with just a housekeeper most of the time. When he was home, he had very high expectations of her and was so hard on her, but Rafe couldn't see it. She loved him, she craved his love, and she always jumped when he said jump. She's learned her control stuff from him. He screwed her up so bad!

"He was all she had," Eden reminded her, "and whenever I saw them together, they were happy. This isn't his fault."

"He was so demanding and hard on her, but she just craved his attention and love," said Letty sadly.

"I don't know, Letty, he seemed nice," Eden assured her. "He was so accepting of Rafe and me."

"It's because she was just like him," insisted Letty. She could never understand why no one else saw it, or if they did, they ignored it. "Under all their surface affection, they were in constant competition, even if they wouldn't admit it to themselves. I really think it's why Rafe finally came to California, so she wouldn't have to compete for women or love with her dad. They were both *Lotharios* when it came to women. I know at times he was very jealous but, at the same time, proud of Rafe's prowess."

"I believe it," Abby piped in knowingly. "I mean, can you imagine the male twin of Rafe? The women of New York were definitely not safe with both of them there."

"So, her being controlling at times is possibly just a learned behavior she has for showing love," Greer signed, and Beth interpreted. She wanted to bring the conversation back to the present. "She wants your life to be perfect, and her definition of perfect has been proven wrong."

"Yeah," agreed Abby, "if she weren't a perfectionist, we wouldn't have this list."

"Wait," said Greer as she looked over the timeline and started signing to Beth. "I think I've figured this out. Look, here is her legend, and it looks like she used a number sequence coding technique. So this timeline goes back," Beth paused waiting for Greer, "over twenty-five years."

"Twenty-five years!" exclaimed Abby, "No wonder it's so thick!"

"It's a timeline of her life," said Greer as she looked at marked significant events. "Okay, here is this year. Oh my god. This is not good," warned Greer and looked at everyone with concern.

43

WITH A SMALL duffle bag over her shoulder, Rafe Salvaggio walked down the sidewalk that ran in front of her and Jude's houses. She stopped in front of Jude's house and stood motionless. After a while, she made her way to Jude's front door and knocked.

"Hey, Rafe." Jude smiled as she opened the door and then took in Rafe's unkempt appearance. Her expression changed to one of confusion. "Is everything okay?"

"Everything is fine," said Rafe calmly. "Can I come in?"

"Sure." Jude opened the door wide and let Rafe inside. They sat down in the living room. "What's up?"

"I..." Rafe started then looked at Jude thoughtfully for a minute. "I'm going away, and I just thought maybe you'd like to come with me."

"Where are you going?" asked Jude on alert because she knew this was something Eden was concerned about.

"I was thinking Canada or Mexico." Rafe forced a smile. "I thought I'd let you choose. I was going to Canada, but I thought maybe you wouldn't want to go there. I remember you saying you didn't go with us to Canada because you didn't like the cold."

"Why do you want me to go with you?" asked Jude unsure what to do.

"We..." Rafe paused, "we have a lot in common. I just thought you'd like a chance to start over, too."

"Start over?" Jude said and looked around. "Rafe, I like it here, plus I don't really have the money to go anywhere."

"Oh, don't worry about money," said Rafe patting her duffle bag. "I have plenty to last for a while. I'll give you some."

"You're going to give me your money?" asked Jude in shock.

"Sure, why not," said Rafe nonchalantly. "I have plenty."

"How much money do you have?" Jude asked cautiously.

Rafe looked at Jude for a while then took a breath. "I have two hundred fifty thousand dollars," she revealed quietly and patted her small duffle bag.

"My god!" Jude blurted as she stood up in shock. "You have a quarter of a million dollars in your bag?" Jude sat back down. "Rafe, you can't carry so much money around on you!"

"Why not?" asked Rafe with a slight frown. "It's mine."

"What if someone robs you?" asked Jude concerned.

"Only you know I have it," she answered, and her lips quirked slightly. "Don't worry, I can get more."

"You can get—" Jude stopped stunned. "Where did you get all the money? Did you rob a bank?"

"No." Rafe laughed dryly. "I sold some art. When I was put on leave from the Conservatory, I took some to auction. I took a lot of it out of the little gallery I had in the house when I turned it into Bronte's room. I didn't want to just store it in a dark storage room. It sold last weekend, and I got the money Monday."

"They gave it to you all in cash?" Jude asked surprised.

"No, of course not." Rafe flashed a brief smile. "I cashed the checks at the bank."

"It's a lot of money," said Jude nervously.

"I know. I was pleased with the sale. It all sold for the high end of what it appraised for, and the broker gave me a good deal on her fees. I think she's hoping for more business," said Rafe and patted the duffle bag.

"I guess," Jude mused and looked at Rafe then the bag of money. "You know, I don't think you can leave the country with so much money. I think you can only take about ten thousand in currency out of the country."

"It's okay," Rafe assured her with a wink. "I only have twenty thousand in cash and the rest is in traveler's checks and a few pre-loaded credit cards. I'll give you ten thousand to carry, and we'll be okay."

"Does Eden know about this?" asked Jude concerned.

Rafe frowned. "No. It's my art."

Well," Jude hesitated, "you said you had more money. So what do you mean?"

"Oh, well, this is just some ready cash," said Rafe casually. "I have a lot more cash in my bank and investment accounts."

"A lot more?" asked Jude

"Yeah..." Rafe hesitated and bit her lip. She thought it was best not to tell her the truth about what Jake called her obscene amount of money she had inherited. They would not need much anyway. "Maybe a few million," she said offhandedly. "We can live anywhere we want to go."

"A *few* million?" said Jude dumbfounded, wondering how many if Rafe's mind constituted a few.

"Yeah, but don't worry about it," said Rafe knowing she had a lot more than she confessed to having. "If we need more money than we have in this bag, I'll just arrange to get more."

"Okay, well—" Jude scratched her head. "I mean, does Eden know you're going and everything?"

"Letty's going to tell her," Rafe answered with a nod. "Will you come?"

"I don't know, Rafe," said Jude nervously. "Will you give me a bit to think about it?"

"I guess," said Rafe thoughtfully. "Sure, it's a big decision."

"Yeah, it is," Jude agreed. She looked Rafe over, taking in her disheveled hair and wrinkled clothes. "Are you taking a suitcase or anything?"

"No," said Rafe with a shrug and patted the bag. "Just what I have from the hotel."

"Maybe you should go get some things from the house," Jude suggested. "Eden's not there, so maybe you could change your clothes and take a shower. It'll make you feel better for the trip."

"She's not there?" asked Rafe and hesitated. "Is she okay? Where is she?" she asked, worried something might have happened.

"Abby came and got her this morning. It's okay," Jude told her reassuringly as she saw how worried she had become. "She's taking her and Flynn to get her car keys at the hotel, and then they're going to get her car."

"She shouldn't be driving," said Rafe upset. She pulled Eden's keys out of her bag and held them up. "Plus I have her keys."

"Well, maybe when you go pack, you can leave them at the house," suggested Jude hoping Rafe would go so she could call Abby.

Rafe looked around and thought about it. "Okay," she agreed as she stood. "You should pack first, and don't forget your passport. Are you coming?"

Jude hesitated then stood slowly. "Okay," she agreed. She headed to her room, and Rafe followed her closely. "Are you sure you want to do this?" she asked as she shoved some clothes in a bag and grabbed her passport.

"I'm sure," said Rafe as she looked at Jude intently. "Let's go get my stuff now."

They walked out and went over to Rafe's house using Eden's keys to get inside. Rafe walked through the house and left the keys on the kitchen counter. "I'll go pack some stuff. I don't have time to take a shower. We have to go."

"Okay, I'll wait here," said Jude. "No problem."

She watched Rafe walk into her room, and then she pulled out her cellular phone and dialed.

"Abby," she whispered. "Abby, where are you guys? I have no idea where she was last night," she hissed, "but you can stop trying to figure out where she is. She's with me. Abby, something's really wrong," Jude whispered frantically. "She looks like hell. I think she's sick. She's freaking me out! She wants me to go to Canada or Mexico. And Abby, she just very calmly told me she has a quarter of a million dollars in her bag!" Jude listened to Abby yelling on the phone. "She says she sold some paintings. I don't know if I can stop her. She had me pack a bag and take my passport. Okay, okay, I won't leave her side. I'll call you back when I can." She hung up the phone and shoved it in her pocket.

Rafe had freshened up, put on some clean, comfortable clothes, and walked out of her room with a small suitcase. "Okay, I'm ready," she said calmly. She pulled a small letter sized box out of her duffle bag and placed it on the floor in front of Eden's door. "Let's go."

"What's in the box?" asked Jude looking toward the box.

"It explains everything," said Rafe. "I'm leaving her a copy in case Letty forgets to show Eden the one I gave her." She looked over and saw her box of photography supplies. She opened it, took a few things out of it, and put them in her camera bag.

"Letty knows you're leaving?" asked Jude hesitantly.

"Yes, I told her last night," said Rafe. She looked at Jude and smiled. "I already told you." She walked out the door with her small suitcase, camera bag, and the duffle bag with the money as Jude followed her.

"Oh, you did?" asked Jude but Rafe did not say anything back. "Where's your car?"

"In storage. Our cab is at the end of the block," said Rafe calmly as they walked down the street. "I didn't know Eden wouldn't be home."

"So," asked Jude warily, "where were you last night?"

"Out," said Rafe flatly.

"Well, you should tell me where you were," said Jude. "We're in this together now."

Rafe stopped and looked at Jude. "I was at the beach," she said and smiled because Jude was right, they were in this together.

"With a quarter of a million dollars?" asked Jude troubled.

"You should keep it down," said Rafe as she looked around.

Jude looked around like Rafe did to see if anyone heard her. "Yeah," she agreed as they walked to the cab, loaded their luggage, and got in.

"LAX," she told the driver then smiled at Jude. "So, Canada or Mexico?" asked Rafe as the cab driver pulled away.

44

INSIDE THE WILSHIRE Hotel, Eden Kingsley and the group had moved up to Greer Noble's room. Rafe's list and timeline were spread out across one of the beds. Eden, Greer, and Beth were interpreting the timeline while Letty watched over Bronte. Flynn and Abby were sitting nearby going over the list to see if they could find anything useful.

They jumped as Abby's phone rang. Abby snatched it up quickly. They had all looked up at Abby as she talked on the phone and waited impatiently for her to tell them what was happening because they could tell the call was about Rafe.

Abby hung up her phone and turned to look at them. "It was Jude," she announced. "Rafe's with her!"

"Is she okay?" asked Eden frantically wishing she could have talked to Jude herself.

"She's at the house, and Jude said she was acting strange and looks sick," Abby relayed. "She said Rafe asked her to go to Canada or Mexico. Eden," Abby looked at her troubled, "Jude said she has a quarter of a million dollars on her."

"What!" Eden said shocked. "Where did she get that kind of money?"

"She told Jude she sold some art," said Abby uneasily.

"I need to get out of here," said Eden as she quickly gathered her things. "You have to take me home, Abby! I need to see if I can get to the house before she leaves."

45

THE CAR WAS barely stopped when Eden Kingsley quickly opened the door to get out ignoring the pain from her injuries. She wanted to find Rafe. Eden got to the front door, and it was locked. She hit the door in frustration because Rafe had her keys.

"I'll check the back," suggested Abby and carried Bronte around the house. She found the sliding door unlocked and rushed to let Eden inside.

They were too late. Rafe and Jude were gone. Abby released Bronte to play with her toys as Eden searched frantically through the house. Eden found out Rafe had packed some clothes and her bathroom things as well as some of the items out of the box of photo equipment that Flynn had brought back over. She stopped looking in defeat when she found the small box in front of her door with a copy of the information Rafe gave to Letty inside.

Eden looked at Abby who had been following her and burst into tears again. "They're gone," she cried. "Why didn't Jude keep her here?"

"I'm sorry," said Abby and hugged her gently. "You know Rafe. She probably just ran right over Jude." She held up a set of keys. "At least I found your keys. They were on the kitchen island."

Letty walked in the door with Flynn close behind her. She could tell by Abby and Eden's demeanor that Rafe wasn't there. "I called Ephraim," she said. "He should be here soon." She looked over at Bronte who was playing, and sadness filled her. She hoped Eden would still let them be in the baby's life if Rafe had left for good. "Greer said she and Beth would be here as soon as they're checked out of the hotel."

"I called Julia," said Abby and led Eden into the living room to sit down.

"What's in the box?" asked Flynn as he sat on the floor with Bronte.

Eden took the lid off the box and pulled out the pages. "It looks like another copy of the list and timeline," she said and dried the tears on her face.

Letty took the box from Eden gently. "I'll put it in the dining room," she said and took it to the table just as Greer walked in with Beth. Letty pulled them to the side. "She's not here," she told them, and they understood Eden was taking it hard. "She left another copy of those papers."

Greer looked at the box Letty had nodded toward on the table. "I think we should take a better look at it. It seems very important to Rafe."

As they spread the papers across the dining room table, Julia and Ephraim made it to the house. Letty kissed Ephraim hello then went into the kitchen to make some drinks. It was something she knew how to do well, and it calmed her.

Eden went into the dining room and saw Julia at the table along with Greer and Beth. She sat down next to Julia trying to contain her anxiety as Greer laid out the timeline and other information across it.

"Should we check the airport to see if her car is there?" she asked hopefully. "Maybe we can get to her before she gets on a plane."

"I can go if you want," offered Ephraim as he held Bronte, and she showed him her toy kitchen utensils. He watched Eden nod. "Okay, I'll call you if I find her car or anything." He handed Bronte to Flynn who took her back with her toys. After saying goodbye to Letty, he took off for the airport.

Letty brought Eden a cup of hot tea then sighed as she sat down. "I put on coffee too. It should be ready soon."

"We need to know more of what Rafe said if you can remember, Letty. Maybe it'll help us find her," voiced Greer.

Letty thought about last night and tried to remember everything Rafe had told her. "She just sounded so out of it," she said with worry. "She was telling me how she felt guilty for everyone. You, Eden," she said putting her hand on her arm, "and her mamma and papa, and her friend."

"Did she say why?" asked Greer.

"Not really. She just said everything was her fault because they all kept secrets from her," Letty revealed.

"Secrets?" asked Eden troubled as she held her warm cup. "I know I was keeping things from her, but what did her parents and her friend keep from her?"

"Well, I don't know if all of you know this, but, Rafe, she saw her mother die in an accident," said Letty sadly.

"She said a driver ran a light and hit her," Eden said. She looked over at the sound of Bronte's laughter in the living room as she played with Flynn. "I didn't know she saw it happen, though," she said turning her attention back to the table.

"She didn't. I was told she saw her right after. It's part of what she was talking about. She talked about how her mother was lying so still in the street and the twisted bicycle..." Letty said recalling the conversation. "She said if she had been better, her mamma would still be alive. I'm not sure what secret Rafe was talking about, though."

"What about her father and her friend? What was her friend's name?" asked Eden then took a small sip of her tea as Abby joined the table.

"Brettito. He was a little boy she and her other friend Gabri were friends with," said Letty sadly. "I don't know what secrets they had either. She only mentioned him a few times when she first moved to New York, but it was just in passing. She never really talked to me about him." She shook her head sadly.

"I think I know that name," said Eden before Letty could continue. "Hold on," she said as she set her cup down then went to her bedroom. Inside, Eden went to her jewelry box and took out a crumpled piece of stationery she had folded up so it would fit. She went back out and sat next to Letty. "Rafe wrote this," she said and handed it to Letty. She looked at Abby and Julia, as she felt guilty. "I found it with Bronte's things when we were in Canada. When I read it, I..." she paused. "It was when I knew how much keeping Bronte from her was hurting her. I kept it and read it every time Jake pressured me about the adoption. I would read it, and it helped me stand up to him," she confessed.

"I don't remember Rafe talking about Brettito when she came to live in New York," said Julia wondering why Rafe never mentioned her friend who had died.

"I asked her father about it when she mentioned his death to me when they first moved here," said Letty. "He only told me, not quite a year after Rafe's mother died, the boy died in an accident." Letty closed her eyes and decided to tell them everything she knew. "But when..." she hesitated then started again, "when her father told my parents about it, I overheard him. He told them the kids were at some sort of festival, and Rafe and Gabri saw the aftermath. Apparently, the boy was caught up with a group of kids who robbed a store, and he was shot in the street." She paused, knowing Rafe never talked about what had happened to her friend or how it affected her, but she thought they might need to know. "He told my parents when he found Rafe, he thought she had been hurt too because she was covered in her friend's blood. He said the boy bled out in the street, and when Rafe got to the scene and watched him being taken away, she had been standing in his blood. When she realized it, she just lost it and fell into the street and into all of the blood. She was covered in it. Her father said she was screaming and the blood was dripping from her hair and clothes when Gabri and another man pulled her out. When he got there, she had completely shut down."

Letty stopped and could see the looks of shock on her friend's faces but continued. "She was really affected badly by his death so soon after her mother's. I don't know much more, but apparently, Rafe was inconsolable and shut down for a long time. He said only her friend Gabri could get her to do anything for a while, including eating and getting out of bed."

"My god!" said Eden shaking in distress. "I can't imagine being a kid and seeing something so horrible and being able to cope." New tears streamed down her face for the new things she was learning about the woman she loved. She didn't understand why Rafe had never told her about that time in her life.

"I can't believe she never spoke of it to me," said Julia astounded by what Letty had revealed. "Though, really, she doesn't speak about her past much at all."

Greer looked at the letter on the table and wished Rafe had felt close enough to tell her about her mother and her childhood friend. "She's been holding in a lot of grief for a long time," she said with concern, "and with all the other things, including the hostage situation, they must have built onto each other." She looked at all Rafe's friends and realized another reason Rafe probably hadn't been able to leave was because they were her family too. "She holds a lot inside her," said Greer as she felt her heart was breaking for Rafe. "It's probably a big reason for some of her control issues," Beth began interpreting. "She probably learned to hide her feelings to cope. Now she's lost the control she thought she had and everything is surfacing."

Abby rubbed Eden's back lightly wanting to help her friend and worrying about Rafe. She wished there was more she could do. "Jude or Ephraim will call us, and we'll find her," she said trying to sound hopeful. "I just hope they call soon."

Greer looked at the timeline as she thought about what was happening with Rafe. "I think Rafe has a deeper problem. I think she may have BPD." She thought about all the things happening with Rafe. "I have to be right," she said. "Everything points to it. We have to get her help right away before something bad happens."

"So, what's BPD?" asked Abby doubtfully.

Greer nodded to Beth and began signing. "Brief Psychotic Disorder. She's showing some classic signs based on what Letty said and what we've all observed. She has a lack of emotional response. This explains her sudden calmness. She's hallucinating, about death in her case. She's making strange statements about guilt and wanting to leave the country. Even her whole conversation with Letty, and the way it didn't make a lot of sense could be a symptom. This timeline and list could be part of it too."

"She's gone crazy?" Abby asked shaken. She could not imagine Rafe not being in control at all times.

"No, she hasn't gone crazy," said Greer. "It's just everything has caught up with her. This last traumatic event with Eden just pushed her over the edge. Look at this timeline. It's perfect."

"Well, like I've said before, she's a perfectionist," said Abby shaking her head.

"Right," voiced Greer. "It's perfect, as far as we know, except she left off what happened at the Conservatory. It's hard to know if she left anything else off because we don't know all of her history."

"Why would she leave it off?" asked Eden concerned.

"Because, the real underlying problem might be that she's been suffering from PTSD, Post-Traumatic Stress Disorder, for a long time." Beth voiced for Greer. "Do any of you know if she went to any of the counseling sessions provided by the school?"

"I didn't even know they offered any," admitted Abby.

"Me either," said Flynn as he followed Bronte into the dining room.

"I..." Eden swallowed guiltily, "I didn't know." She watched Flynn sweep Bronte up and take her back into the living room.

"What the hell did she do after I left?" Greer asked for herself, angrily.

"She just stayed home," said Abby in shame. "She didn't want to go anywhere or see anyone."

"I can't believe you people!" Greer shouted. "One of your friends goes through something where there is a high chance they will die and you just..." she shook her head in disbelief, "just do nothing for her!" She glared at Eden. "Do you know she wanted to die? She was practically begging the guy to shoot her! She wanted to die!" she screamed.

"She..." started Eden unnerved, "wanted to..." she couldn't speak. She had no idea about anything Greer was talking about. Eden only knew Rafe accused her of wanting her to die. She covered her face with her hands in misery. "I didn't know," she said, stricken with guilt.

"This is unbelievable!" Greer shouted and signed angrily to Beth who interpreted. "I was wondering how she had time to make something like this timeline. She must have been working on it for months. It explains her not ever talking about it and her avoidance of you all for a month. Now, with this new trauma, her avoidance of Eden. Letty, it even explains her statement about feeling the gun on her. She has felt a gun on her in those places. She's reliving it and doesn't even realize it."

"I wonder if it's the reason she wouldn't let me come into her room, and why she was always reluctant to stay the whole night with me," Eden revealed as she tried to wipe away her tears.

"You're telling me she has never spent an entire night with you?" asked Greer shocked.

"Well," said Eden uneasily, "she was there when I went to sleep," she paused, "but I only know of maybe one or two times when she was there when I woke up." She rubbed the back of her neck anxiously. "I just thought it was because she was still not sure of me."

"What other things did she do making you think her not being sure was the reason she was doing them?" asked Greer concerned, hoping to get more information to help diagnose Rafe.

"I don't know," said Eden hesitantly and licked her dry lips. "She, we never," she looked at Greer sadly. "We never stayed in her room. She kept the door locked."

Greer immediately started signing for Beth to interpret. "Are you telling me you've never been in her room since you got back together with her?" Eden nodded, and Greer looked at Beth with concern and signed for her only. "My god, Beth. How do I tell her I may have been the last person, the only person Rafe has allowed in her room?"

Beth signed back, "You don't. What good would it do?"

Greer nodded in agreement and turned back to Eden. "What else did she do?"

Eden took a deep breath to clear her mind. "She would go out taking pictures and be gone for hours, who knows where," she hesitated, "but it seemed like she didn't come back with many pictures. At least I didn't see a lot, I mean, there were a few."

"She went out running a lot and said she had to do it alone," Flynn added following Bronte again. "We started lifting weights, and we worked on the chase lounge project too. She didn't want anyone to know about the project. Oh," Flynn remembered, "we talked about war and strategy a lot."

"War and strategy?" scoffed Abby as Flynn nodded. "I don't get it."

Eden looked down and put her face in her hands then looked up at Greer. "She was—" She stopped. "It was all so different when we were together. But Rafe said she had changed, and she had said it before," she stammered, "so I just thought," she looked at Greer uneasily. "Do you really think this is the reason she didn't want me in her room?"

Greer rubbed her temples then signed quickly. "It's possible," relayed Beth. "It looks like she was always doing a lot of things alone or with just one person at a time to manage people. She changed her behavior when she was drinking it seems.

"And when she smoked pot," added Abby trying to be helpful. "It helped her open up when she was shut down about the article and everything."

Greer nodded as Beth interpreted then added more observations. "She also may have been having nightmares, so she didn't want you in her room, Eden. It's a symptom." She paused to think and look at the papers on the table. "We have to find her. She may become a danger to herself if things get any worse. She's out there somewhere with a quarter of a million dollars having hallucinations and delusions. There's no telling what she might do."

"Jude said she wanted to go to Canada or Mexico," said Abby apprehensively.

"She told me Canada," added Letty and hesitated, "or Italy."

"They're all in totally opposite directions!" shouted Eden angry and afraid for Rafe. She felt like her fear was trying to take over, and she worked to fight it and hold herself together.

"Eden, we have to call your therapist Cathcart," Beth relayed for Greer. "I'm not a licensed psychologist in California. I was just a teacher here. We have to get her in somewhere. Who has her medical power of attorney?"

"I do," said Letty then looked at Eden. "She changed it to me a while back."

"I know," said Eden sadly as Letty hugged her.

"Well, we'll need Cathcart and Letty to get her in somewhere," signed Greer for Beth to interpret, "and possibly to help file a police report so they'll look for her under a medical emergency."

"Wait," interrupted Letty and looked at Greer and Eden. "If we do this, will it hurt her job or anything? And how will it affect the adoption? Maybe we should try to find her first."

Greer began signing again, her frustration showing. "Letty," Beth interpreted, "I'm sorry to say this, but if we don't find her soon, none of that will matter! We don't know how bad things really are for her!" Greer looked at everyone then at Eden and signed for Beth to interpret again. "I'm sorry. I need to take a timeout. I'm so angry with all of you right now, I'm afraid I'll say something I'll regret!" She walked out of the front door leaving everyone stunned.

"You know," said Beth apologetically, "she'll be okay. Greer just really does love Rafe, and she can't stand seeing her in pain. Greer was upset she had to leave Rafe back then. She probably thinks most of this is her fault for not staying. Rafe asked her to stay, and she may be feeling guilty. Just..." she paused, "give her some time."

"We know she loves her, and she's right," Letty assured her feeling upset herself. "I'm her cousin and only blood relative she's got now, and I didn't even look in on her. Greer told me Rafe needed her friends and family around. It's why she had me make sure everyone was here at the house after what happened at the school."

"We just never think about Rafe being the one who needs help," admitted Abby. "She's the strong one."

"She isn't strong, Abby," said Eden as she shook her head in misery. "She's just good at hiding her fear and other emotions. I was so wrapped up in my own problems that I didn't even consider Rafe was going through this. I should have seen it. I know her best," she said, angry at herself. "I'm supposed to know her best, but I don't know anything." She broke down in tears at yet another failure heaped on her shoulders.

"We know now," Letty assured her and hugged her again. "Let's just get things fixed and not think about what we can't change."

"I'll try to call Jude back and see if she can tell us where they are," offered Abby wanting to do anything to help her friends. She dialed her phone. "Voice mail," she said and waited to leave a message. "Jude, it's Abby. Listen, we need to know exactly where you are and where you're going. If you can, try to keep Rafe in town as long as possible. We're getting her help. Don't be surprised if the police pull you over. We may be putting out an emergency medical alert on her. Whatever you do, don't let her out of your sight!"

46

AT LAX AIRPORT, Rafe Salvaggio and Jude Atwood were dropped off at their terminal. They took their luggage and Rafe's camera case out of the trunk of the cab, and then Rafe paid the cab driver and gave him a large tip with a happy smile. "Thanks for driving me around, and your patience," she told him as they shook hands. She slung the duffle bag over her shoulder and then led Jude inside the airport.

"Are you sure you want to do this?" asked Jude worried as she grabbed their luggage. She didn't know when exactly it happened, but now, Rafe seemed like she was back to her normal self and in a very good mood. Jude hoped she could convince Rafe to stay in the country. "We could go somewhere in the States," she suggested. "We don't have to leave the country."

"I'm sure," said Rafe as she smiled at Jude. "Just think of it as a great adventure. Have you decided where you'd like to go?"

Jude rubbed the back of her neck and sighed praying they couldn't buy tickets with this short of notice. "Okay," she nodded, "I guess Mexico."

"Great! Come on." Rafe and started walking to the airline ticket counter.

Jude followed Rafe with the luggage, except the duffle bag. Rafe had it, and it held the money. "I don't think we can get tickets with this short of notice," said Jude hoping it was true.

"I've got everything taken care of." Rafe smiled as she turned her head and winked at Jude. "Give me your passport." Jude pulled her passport from her pocket and gave it to Rafe. "Wait here," she directed and walked up to the self-check-in kiosk. Rafe was there a few minutes then walked back to Jude. "Here you go," she said and handed Jude her passport along with a ticket and boarding pass. "Let's get to our gate."

Jude looked at the ticket in shock then followed Rafe. "How..." she stammered, "how did you know I'd pick Mexico?"

"I didn't," said Rafe casually. "I booked both places when I decided I was going. I still have a good travel agency." They got through security and to the waiting area and sat down. Rafe looked at her watch and smiled at Jude. "In a little less than five hours, we'll be in beautiful Cancun, Mexico. You'll love the resort I booked. I talked to the manager directly, and everything will be ready for us."

Jude couldn't believe the situation she had gotten into so fast. "You planned everything, for two places?" she asked, and Rafe just smiled and nodded. "Rafe," said Jude cautiously, "I've got to make a few calls and check my voicemail before we take off," she said and took out her cellular phone. It had been buzzing in silent mode so she knew there were messages. They were probably all from Abby.

"Jude, we're starting over." Rafe frowned as she took Jude's phone. "There's no one you need to call and no one whose messages you have to listen to," she said then turned off Jude's phone and put it in her bag. She wished she had made her leave it at home as she had her own. "We're free of our old life." She smiled as she sat back to relax and wait to board the plane.

"Right," said Jude uneasily and forced a smile, "free."

Outside the airport, Ephraim drove around the parking lots and terminals looking for Rafe's car not knowing she hadn't taken her car to the airport, and she was already inside about to board her flight.

47

EDEN KINGSLEY AND the rest of the worried group were spread out in the living room and dining room back at her and Rafe's house. They had been trying to figure out what to do about Rafe and waiting anxiously for a phone call from Jude. Ephraim had called, and he hadn't seen Rafe's car anywhere at the airport.

As they continued to discuss the situation, everyone was in a high state of anxiety. Eden could feel the thickness of emotion around her, and it compounded her own anxiety. She did her best to keep herself above water as she thought about everything happening and Rafe's behavior.

"She's been going through all of this for months, and I couldn't even see it," lamented Eden as she took a pill for her pain. "Looking back now it's so clear. I don't blame Greer for being angry. I've failed Rafe. I've failed her so badly," she croaked and broke down in tears losing the composure she had been trying to maintain.

"We can't keep thinking like this," said Letty as she held Bronte. "We have to concentrate on getting her back and getting her help."

Greer walked back into the house followed closely by Beth. "Hi, I'm back," announced Greer. "Listen," she looked at everyone, "I'm sorry I got so angry. I think I'm most angry at Rafe for not going to counseling. I'm sure she thought she was too busy to go or thought she didn't need it."

"I understand," sobbed Eden to Greer through her tears. "Everything has just been so hard. Harder than I ever even imagined things could be for her, and for us."

"I've been thinking about the situation," said Greer. "Letty, I think you should talk to Rafe's lawyer."

"Her lawyer?" asked Letty in surprise. "Why?"

Greer signed, and Beth relayed her words. "To find out if Rafe signed a release for the counseling services. If she didn't, the school and the counseling office should pay for whatever treatment she'll need. If she did, we need someone to review her exit questionnaire and make sure something wasn't overlooked or if they just failed to properly review it."

"I'll call Katheryn and leave her a message explaining I need to talk with her as soon as possible," Letty volunteered as she put Bronte on the floor to play. She could see Eden might not be able to handle things at the moment.

"Letty, tell her I'll be there too," Eden whispered hoarsely as she watched Bronte. "I need to talk to her about something."

"You..." started Letty worried, "you're still going to go through with the adoption, aren't you?"

"Yes," she assured her. "It's not about the adoption. I'll tell you about it later."

"I've left a bunch of messages and Jude isn't answering," Abby informed them irritated.

"I'll call Cathcart and see if he can meet with us in the morning too," Eden said trying to controlling her emotions. "I hope Rafe and Jude are going to be okay."

"Eden, they have time, money, and good looks," said Julia. "What could go wrong?"

"Exactly," exclaimed Abby sarcastically. "They have too much money, too much time, and they are both too damn hot for their own good. Mexico or Canada," she shook her head. "I think I'm more worried about the people there than those two. I know Jude will do her best to keep Rafe safe." She looked at Eden as another thought crossed her mind. "Are you worried about her," she hesitated, "you know," she wiggled her eyebrows, "hooking up?"

Eden cringed. "Please, Abby, I don't even want to think about the possibility."

"I'm with Eden," said Greer after Beth relayed the conversation.

48

RAFE SALVAGGIO AND Jude Atwood had arrived at Nizuc Luxury Resort & Spa in Cancun, Mexico. The hotel manager took them to Rafe's suite first, and Jude was overwhelmed by the room. It was a luxury Garden Pool Villa with a lounge pavilion connected to a luxurious bedroom suite. The suite was set in a private tropical garden with an infinity pool and waterfall. Inside it had a king bed draped in fine Egyptian cotton linens and blackout curtains in case Rafe wanted to sleep all day and be up all night. The bathroom had a freestanding deep soaking tub with a separate rainfall shower, and there was an outdoor shower too. But what impressed Jude most was it came with a 24-hour butler service.

When the manager walked them to Jude's room, Jude was excited to see inside. The manager opened the door to the Ocean Suite. She had a spectacular view of the ocean with a king sized bed, and it had a private terrace. Rafe told her it was an adult only suite and winked, then told her that she thought she might like a space with privacy. Jude was excited and impressed with how Rafe went on adventures.

In no time, the pair had taken showers and changed into their swimming suits. Rafe, showing off a lot of skin and her muscles in her black bikini, made her way out of the hotel casually with Jude following in her board shorts and a tank top. The pair turned a lot of heads as they walked through the hotel and onto the beach. Jude couldn't help but grin at some of the expressions people had on their faces as they watched Rafe walk by and how Rafe ignored all of them. There were quite a few who took the vision of Jude in too, and she blessed them with a small smile.

They found beach chairs and sat down to relax. Jude watched Rafe as she smiled appreciatively at some of the women who walked by and ignored a couple of guys who tried to get her attention. She knew she needed to find out what more Rafe had planned and had to call Abby back somehow.

"So," began Jude warily, "what are we going to do here, Rafe?"

"What do you mean?" asked Rafe as she looked out at the ocean.

"I mean," said Jude as she leaned back in her chair, "are we just going to be beach bums or are we going to get jobs? It really doesn't matter to me, but it would be nice to know."

"Jude, Jude, Jude," chanted Rafe with a smile. "You should know by now I don't go anywhere without a plan."

"So, you do have a plan?"

"I do," Rafe affirmed as she laid her head back and closed her eyes.

Jude waited for Rafe to say more, but after a while, she got impatient. "Do you mind letting me in on the plan?" she asked as she watched another girl strike out into the ocean with a bikini barely covering her.

Rafe opened her eyes and looked at Jude, then followed her gaze and saw what she was looking at in the distance. She smiled and sat up. "No problem," she said, and Jude looked over at her with interest. "I think we'll stay here a week and relax, then head to Puerto Vallarta. I know someone there who has a hotel catering to artists and holds a lot of different retreats and workshops."

"So," said Jude confused, "we're going to stay there?"

"We'll go," answered Rafe, "and I'll talk to the owners about possibly working for them or becoming a partner." Rafe shrugged because it didn't really matter to her what they did or where they ended up. "I've got great contacts, and I can get a lot of people to come to Mexico for their retreats. I was also thinking about buying a building to restore. We could live in part, and I can open a gallery for work created on the retreats and by some local artists. I may even put in some of my own photography."

"Wow." Jude was impressed with her plan. "What about me?"

"I've been thinking a lot about you," said Rafe seriously. "I've been watching you for a while."

"You have?" asked Jude with a nervous laugh. "What have you been watching me do?"

"I have." Rafe smiled. "I watched the way you drew pictures for your business fliers, and how you helped with Annie's art classes, and the work you did when Annie gave you art lessons."

"So you're going to set me up with some kid art class?" asked Jude doubtfully. "I don't think me being a teacher would go over very well."

Rafe laughed. "No, I've been watching your process."

"My process?" asked Jude confused.

Rafe nodded thoughtfully. "I think you're a natural artist."

"You do?" asked Jude surprised.

"Yes," said Rafe earnestly. "I saw the way you looked at the projects you did for your business and made drawings for the messages you wanted to convey. The drawings were really very good. Also, the art you did on your own when Annie gave you assignments was impressive. You worked just like an artist does when they begin a painting or other project."

"So, you think I should become a painter?" asked Jude excited.

"Well, I think you should try several mediums to see what happens," suggested Rafe. "You've conquered art for marketing and for fun. Now you can try to see what you can do on a larger scale, for the masses, for the next generation."

"Wait a minute," said Jude feeling doubtful. "I don't know. What if I'm no good? How am I supposed to make money to live?"

"You'll be good," declared Rafe. "You'll be great! I'll be your patron."

"My patron? What's a patron?" asked Jude curiously.

"A patron gives financial support to an artist so they can work on their art," Rafe explained.

"So," Jude hesitated, "you're telling me all I have to do is to make art, and you're going to support me?"

"Well, not exactly," Rafe answered with a smile. "In return for the support, I keep the income from your work until it exceeds what I pay out. The arrangement lasts until you decide you can go out on your own and make a living or until you decide you don't want to be an artist."

"Sounds fair I guess," said Jude as she nodded. "What if I'm terrible?"

"I lose a little money, and you have to find another job," said Rafe and shrugged. "It's an investment and a risk for us both. For me money, for you time and talent. But I think you'll be surprised. I know you can be great from what I've seen you do."

"But," said Jude doubtfully, "it was mostly finger paints and a pencil."

"But its fiber or clay or paint," argued Rafe. "The medium isn't the art. What makes it art is what the artist does with the medium."

"I've never had any real art lessons," said Jude worried, "just Annie."

"You've been to massage school and know a lot about touch and the human body, and I'm sure Annie taught you about texture and color and a lot more. Give yourself a chance. What do you have to lose?"

Jude thought about it for a while. "Okay, I'll do it." Jude smiled liking the idea of being an artist. "You really do have plans."

"Yes, but right now, my plan is to study at your feet." Rafe winked.

"What?" Jude asked surprised. "Study at my feet?"

"I'm also working on some new pickup lines," Rafe claimed. "It's been a while."

"I thought you said you didn't want to be with anyone again," said Jude wondering what Eden was going to do when she found out.

Jude!" Rafe laughed and looked at her slyly. "I said I didn't want to be with anyone again, not that I didn't want to 'be' with anyone again, you know?" She winked again.

"Oh!" Jude said when she got it. "Okay, okay!" She laughed. "So, why do you need a new line?"

"Well, I just think the other one I had is kind of overused." Rafe sighed. "New life, new line," she joked.

"Okay," said Jude, torn because she was happy Rafe seemed to be better but nervous because she knew everyone was looking for her. "Hey, you want to walk over to the bar with me? I need a Corona."

"You don't have to drink Corona just because we're in Mexico," Rafe informed her.

"I know, but I like it."

Rafe put on her cover up but let it hang open, and they walked to the nearby bar with eyes following them. At the crowded outdoor bar, Jude went to get them drinks while Rafe secured a table. It took a while, but Jude was finally able to get their drinks and made her way toward Rafe. She spotted Rafe at a table sitting very close to a beautiful, well-endowed, blond-haired woman with big blue eyes. Jude stopped behind them and listened to their conversation.

"So, now what are you thinking?" asked the girl as she smiled sweetly at Rafe.

"No, no, you don't want to know what is in my mind, Shannon," Rafe said in a heavy Italian accent and laughed shyly. "*Non è nulla,*" she said absently in Italian. "It is nothing," Rafe repeated in her accented English and looked into her eyes. "*Esso renderà i tuoi occhi blu avrete bisogno di lasciare me,*" she said softly and paused, pretending to think of the words in English. "It will make your blue eyes want to leave me," she translated sadly.

"Oh, no," said Shannon not wanting Rafe to feel sad and feeling the need to touch her. She put her hand on Rafe's arm, entranced by her accent and the way she looked at her. "Now, I have to know. Tell me," she said leaning close.

"Rain," said Rafe as she looked down at the table. "Summer rain mostly."

Shannon dipped her head down so she could look into Rafe's gray-blue eyes. "Rain?" she repeated with a melodic laugh. "What's so bad about rain? It sounds nice," she said thinking it sounded especially nice in her beautiful accent.

Rafe lifted her head and looked intently into her blue eyes. "Summer rain," she said softly. "*Che cade,*" Rafe said and shook her head. "Sorry, I mean falling. You are so beautiful to make me forget my English," she said and smiled slyly.

"It's okay," said Shannon. "Go on, summer rain, falling," she encouraged her.

"Si, falling," she said softly. "Falling lightly down on your hair and face," Rafe said as she used her finger to lightly trace the trail she had described in a soft, sultry voice. "I see one small raindrop on your eyelashes, and how it shines before you blink, and it falls to your face. It ends up running down your smooth wet cheek, down under your chin and then your neck." She took her hand away from her neck when it met her chest. "Until it disappears down your shirt."

Rafe smiled and quickly looked at Shannon's shirt, then back to her eyes, and leaned in and whispered in her ear, "I'm thinking about how I'd like to follow it," she purred heavily. "I can smell the rain and scent of your skin. I see the light steam rising from your warm skin as the cool rain covers you like a blanket of tiny drops." She pulled away and smiled playfully. "Still, the one drop hiding under your clothes calls me to follow." Rafe gave a sad look. "And I want to," she breathed in her ear, "but I stop myself."

"Why?" asked Shannon entranced feeling a tingling sensation run through her body as Rafe breathed on her softly.

"Because," Rafe whispered in her ear again and pretended to fight for English words, "it's only in my mind, and I want to experience it for real," she paused, "not in the fantasy." She smiled and winked then touched Shannon's nose lightly.

"You are crazy!" said Shannon as she sat back and laughed.

"I know!" Rafe laughed with her. "This is why I try to keep my thoughts to myself."

Shannon looked over where her friends were seated then back at Rafe then leaned closer. "I liked it, you know," she whispered.

"*Davvero?*" asked Rafe with an arched brow. "You did?"

"Yeah," said Shannon as she touched Rafe's hand again, "you can think of me in the rain anytime."

"*Grazie,*" said Rafe and looked into her eyes. "Thank you."

"No problem," said Shannon then bit her lip as she looked down away from Rafe's gaze, "and I don't want to leave," she said shyly.

"I'm glad," whispered Rafe as she put her hand over Shannon's then looked across the bar at nothing in particular.

"You're doing it again, aren't you?" asked Shannon as she watched Rafe.

"*Che cosa*? What do you mean?" asked Rafe as she brought her attention back to Shannon.

"You have a faraway look in your eyes again," said Shannon softly, "like you're somewhere else."

"I am," Rafe confessed. "Will you keep me here? It's really where I want to be." Rafe gave her a half smile.

"How? How can I keep you here?" asked Shannon as she smiled in anticipation.

Rafe looked down and hesitated then looked up at her with raw passion. "*Baciami.* Kiss me."

Shannon took a sharp breath. "Kiss you?"

"*Si,*" Rafe nodded and leaned closer, "*Baciami, bella.*"

Jude thought this was a good place to interrupt for Eden's sake. "Hey, Rafe!" she called and sat down. "Here's your beer." She set the beer down in front of Rafe and looked at Shannon. "Hi, I'm Jude," she said and reached out to shake her hand.

"Hi," said Shannon disappointed the moment was lost. "Shannon," she said and shook Jude's hand.

"You here long?" asked Jude and took a drink of her beer.

"I leave tomorrow," said Shannon then pointed to a group across the bar. "My group is over there."

Jude looked over at the group of men and women she pointed toward. "Oh, where are you from?"

"We're here from Indiana," shared Shannon proudly.

Jude looked at Shannon then at Rafe and saw her wink. "Indiana?" asked Jude surprised.

"Yes." Shannon laughed. "I'm an Indy girl."

"Seems like I was right about Midwestern girls turning up everywhere I go," said Rafe continuing her accent.

"Yeah," said Jude, "it's so weird. It was something we talked about, and now we meet someone from there."

"It is," agreed Rafe and took a drink of her beer. "I stole Shannon here from one of her more intoxicated travel mates."

Shannon looked over at the group across the bar. "He's such an ass," she said annoyed.

"Rafe, you're always stealing someone," Jude teased. "Remember how you stole Eden from the guy she was seeing in college?"

"Eden?" asked Shannon curiously. "Do tell!"

"It was in my other life." Rafe frowned and tried to wave the subject away.

"Who was she?" asked Shannon.

"She's just a woman we knew," said Jude noting Rafe's dark look, "from the Midwest, but she's in Los Angeles now," she finished weakly.

"Oh," said Shannon wanting to stay and hear more but saw her group starting to leave. "Well, it looks like my group is leaving, and I kind of have to stick with the group tonight." She shook Rafe's hand warmly with both hands. "I hope I'll see you again sometime." She leaned in and kissed Rafe next to her mouth.

"Me too." Rafe quickly kissed her back and arched her brow. "*Arrivederci*," she said as Shannon released her hand. "Have a safe trip home if I don't see you, *bella*." Rafe watched Shannon saunter away clearly hoping she was still looking.

"Sorry, Rafe," said Jude nervously. "I didn't mean to run her off. I just didn't think." She shrugged and watched as Rafe just calmly took a drink of her beer. "I heard your line," she said making Rafe smiled. "Pretty good." Jude laughed. "The accent was a nice touch."

"Don't worry, Jude. I didn't lose her," Rafe said dropping her accent as she looked slyly at Jude. She opened her hand and showed Jude a folded up napkin with a note and a number. "I guess the line wasn't too bad for something last minute." She sighed then wadded up the napkin and threw it onto the table.

"Aren't you going to keep her number?" asked Jude curiously.

"No, she's into men. She's just another curious Midwestern girl, and I don't do curious anymore," she paused, "or Midwestern girls."

"But—" Jude stammered. "You had her." She looked at Rafe then remembered Eden was looking for her. "I mean, I do curious, and I don't care where she's from. Can I have it?"

"Sure." Rafe laughed softly, gave the napkin to Jude, and then frowned at the pain in her head.

Jude looked at Rafe and could tell something was wrong. "I was just wondering," she started warily, "what about everyone back home. Eden, Letty, and all of them."

"What about them?" Rafe asked as she took another sip of her beer and looked out at the ocean.

"Well, won't Eden miss you? She loves you. Does she know you aren't together anymore?"

"Of course, she knows." Rafe laughed sullenly. "She knew the day I left and met Greer at the hotel."

"Oh," said Jude with a nod. "Well, what about Greer? Does she know you aren't going with her?"

Rafe looked out at the ocean silently for a moment. "She should know by now," she said softly and sat her drink on the table. She closed her eyes wishing the pain in her head would go away. "I'm going to head back to my room. I think I may get dressed and take the manager up on her drinks offer," she lied, trying to be in the adventure for Jude. "Oh, I put the money in the safe so here's my room key in case you need any. You remember the code, right?"

"Right," said Jude with a nod, noticing Rafe's hand shaking as she handed her the key. As Rafe walked away Jude watched her pressing her hand against her head again.

49

AFTER EXPLORING THE hotel and the beach, then finding and talking with Shannon for a while, Jude Atwood made her way up to Rafe's room. She was hoping Rafe had left to go have drinks with her manager friend. Using the spare key to get into the room she was surprised to see Rafe was there sleeping. Rafe called out incoherently in her sleep as Jude quickly searched through Rafe's bag for the cellular phone. She wanted to hurry and call Abby then go have some private time with Shannon. When she finally found the phone, she turned to leave and stopped short at a familiar voice.

Rafe had opened her eyes wide as she startled awake from her nightmare, "Jude," she said softly as she recognized her. "Jude, what are you doing here?" she whispered hoarsely.

Startled, Jude turned back around and looked at Rafe. She saw her shining eyes and the wet curls sticking to her face and could tell she had been sweating and having a nightmare. "I..." Jude stammered because she was caught. She quickly hid her cellular phone behind her back. "I just needed some money. You said I could take what I needed from the safe, and I wanted to go into town with Shannon."

Rafe sat up and put her feet on the floor then ran her hand through her sweat-dampened hair. "Okay, sure," she said then looked up at Jude. "We may be leaving tomorrow."

"I thought we were going to stay for a week," said Jude in surprise noticing the dark circles around Rafe's eyes and her paleness.

"I know, but I think we need to go," said Rafe shakily. "I'm thinking about Italy."

"Italy?" Jude repeated desperate to find a way to stay.

"Yes," Rafe mumbled. "I can hear them calling me back."

Jude looked at her not sure she heard her right, still reeling about Rafe wanting to go to Italy. "Can, can we talk about it in the morning? We just left the country, now you want to leave the continent. I don't know, Rafe. Let's just sleep on it and take a day to make sure."

"I understand," said Rafe thickly as she frowned. "You're afraid." She looked at Jude shakily. "Okay, I'll give you a day to think about it, but then I'm leaving. I hope you'll come with me."

"You just go back to sleep," Jude soothed her as she helped Rafe lay back down. "You've had a long day. This is a big decision. I guess I just need to get used to the idea."

"Just think of it as an adventure," said Rafe and closed her eyes.

Outside the room, Jude closed the door softly and made her way back to her own room. She tried her phone but couldn't get a signal, so she made her way to the common area just in case Rafe decided to look for her in her room. Jude went through the phonebook on her phone, then picked up the lobby phone, and dialed. She gave the long distance operator the number and waited as the call was placed.

"Abby? Abby, it's Jude. Accept the charges," she said for the recording then listened as the call was connected and charges were accepted.

"Jude!" yelled Abby as the call was connected. "Where the hell are you? I've been calling you all fucking day! Is Rafe still with you?"

"Abby, just listen," said Jude frantically. "I couldn't call you. Rafe took my phone. We're in Mexico."

"Mexico!" Abby screeched. "Jude, I told you to keep her in town!"

"Jude, how is she?" Eden's voice came over the phone as she took it from Abby. "What's happening? How did you get to Mexico so fast?"

"She's okay," Jude reassured her. "You should see the resort and the rooms she got us. We're living like kings!" Jude told her excitedly. "She was great today. She seemed like her old self, but then..." Jude hesitated.

"Oh, my god," Eden said fearfully, "then what Jude?"

"Eden, she woke up from a nightmare tonight and now she wants us to go to Italy," Jude explained anxiously. "I'd love to visit there," she laughed weakly, "I mean the girls, whoa! But I really didn't even want to come to Mexico. I want to come home. You have to come and get us, and you have to be here tomorrow. If you're not," Jude paused, "she's going, and I don't know if I can go with her."

"Okay, okay," said Eden trying to stay calm. "Where exactly are you?"

50

HANGING UP THE phone, Eden Kingsley looked at the group of friends who had gathered at Rafe's house. They were all waiting for her to relay the news from Jude. She handed the phone back to Abby and steeled herself for what she knew she had to do. "I have to book a flight to Mexico for tonight," Eden informed as she looked at everyone anxiously.

"How are you going to convince her to come home?" asked Abby worried. "I mean—with all the crazy stuff going on in her head, she'll probably run as soon as she sees you."

"I—" Eden was stopped short by Abby's words. She looked at Greer desperately. Eden never thought she would be asking this woman for help but felt like she had no choice. She had no doubt Greer would know exactly what to do. "How can we do this," she asked worried, "get her back, and get her help?"

"Let's make some calls," said Greer. "We'll get this figured out, hopefully before she does anything else or goes anywhere else."

They made calls to book flights to Mexico. Greer and Beth rebooked their flights in light of the situation with Rafe. Greer knew Rafe needed help that Eden and her friends might not be able to arrange and thought it was best they went with them. She helped them make calls and organized getting the help she was sure Rafe needed. Her heart was aching for Rafe, and she knew Eden was having an even harder time.

51

EARLY MONDAY MORNING, Eden Kingsley was at LAX with Greer, Beth, and Abby holding their tickets for Cancun, Mexico. Greer had made calls to get medical help for Rafe in Mexico while Eden and Letty met with Katheryn for the legal paperwork they would need. Their friends were seeing them off as they waited to go to their gate to catch their flight.

"I'll miss you," cooed Eden as she kissed Bronte. "Mommy will be back soon with Mama. I know you miss her." Bronte looked around for Rafe at the mention of her mama. Eden hugged and kissed her again then handed her to Ephraim. "Thank you, Letty. Don't worry, we'll find her and bring her home."

"I know," said Letty as she hugged Eden. "I know you will. Thank you for doing this and for what you're doing for Rafe," she said as she took Bronte from Ephraim. "It will mean so much to her, I know it will."

"I'm doing it for both of us, for all of us," said Eden determined not to cry. "So we can be the family of her dreams and mine.

"We are a family," Letty affirmed to her as tears ran down her cheeks. She looked at the travelers. "I guess you should get to your gate. I wish we could have gotten you on a flight last night."

"I know," said Abby frustrated, "I tried, but this six-thirty flight was the earliest one I could get us all on."

"It's okay. It gave Greer time to arrange everything with the doctor," Eden told Letty as they all walked toward their gate, "and we've talked to the owner of the resort who helped us find rooms for everyone. We have all the legal paperwork we need, and the doctor Greer called is meeting us there later today. Greer was afraid we wouldn't be able to get Rafe to her here in the States, so she arranged for her to go to Rafe in Mexico."

"It's lucky Greer knows her," said Abby impressed. "Not many psychiatrists make house calls to Mexico."

"I just hope Rafe doesn't hate me for signing those papers to do this," said Letty uneasily. "But we have to get to her. She isn't thinking clearly. She needs this help."

"She won't, Letty. It had to be done," said Eden reassuringly. She hugged Letty and kissed Bronte again when they arrived at their gate.

"I know she loves you," Letty whispered to Eden. "She loves you so much."

"I just hope you're right," said Eden anxiously, "because I really do love her, very much." She followed the others through the security line anxious to get to Rafe.

52

FINALLY ARRIVING IN Cancun, Mexico Eden Kingsley along with Abby, Greer, and Beth checked in to their accommodations and then called the doctor to make sure everything was ready for Rafe.

After meeting the doctor and all the arrangements were confirmed, they went straight to the resort looking for Rafe and Jude. At the resort, while Abby went to tell the manager they were there, the others knocked on Rafe's door. There was no answer, so they went to Jude's room. There was no response there either, so they decided to try Rafe's door one more time.

"Where is she?" demanded Eden as she pounded on Rafe's door again frustrated.

"The manager said she went out before lunch with a big group and hasn't come back yet," relayed Abby breathlessly as she ran up to the group. "There really aren't very many places she could be," she assured them. "Beach, bar, restaurant, here."

"Abby, Cancun isn't just this little spot. There are a lot of places she could be," Beth told her. "Museums, attractions, excursions... Does she scuba dive or fish?

"Rafe? No way!" Abby scoffed.

"I knew we should have come straight here," said Eden in frustration.

"We should go see if she took a shuttle somewhere if she's with a group," Beth suggested.

They made their way down to the lobby and found a shuttle driver. "Excuse me," said Eden as she stopped the driver, "*¿Has vistas dos mujeres que iban con un grupo grande hace una hora?*"

"You speak Spanish!" said Abby in surprise.

"Just what I can remember from college, and very badly," said Eden as she waved Abby back and looked at the driver who was nodding as he smiled at her. "*¿Donde?*"

"*En el puente*," said the driver as he shook his head and walked away. "*Turistas locos*," he muttered.

"What! Did he just call us something bad?" demanded Abby.

"No, calm down, Abby," said Eden as she tried to remember her college Spanish. "He said at the bridge," Eden relayed when she figured it out. "What bridge?" Eden asked, exasperated.

"I'll go talk to the manager again," said Abby and headed off.

"Maybe we should just wait until she comes back," suggested Greer after Beth told her the conversations.

"What if she's not coming back?" asked Eden as she looked at Greer with fear in her eyes. "What if they're on a plane right now? We can't wait."

"Hey, guys," called Abby as she came back. "She gave me directions to the bridge. Let's go."

53

WHEN THEY REACHED the abandoned wooden train bridge, Eden Kingsley and the rest of the group were horrified at its decrepit and dilapidated condition. There were several people standing on it. A few young people were looking over the edge while a few older men were sitting around their food and craft stands talking. The water was very far below the old train bridge, and it was almost dizzying to watch the rushing water below. They spotted Rafe and Jude among the younger group who were looking over the edge.

Rafe was sitting on the rail with her feet dangling over the edge. She was nervously rocking back and forth.

"You don't have to do this," Jude said, obviously worried. "Please, Rafe."

"Just back up Jude, don't touch me," Rafe warned, annoyed. "I do have to do this," she said as she stepped down onto the outer edge of the bridge and held the rail tightly, her fists white from her grip.

"Rafe," Jude pleaded. "This—" she stopped fearfully. "Please, I don't know if I like this. Please, come back over. Don't do it. Let's go back," she begged.

"I can't," Rafe said as she smiled nervously hoping that Jude would understand. "I have to jump. I can't turn back now. I just need to let go."

Eden and the group had watched in horror as Rafe climbed over the rail. Eden began running toward Rafe with everyone following her. "Rafe! Jude!" Eden called frantically. "What are you doing? No!"

"Eden?" Jude gulped in surprise.

Rafe snapped her head up. "Ede?" She didn't know how Eden could be there. She should be far away.

"What are you doing?" cried Eden, upset as she pushed through the crowd to get to them.

"Eden, don't. It's okay," Jude tried to reassure her.

"What are you doing here?" asked Rafe aggravated as she re-gripped the rail.

"I—" Eden panted, in pain from her run, and took in the full scope of Rafe's precarious position. "I came for you," she said horrified that Rafe was on the wrong side of the railing.

Rafe looked at the river below her then back at Eden. "You should go home," she said firmly.

"Goddamn it, Rafe! What are you doing?" screamed Eden. "Get back over the railing!"

"No," said Rafe as she looked at Eden with a frown and shook her head. "Stop telling me what to do!"

"Eden, don't!" Jude cautioned her.

"Rafe," squeaked Abby as she joined Eden, shaking. "Come on," she begged.

"Rafe! Stop!" said Greer with wide eyes.

"Get over here!" demanded Eden and snatched for Rafe's wrist.

"Stop it, Ede!" Rafe yelled and pulled her hand away from her. Rafe looked at Eden in surprise as she lost her balance.

Eden watched as Rafe tried to reach for the rail and missed then fell back and disappeared. "No!" Eden screamed in anguish. "Rafe! Oh, my god! Oh, my god!"

"Shit," screamed Abby as she stared in disbelief. "Oh shit! No!"

"No! Rafe!" Greer yelled in terror along with them.

"No!" Eden cried out in a long horror filled scream as her knees weakened and bent.

"Eden, stop it!" Jude yelled as she caught Eden and took her by the shoulders.

"I've killed her," Eden burst into a flood of tears and tried to look over the edge of the bridge.

"Eden, Eden, it's okay," said Jude as she pulled Eden away from the edge. "Look," she said and pointed to the bottom of the railing where a cable and rope were tied. "It's just a bungee jump. She shouldn't die. I hope," Jude said weakly.

Eden broke away from Jude and rushed to the railing to look over the edge of the bridge with Abby and the others. They heard Rafe whooping and laughing as she dangled and bounced over the water below.

"I'm going to freaking kill her!" Eden screamed angrily.

"Not if I get to her first!" roared Abby holding her chest.

"She's freaking laughing!" fumed Eden annoyed.

"What's happening?" asked Greer and Beth signed everything to her. "Son of a bitch!" voiced Greer, torn between relief and anger. "She almost gave me a heart attack!"

"Eden," said Jude nervously, "she just wanted to try it," she tried to explain. "She—"

"Shut it, Jude!" Abby angrily cut her off. "She's fucking dead meat!"

"How could you let her do this?" Eden asked Jude as she looked at her in dismay and took in the clearly not certified, or anything else, equipment and people running the jump. "This can't be safe!"

"I—" Jude started hesitantly. "Eden, I couldn't stop her," she said weakly. "It's Rafe."

Abby watched Rafe as she was recovered by a boat below then got into a jeep on shore. "Where's she going?"

"To the resort, I guess," said Jude as she shrugged. "No reason to come all the way back up here. I'm next," she said as a man pulled up the bungee rope. "Plus, we already paid."

"Oh, no you don't," Eden said fiercely as she seized Jude by her shirt. "This is insane!"

"Oh, man!" said Jude disappointed as she was dragged from the railing by Eden. "She made it," Jude reminded them, "so I'll be okay. I just couldn't go first," she explained.

Abby grasped Jude and helped Eden drag her off the rickety bridge. "What the hell is wrong with you two!" screeched Abby.

54

THE DRIVE BACK to the resort was not nearly long enough to diminish Eden Kingsley's temper. The group made it back to Rafe's room, dragging a disgruntled and admonished Jude with them.

"Rafe! Rafe, open the door." Eden beat on Rafe's door angrily. "I know you're in there! What did you think you were doing! You could have been killed!" There was no response, and Eden slapped the door. "Rafe, goddamn it! Let me in!"

"Jude, use your key," Abby demanded. Eden's use of foul language completely justified in her mind, even though it was shocking. "I'm going to give her a piece of my mind!"

"I don't know." Jude shifted from foot to foot concerned because Eden was swearing, and Abby looked like she was going to commit murder. "I don't think yelling at her is going to help. If I open the door, she could be mad. Maybe you should calm down first."

"Eden, she's right," said Greer calmly. "Let's all calm down. She's fine. She's not hurt," she reminded Eden. "Let's just take a step back."

"Jude, open the door!" Eden demanded, and Jude hesitantly unlocked the door. Eden tried to get in, but Rafe had put the chain lock in place. "Dang it, Rafe!" she yelled through the crack in the door. "Rafe, this is serious. Let me in!"

"I'm taking a shower," said Rafe through the door. "Go away," she said irritably and tried to close the door.

"A shower," Abby yelped exasperated. "Great! No excuses, Rafe! Let us in! We aren't going anywhere!"

"Well, I might be," said Rafe annoyed. "You should just go back home," she told them and walked away from the door.

Eden watched Rafe walk away from the door and saw she was half-naked and heading for the shower. "Rafe! Come back, and open the door!" she demanded.

"Eden, please," said Greer. "This is getting nowhere, and it's not helping anything."

"What are we supposed to do?" asked Eden helplessly and started to shake from the pain of her injuries. "We have to get her to the appointment."

"I know, but arguing with her right now isn't helping," Greer pointed out. "You're upset, and you've had a bad scare," she said as she looked at everyone. "We all have. Let's just try something different."

"Like what?" Eden asked anxiously. "If we leave, she's going to find a way to take off. You know she is!"

"I know," Greer acknowledged. "I don't think we should all leave. Maybe she'll talk to just one of us."

"You know it won't be me right now," said Eden with tears in her eyes. "You're talking about you. You want to talk to her alone," Eden said distraught.

"I think I should try," said Greer after Beth signed what Eden had said through her tears. "Eden, she needs to get this help. I'm not cutting you out, I promise. I just want to get her to the appointment too."

"Come on, Eden," encouraged Abby as she hugged Eden. "She's right. Let her try. You really need to take your meds. You're getting pale."

"Okay," Eden nodded as she leaned on Abby weakly fighting to control her emotions and desperate for any kind of help even if it was from Greer. "Okay."

"Jude, take them to the lobby area, and we'll meet you there, with or without her, in a little while," Beth interpreted for Greer. "Okay?" voiced Greer and watched Eden nod again while Abby and Jude led her away.

"So, what do we do?" signed Beth.

"Tell her I made everyone leave," Greer signed back. "Tell her I'm glad she finally made up her mind about Eden, and we need to talk. Tell her I love her," she signed and looked at Beth determinedly.

"What?" Beth signed quickly with shock on her face. "Greer, you can't do this to Eden. She trusts you!"

"Beth, just say it!" Greer voiced and looked at her firmly. Beth sighed heavily then interpreted what Greer said through the door.

Rafe closed the door and began to unlatch the chain lock. Greer smirked at Beth.

"Rafe, I'm happy to see you," said Greer as the door opened.

"Come in," Rafe said as she looked suspiciously out the door. "Hurry before they come back."

"I'm so glad I found you," said Greer as she entered the room and found Rafe wrapped in a towel. "Why did you come to Mexico?"

"To get away." Rafe frowned as she locked the door. "I guess it wasn't far enough," she said as she dropped her towel and walked naked to the outside shower.

Greer looked over at Beth who blushed and looked away from Rafe. Greer motioned to Beth, and they followed Rafe to the edge of the shower. Beth stood to the side where she could hear Rafe and still be able to sign to Greer. "Everyone's been very worried about you," said Greer as she watched Rafe soap her beautifully toned body under the rain shower.

"Well," said Rafe as she bent her head back to wet her hair, "they shouldn't. I'm fine."

"Are you fine?" asked Greer. Rafe ignored the question as she washed her hair and then rinsed off. "Rafe, we need to talk."

"There's nothing to talk about." Rafe grabbed a towel from the shelf and dried herself. "I'm sorry I didn't tell you in person," she said as she wrapped the towel around herself and walked toward the bedroom, "but I had to go."

"I know you think you had to go," said Greer as she and Beth followed. "I'm not angry with you. I love you."

"Eden is." Rafe quickly put on her underclothes. "She just doesn't understand." She pulled her shirt over her head then looked at Greer sadly. "I love you, too. I'm sorry about everything, but I have to get away." She put on her jeans then started quickly packing her things in her duffle bag and suitcase.

"Rafe, I need you to sit down," said Greer as she sat on the edge of the bed, and Beth stood at the door. "I need you to stop packing and listen to me."

"I'm sorry," said Rafe sadly as she opened the safe. She took out her money and passport and put them in the duffle bag. "I don't have a lot of time. I'm catching a flight for my first leg to Italy."

"Please, don't go," Greer pleaded as Rafe put on her shoes. "I need you to talk to someone." She hesitated. "A doctor."

"I'm not sick," Rafe chuckled as she started to comb out her hair.

"I know," said Greer cautiously. "It's not that kind of doctor. She's a psychiatrist."

"I'm not talking to another fucking psychiatrist about Eden and relationship issues," said Rafe angry and annoyed. "It's a waste of time."

"Rafe, it's not about your relationship with her."

"What's it about then?" asked Rafe in frustration. She stopped combing her hair and looked at Greer. "Why did everyone have to come all the way here to find me?"

"The doctor needs to talk to you about what happened at the school," Greer explained gently.

Rafe looked away from Greer then sat down on the bed and put her head in her hands. "I don't want to talk about that either." She lifted her hand and rubbed her temple. "I'm getting a headache," she said then got up and searched through her bag for some aspirin.

Greer looked at Beth as she signed what Rafe said then looked at Rafe. "Is that why you didn't go to the counseling sessions?" asked Greer softly. "You didn't want to talk about it?" Rafe went to the refrigerator, got out a bottle of water, and didn't answer. "Rafe?"

"They asked too many personal questions." Rafe took her pills. "I'm not talking about," she frowned at Greer, "*things*," she said angrily, "in front of students."

"Ah, so you didn't like the group sessions," said Greer as she finally understood what happened.

"No, I didn't," Rafe said hotly, glad to talk about something that was not just a blur making her head ache. "The therapist was an ass!"

"He was just doing his job," Greer reminded her. "But I agree he should have had private sessions for you."

"He should have." Rafe nodded righteously. "But I didn't need him anyway. I'm fine."

"You're fine?" asked Greer sadly. "Rafe, can't you see what you're doing?"

"What?" Rafe frowned. "I'm not doing anything. I'm just starting over. People do it all the time," she said and sat down next to Greer. "Will you come with me? I love you," she said and looked at her pleadingly wanting to talk about anything else.

"What about all you've worked for?" asked Greer avoiding Rafe's question. "You're going to give up your job at the Conservatory, your love and life with Eden, and your relationship with Bronte?"

"I have to," said Rafe as she took Greer's hand. "I have to let go."

"You don't have to." Greer sighed. "Rafe, the reason you're having bad dreams—"

"How do you know I've had dreams?" demanded Rafe as she looked at Greer in confusion. "Just stop," she said and held her hands out. "I don't want to talk about it." She began packing again then looked at Greer with suspicion. "How did you know where I was?"

"Well," Greer started to explain.

"Jude!" Rafe shook her head feeling betrayed. "Jude told you!"

"How do you know?" asked Greer in surprise.

"Her phone is gone," said Rafe as she stuffed more things into her bag. "She called and told you where we were. It's okay." She sighed and shook her head. "She's just scared. I guess she needs to go back with you when you leave. I'll go on my own."

"You're not scared?" asked Greer curiously.

"No, why would I be afraid?"

"You're not afraid to go, but..." Greer was treading carefully, "you're afraid to stay. Is it because of the nightmares?"

"I told you," said Rafe irritated, "I don't want to talk about it—or Eden."

"Eden loves you," Greer reminded her. "It's why she's here."

"Greer," Rafe closed her eyes and calmed herself, "she doesn't need me anymore."

"So your reason for leaving is because she doesn't need you?" Greer asked calmly.

"The things I've done caused her to make too many mistakes," Rafe said as she zipped up her bag.

"I agree, she did make mistakes," she said softly as she looked at Rafe, "some monumental mistakes. Both of you suffered because of them. But it wasn't something she did in malice," Greer explained. "Her intent was benevolent. So you have to take it into consideration."

"The only thing I have to take into consideration is the mistakes she made were my fault because she was angry with me and—" she stopped not wanting to talk about the fact Eden really didn't love her anymore. "She's just better off without me."

"Her mistakes weren't your fault," said Greer as she shook her head. "Don't try to take away her right to make choices or even mistakes. Even if Eden was angry with you, she's responsible for the things she does and choices she makes. Don't belittle her, Rafe."

"It doesn't matter," Rafe said and sat next to Greer wanting her to understand. "She still just doesn't need me."

"So, you think because she doesn't need you, you can't love her," Greer said trying to understand, "or she doesn't love you?

"Yes, maybe, I don't know," said Rafe as she rubbed her head. "I just don't want her trying to protect me again."

"You don't want her to protect you?" Greer asked hoping Rafe would expand on it.

"No," said Rafe flatly.

"But it's okay if you protect her?" asked Greer cautiously.

"What?" Rafe asked with a frown.

"You're doing what you think is best for her by not being with her," said Greer calmly, "protecting her from yourself. Double standard?"

"No," Rafe disagreed. "It's different because I'm protecting myself too."

"What exactly are you protecting yourself from?" asked Greer curiously. "Eden?'

"Greer," Rafe looked at her sadly, "why are you doing this? Don't you want to be with me? I love you, you know."

"I know, and I do love you, Rafe," Greer sighed, "but this is wrong, and I can see you know it's wrong. I can see you're doing your best to convince yourself you shouldn't love Eden," she paused, "but you do."

"I love you," Rafe said softly.

"Why are you forcing her to fight when you want to take her back?" Greer asked as she touched Rafe's arm.

"I don't," Rafe insisted. "I'm not forcing her to fight," she said and pulled away from her. "She's just—" she shook her head, "going crazy!"

"Rafe," Greer said touching her on her arm again, "she told me she's never had to fight before. She's just doing whatever she thinks will get you back."

"Well, she sucks at it because the things she's doing don't make me want to come back," Rafe said irritably. "She's just pissing me off."

"Well, I think Eden is more of a peacemaker than a fighter," Greer observed, "more of a negotiator or mediator."

"What are you saying?"

"Rafe, she's letting me talk to you," Greer reminded her, "so she's compromising her own fears and insecurities. Right now, I'm sure she's probably in physical pain from her anxiety about me talking with you. She loves you enough to try something that scares the shit out of her," she paused, "me alone with you. For all she knows, I'm in here seducing you!"

"Will you?" Rafe smiled and leaned into her.

"No," said Greer and pushed her back firmly. "I told you, I don't want you to put your love for her on a shelf."

"I know," Rafe said, disappointed. "It's like you said, you need all of me, and right now, I don't know if I have all of me here to give to you—or to her. I don't want to hurt," she said defiantly, "and I don't want to hurt anyone else. I'm not meant to have happiness, I guess." She shrugged and calmed herself. "Part of me is gone," she said sadly, "and I'm not sure how to get it back."

"This is why I think you need to talk to the doctor," Greer encouraged her. "I know her, Rafe. She's a good friend, and I'm sure she can help you."

"I hate therapists!" Rafe said as her emotions swirled back into anger. "They all think they know me! They don't!"

"Rafe, she's here to talk to you," Greer said firmly, "about what happened at the school, nothing more unless you want to talk about something else. Just meet her, please. Just try," she pleaded.

"But Greer, I don't need to talk about it," Rafe told her and hoped she would see reason. "I told you!"

"Do it for me," Greer pressed. "I want you to get that part of you back that you think is missing. She can help with the nightmares too. Then, after you talk to her," Greer shrugged, "you can go if you still want to. Okay? I love you, Rafe. You said you love me," she said and rubbed her arm again, "then show me. Do this one thing for me."

Rafe rubbed her temples as the pain in her head grew. "I... I don't want to see them," she said, "her," she clarified, "Eden. I can't."

"You don't have to see Eden," Greer assured her and rubbed her back to comfort her. "It can be just you and me. Okay? Do this, and then you can go to Italy if you still want to go. I want you to be happy. I want your nightmares to stop, and I want you to get back to being you. Will you do it for me?"

"I—" she stopped trying to think things through. "Will you stay with me?"

"I'll stay for you," Greer promised. "I want to help you."

"No," said Rafe as she shook her head, "will you stay with me, not for me. Please, stay and be with me, Greer."

"Rafe, I can't tell you I can be with you right now," Greer told her truthfully. "I'm sorry," she said and hugged her. "I'll stay for you right now. After you see the doctor, then we'll talk about the other." She looked into Rafe's sad eyes, "Okay? I don't want us to make such a big decision right now. It's too important. Let's get you ready to go. I'll get your bag ready. You go brush out your hair before it's totally dry and pack your bathroom things."

"Okay," Rafe relented as she felt the warmth of Greer's arms around her. She held her a bit longer then got up feeling defeated and went into the bathroom.

Greer led Beth back out into the sitting room and signed to her. "Go tell them to leave and meet us at the hospital. Don't let any of them come to the room. Make sure they're on their way, and then come back. I'm afraid she'll change her mind if she sees them or Eden. Do it quickly because I need you to call the doctor about what's happening too."

Beth nodded and left the room to go find Eden and the others.

55

A LUXURY TAXI pulled up to the hospital. The driver opened the door and Greer Noble led Rafe Salvaggio inside with her luggage as Beth followed. They were greeted by the staff that had been eagerly waiting for them. Eden and the others were gathered in a private waiting room. After speaking with Beth, the doctor had arranged everything to be prepared so Rafe could go straight to her room upon her arrival without seeing Eden or the others. Greer and Beth went to the room with Rafe to help her get settled.

"So," said Rafe as she put her bag beside the bed, "why do I have a room? I thought I was just going to talk to her."

"Well, you are," said Greer carefully. "The room is just in case things go longer than expected."

"I won't need it." Rafe looked around unhappily at the sterile room. "There's not much to talk about."

"It's just in case, Rafe," Greer said as the doctor walked into the room.

"Hello, I'm Dr. Baker. You can call me Kate." She shook Rafe's hand. "I'm glad to see you made it."

"Hello," Rafe greeted the doctor, "Rafe Salvaggio. Can we just get this over with? I have a plane to catch."

"Sure, have a seat," said Kate as she pointed to the chair. "Greer, I'll come and get you when we're finished, okay?" Kate signed and spoke.

"Okay, thanks, Kate," said Greer as she and Beth left the room and closed the door.

"So, I've been told you've been having some problems," said Kate as she sat across from Rafe. "Nightmares maybe?" she asked, and Rafe nodded. "Also, you feel like you have to leave your home and family. I looked at the timeline you gave Greer. Did you know you left out what happened at the school?"

"I didn't leave anything important out," said Rafe defensively, not liking that the doctor had been looking at her personal information.

"So, you don't think what happened was important?" asked Kate calmly.

"No," said Rafe flatly.

"Can you tell me about it? Tell me what happened?" Kate waited as Rafe remained silent. "Maybe I can help you," offered Kate. "I read the reports. There was a young man with a gun," she started.

"You know, I think this is a waste of time," Rafe said as she stood up. She couldn't talk about that time. It was all gone from her mind, and it hurt trying to remember. It even hurt to hear others talk about it. It was best to just leave it all in the darkness. "Tell Greer I couldn't do it. I have to go."

"Rafe, you can't leave," Kate told her calmly.

"Why not?" asked Rafe becoming frustrated.

"Because," Kate began delicately, "your cousin Letty has used her power of attorney to give me permission to keep you here if I think it's necessary."

"What?" Rafe erupted. "She fucking can't do this! Those papers are for emergencies! In case I'm unconscious or something! You can't fucking keep me here!" she roared.

"This is an emergency," Kate said calmly. "You may not know it or believe it, but you're having a medical problem, and it's keeping you from thinking clearly."

"All you fucking therapists think everyone is crazy!" Rafe fumed. "I'm not crazy! I know exactly what I'm doing!" she yelled as she paced. "Just because I don't want to talk about—" she fought for her words, "*things,*—" she spat, "doesn't mean I'm crazy! She had no right to do this!"

"Calm down," Kate said softly. "No one said you were crazy. You're not crazy. You're hurt, and you're suffering. Your cousin wants to help you. Your friends and Greer want to help you. Your partner, Eden, wants to help you."

Rafe stopped pacing and turned her anger onto Kate. "She's not my partner anymore!" Rafe growled. "Don't call her that!"

"I'm sorry," said Kate evenly and watched as Rafe paced the room. When Rafe sat back down, she pressed on. "Eden told me she loved you and you were her partner," she explained. "She said when she was hurt, you came and helped her," she reminded Rafe. "She wants to help you too."

"I had to help her." Rafe hesitated not wanting to think about Eden or what happened to her. "I... I was the decision maker on her medical power of attorney," she said defensively. "I had to go."

"Yes, you did." Kate nodded. "But you also went because you love her." Kate waited to see if Rafe would respond, and when she didn't, she continued. "Did you know all the time the two of you were apart, she left you as her decision maker? She told me you're the only person she would trust with her life."

"When did you talk to her? How do you know all of this?" Rafe asked suspiciously. "She shouldn't trust me," Rafe said vehemently. "She should get it all changed."

"I talked to her and Greer yesterday on the phone," Kate told her calmly, "and I talked to her today when she got to the hospital."

"She's here?" asked Rafe distressed then got up and picked up her duffle bag. "I have to go."

"You can't go, Rafe." The doctor got up and took Rafe's bag, putting it back by the bed then walked over to stand in front of the door.

"You can't let her near me," Rafe begged her with fear in her eyes. "You have to make her go home," she said frantically. Rafe fumed as she wandered around the room looking for a way out and mumbling under her breath. She looked in the bathroom then tried to open the window, but it was sealed shut. She stepped in front of the doctor and looked past her at the door.

Kate could see Rafe wanted to go out the door but could tell by what she was mumbling to herself that she was stopped by the thought Eden might be just outside.

"You have to get her out of here," Rafe roared as she realized there was no way out. She angrily paced the room again while holding one hand to her chest and the other to her head. "You have to get her away from me," Rafe said as sweat began to run down her face, and she began to shake. She went to the window and held on to the ledge, willing herself into calmness. She turned to Kate with a fevered look in her eyes. "If you don't, I'm leaving, and there is nothing you can do to stop me!" she said angrily and began to pace again. "I'm not talking to you until you make her go home," she declared then sat down and crossed her arms defensively.

"Okay, Rafe. I'll go talk to her," Kate said calmly. She was concerned with Rafe's reaction to Eden being there and wondered what her plan was for leaving if she couldn't even walk out the door of the room. "I'm going to have the nurse bring some medication to you. It will help you calm down," she said softly. "I'll also get something to help your nightmares. It may not work the first night because it needs to make its way through your body, but it will help you." She waited for Rafe to acknowledge her, but Rafe didn't move or speak. "I need to know you'll take the medication for me, Rafe. You don't have to speak, just nod," she said and waited for her to respond. "If you don't agree, I'm not sure I should have Eden leave," she said firmly. Rafe looked at her angrily then nodded. "Okay," Kate said somberly. "I'll be back in a little while and let you know what's going on."

56

WALKING INTO THE waiting area, Dr. Kate Baker found Greer and the group of Rafe's friends. They all stood and then gathered around her wanting to know what was happening with Rafe.

"How is she?" Eden asked, desperate for any news. "Is she going to be okay?"

"She's safe, and I think she'll be fine," Kate reassured them. With the shape Eden was in with her injuries, and everyone's emotional state, she didn't think telling them about Rafe's current state of mind would help anything. Besides, she really couldn't discuss her patient with them. She turned to Greer. "Did you get me the information from the school?"

"Yes, I emailed you their information," Greer confirmed. "They were surprised since no one there noticed she was having problems. Lately, Rafe hasn't been on campus."

"She—" started Eden ashamed and feeling like Greer was blaming her, "she's on leave from the school."

"Well, it explains why she felt she could just leave the country," said Kate surprised. "Why is she on leave?"

"Because," Eden said softly, "because of me."

"Eden, it wasn't all your fault," said Abby sympathetically. "The group trying to stop the adoption published an article suggesting Rafe was corrupt and unethical," she told Kate, "among other things. Luckily, they lost in court."

"Sounds like she's had a lot happen to her in a very short amount of time," said Kate thoughtfully as she recalled everything she had been told by Greer.

"Her life has just been totally fucked up by all the things happening lately," said Abby feeling angry for Rafe.

"This is going to be difficult for you to hear, Eden," said Kate as she prepared to be the bearer of bad news. "Rafe says, as long as you're here, she won't talk to me, and if you don't go home, she'll leave."

"What?" Eden was hurt Rafe wanted her gone. "I don't want to leave," she said upset. "I want to stay and help her," she insisted as tears started leaking from her eyes.

"I know," Kate said seeing how upset the news made her. "But I think the best way you can help her is to do what she wants. She needs to be here."

"What are you going to do? How are you going to help her?" asked Eden as she wiped her tears and tried to calm herself and quell the anxiety tearing its way through every inch of her body.

"Eden, I'm sorry," said Kate gently seeing her distress. "I can't discuss her treatment with you. I have to respect her privacy, and she hasn't given me permission to tell you anything. On the contrary, she is demanding you leave."

"But Eden is her partner!" Abby said upset. "They have a baby together!"

"I'm sorry, but you don't have her permission or her medical power of attorney," Kate said sympathetically. "I can't even ethically speak to Letty because, though she has a power of attorney, it didn't cover discussion of her medical situation unless it's determined Rafe is incapable of making decisions and speaking for herself. At the moment, she's capable even though she's having some problems. You're lucky your lawyer found a judge who would allow even this temporary medical judgment."

Eden looked at Kate in distress and sat down slowly. "I understand," she said softly feeling helpless and worried. She took a deep calming breath, determined not to cry, and looked up at Kate. "How long will she be here? I can't leave her alone," she fought back her tears. "The..." she cleared her throat, "the adoption court date is a week from tomorrow," she said sadly hoping Rafe could be back in time. Luckily, Katheryn assured her they could file to change the court date if it was necessary.

"She has a lot of bridges she needs to cross, Eden," said Kate gently. "How fast her treatment goes really is up to her."

"Can't we just take her home? Get her a room somewhere close to us?" asked Eden hopefully.

"The way she's acting now tells me the treatment can't wait," said Kate as she shook her head. "She's too much of a flight risk, and according to what you've told me, she's doing dangerous things that are out of character for her. Right now she needs a therapist she feels she can trust, and I'm hoping you'll trust me too," she said gently.

"You're right," said Eden anxiously running her hand through her hair. "Rafe hates anything to do with therapy, so if she trusts you, I think she may do better."

"I'll call some doctors I know in L. A. and see if I can set something up for when she returns," Kate assured her.

You won't see her in L. A.?" asked Eden worried.

"I wish I could, but I'll be in Baltimore," Kate explained.

"Please, just—" she took a shuddering breath, "help her. I need her to come home," she said as the feeling of helplessness ran through her again. "Help her come home."

"I'll do my best for her, Eden," said Kate as she rubbed Eden's shoulder gently. "I promise."

"What if she doesn't change her mind," said Abby apprehensively. "We know she has a shit load of money. You should take it away from her so she can't get very far."

"I'll see about putting it somewhere safe until she's ready to leave," Kate assured her.

"I think it sucks we all have to leave," Jude said upset. "She'll be all alone. Do you think I can stay with her? Then I could let Eden know what's going on."

"Jude, you can't stay!" Abby said in dismay. "You have a business and everything. If you stay, it could mess up things for you."

Jude shrugged. "I can get a job anywhere. Rafe thinks I should become an artist. Besides, I don't have any money to buy a ticket home. Rafe paid for everything."

"Jude, she is out of her mind!" Abby scoffed. "You can't throw your life away on the things she's told you! An artist! Come on Jude. That's just..." she laughed, "just crazy!"

"Fuck you, Abby!" snapped Jude angry and offended. "She didn't seem crazy when we were talking about it. She believes in me. I've only had one other person believe in me like she does! She's not crazy!"

"She's not crazy, Jude," Eden said as she hugged her.

Jude stiffly allowed Eden to give her a hug and her discomfort made her anger at Abby dissipate.

"Don't worry. I'll buy your ticket home," Eden assured her. "Rafe knows art, and if she said she thought you could do it, then you can. But you have to take care of yourself while she's here getting help." She released her from her hug and looked at her sadly. "You can't stop your life."

"Right. And neither can you, Eden," said Kate. "Do this for her. Go home, get back to work, and spend time with your daughter. I'll take good care of her."

"You have too," said Eden desperately. "I don't know what else to do. I wish I could see her, talk to her."

"I know it's hard," said Kate, "but you can help. Let's sit down so you can tell me everything you can about what's been going on so that when I talk to her, I can figure out what things are affecting her most. The more I know, the better. Eden, why don't you come with me first," she said and motioned to a private room. "We can talk in here privately."

"Okay," said Eden, willing to put her trust in Kate. "I'll do anything to help her."

"We will too," said Abby. "If you need us to help, just let us know."

"I will," said Kate. "Thank you." Kate led Eden into the private session room to talk about all the things happening in Rafe's life.

After everyone had talked to Kate as a group, there was an air of helplessness around them. Finally, Eden and the rest of the group made their way out of the hospital with heavy hearts. As they left, Greer and Beth remained in the waiting room with Kate to talk with her privately.

"This is very hard, Kate, for everyone," said Greer as the last of the group left the room. "They're a very tight group, and when one hurts, they all hurt."

"Well, Rafe's going to need a tight-knit group like them when she gets back," Kate signed. "The hardest thing to deal with is she simply believes she doesn't need the help. It amazes me, for all they say happened, she's been able to hide her condition for so long."

"So do you think I was right?" asked Greer. "She has classic signs of PTSD? I'm surprised her employer or anyone else didn't catch this earlier."

"You know I can't answer, Greer," Kate said and signed to her. "All I can say is she is going to need her friends to watch out for her for a while. Make sure she gets to her sessions and talks through things with her therapist, really talks, when she's able," she signed emphatically. "It won't be easy, and it may take a while, but it's going to be the best medicine. There's no telling how long it will take her to be able to talk in a meaningful way. So everyone will have to be very patient with her. Maybe you can help by arranging someone to talk to her friends about dealing with a person with the symptoms you described to me. It may help them deal with what's to come."

"Can I see her before I go?" Greer asked understanding Kate had to maintain patient/doctor confidentiality. "I just want to reassure her, to let her know that just because everyone left, it doesn't mean they aren't still there for her."

"I think reassuring her everyone is on her side is a good idea," said Kate. "Positive reinforcement always helps." They walked toward Rafe's room where the nurse was just leaving, having administered the medication to Rafe. "I have to go check on some things," said Kate. "I'll see you before you leave."

"Okay," said Greer and walked into Rafe's room. "Hey, Rafe." She smiled and hugged her. "Everything's just like you want it."

"They're gone?" asked Rafe suspiciously.

"Yes," Greer reassured her, noting Rafe looked as if she had deteriorated already. She looked pale and haunted. Greer hoped the medication would start helping her. "I have to go too, but if you need anything, please call me, okay? I'm still here for you, and so are all your friends," she paused, "and Eden." She felt Rafe stiffen. Pulling away Rafe went to sit down without responding. "Rafe, you know you're going to have to talk about her. And you're going to have to talk to her again when you go home."

"I don't have a home anymore," Rafe said sadly as she looked at Greer. "If Letty and the doctor ever let me out, can I come to your house?"

"You do have a home," said Greer as she sat across from Rafe and pushed her dark hair from her face. "You're not going to be here forever, and Eden's waiting for you. Your daughter's waiting for you," she reminded her.

"Tell her she doesn't have to fight for me anymore," Rafe said as she leaned back in her chair away from Greer's touch. "She should just go where she'll be happiest.'

"She loves you, Rafe," Greer said definitively. "I know you love her. Things are just..." she hesitated not wanting to upset her, "confusing right now."

"I'm not fighting for her anymore," Rafe said sadly. "I can't."

"She isn't making you fight. She wants you to come home," Greer assured her. "Are you giving up your dream? She hasn't," she said and waited for Rafe to respond. Rafe sat silently and looked at her with a hurt look on her face. "As for me," Greer continued, "if you show up on my doorstep," she paused and looked solemnly at Rafe, "you'd better be sure."

Greer took a breath and prepared herself in case Rafe had an adverse reaction to what she had to say next. She knew Rafe had problems with people keeping secrets, so she wanted to make sure one was not between them.

"Rafe, I've been seeing someone," she said calmly and waited for a reaction, but it didn't come. "I'll admit the relationship is new, and she's probably hurt I went to L. A. when you called. But I didn't know about everything going on and," she paused, "I do love you. But I want someone who will love me totally. If you can't—" She shook her head and waited again for the fallout she expected.

"If I can't, I shouldn't come?" asked Rafe very calmly as she looked down at her hands.

"You know you can come anytime," said Greer very surprised at Rafe's calm reaction, "as a friend, and only a friend, if you can't give me all of you."

57

EDEN KINGSLEY AND her group of friends arrived home safely from Mexico on an afternoon flight. Eden had worried about Rafe all night. She continued to worry all through the flight home, crying off and on trying to deal with her physical pain as well as the pain washing over her from her fears and anxiety. She didn't know what she and Bronte would do if Rafe didn't come home and decided to leave for Italy. She remembered when she was afraid Rafe would go to Italy with Bronte. She knew now her fear was foolish, and this new fear was what was real.

Guilt ran through her for everything happening now and in the past, for everything compounding the stress Rafe was dealing with from leaving her to everything with Jake and the Stewards.

The image of Rafe still wearing her ring in Canada came to her mind. She knew now it meant Rafe had still hoped they would get back together during all those months she was gone with Jake. She could only hope the love Rafe had been holding onto all that time was still there and she would come home. *Rafe has to still love us. She has to come home*, she thought.

Abby did her best to try to console Eden as they left Rafe behind. She knew it was hard for herself, so it had to be even harder for Eden. It seemed so unreal the person she knew for so long who was so strong was hurting in a way no one could understand.

Jude stood by uncomfortably to help where she could and worried Rafe may be angry with her about telling everyone where she was. She hoped when she came home that they could still be friends. They were all happy to be back home but sad and worried they had to leave Rafe behind.

Letty was there to meet them, pushing Bronte in her stroller, anxious to see Rafe and to find out how things went. As they all came down the escalator, Letty looked over the group hopefully.

"Where is she?" Letty asked as they made it to her. "Didn't you find her? What happened?"

"We found her, Letty," said Abby tired and sad. "She's at the hospital, and Dr. Baker is taking care of her."

"Why didn't anyone stay with her?" asked Letty upset and worried.

"The doctor said Rafe wouldn't talk if we were there," Eden said and tried to stay calm. "She said Rafe threatened to leave if we stayed. She thought it would be best to do what she asked."

"This is fucking ridiculous, Eden!" Letty lashed out angrily. "You just left her alone in a hospital in Mexico! That's fucked up! I thought you were bringing her home! I thought you loved her. I should never agreed to not going with you! You should have lied to her and stayed!"

"No, Letty. She's been lied to enough," said Eden starting to shake with guilt and anger. "She had so many things happen. She has to have help so she can get through this. She's where she needs to be."

"The doctor said if she didn't want us there, staying wouldn't be helpful," said Abby trying to help Eden. "We have to make sure everything is good for when she comes home."

"Where's Greer? Did she stay with her?" asked Letty hopefully.

"No, Greer got a different flight so she could get back to Baltimore," said Eden. "But she's going to make us an appointment with another doctor who can help us all understand what Rafe's going through and tell us how we can help her," said Eden hoping to give Letty some kind of positive information. "Help us know what signs we need to look for if she's having problems."

"Signs?" asked Letty confused. "I thought they were helping her. I don't understand."

"It's going to take more than the forty-eight hours the judge gave us to get her through this," said Eden sadly as she picked up Bronte who was reaching out for her from her stroller. "Dr. Baker said she would call and talk with you to let you know what to expect. She said it was up to Rafe how long her treatment would last. All we can do is learn how to help her and be ready when she gets back."

"Yeah," Abby interjected, "Greer said she would have to really talk about how she's feeling and what she's thinking, so we have to know what to do and how to help her. We have to watch for signs she's feeling under stress and having disturbing thoughts."

"There's so much." Eden sighed and then turned her attention to Bronte. "Hey, baby, I missed you," she said and kissed her as the little girl hugged her neck.

"And we have to make sure she doesn't do any more crazy stunts too!" Abby reminded them.

"Stop saying shit, Abby! She's not crazy!" Jude fumed at Abby. "She wanted to do it! It was a challenge. She wanted to experience the falling. I wanted to do it too. People do it all the time, and they aren't crazy!"

"Yes, they are!" Abby declared. "Jude, the freaking bridge was already about to collapse, and she jumped off it! What if those boards broke! So much could have gone wrong!"

"What the hell are you talking about?" asked Letty as she looked at the two bickering women in confusion.

Jude looked at Letty and hesitated, knowing she would be upset. "We went bungee jumping," she explained. "She went first because I couldn't."

"She scared the shit out of all of us is what she did!" Abby told her annoyed. "Eden almost died! So did I!"

"Okay, okay," said Eden trying to calm everyone though she didn't feel calm at all. "Let's just get home," she said and started walking through the airport.

"Did she say anything about me? Was she angry?" asked Letty as she followed Eden, worried about what Rafe was going to do.

"The doctor said she couldn't tell us what she talked about, Letty," said Eden trying to control her frustration. "But you did the right thing. She really needs this help."

"I still think someone should have stayed," Letty fretted. "She's all alone."

"Letty, I'm sorry. I wanted to stay, I did," Eden assured her. "But Rafe wouldn't cooperate if I stayed. I had to do what was best for her. I hope I did what was best for our family."

To be continued in Book Seven – Confronting Darkness...

Salvaggio's
Light
Book Seven
CONFRONTING DARKNESS

C.L. Cattano

NOTES

Translations: For translations of Italian, French and Spanish use: www.Babblefish.com

The chapters in this book were arranged with the intent of saving paper. This chapter style saved 35 pages. Original Total Book Pages 344 — Final Pages 309.

Music mentioned in this book.
No financial incentive was given for the mention of the following artists in this work. The author is a fan and felt mentioning them worked in the story. For the use of their name, credit is given, and links to their work are below.
Enjoy!

Kristy Lee
Website: https://www.kristyleemusic.com
Facebook: https://www.facebook.com/kristyleefans
Twitter: www.twitter.com/kristyleemusic
Instagram: http://www.instagram.com/kristyleemusic
YouTube: https://www.youtube.com/user/kristyleevideo

ABOUT THE AUTHOR

C.L. CATTANO LIVES in the Midwestern U.S. with her partner and their dog somewhere between the city and the forest. With a joy for traveling, she and her partner have visited many countries and have a love for meeting people and learning about the places they visit. When possible, she likes to include references in her work about the things she has learned, the places she has been and people she has met while on her travels and in her everyday life.

Cattano has a variety of creative interests including, but not limited to, creating fine art, writing, photography, and supporting women in the arts. She considers herself a 'Jack of All Trades' dabbling in what she terms the 'whimsies of her soul' that pull her toward happiness and fulfillment.

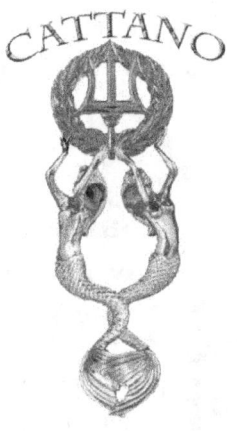

OTHER BOOKS
By C. L. Cattano

Cursed Hearts is a love story that transcends time and gender. Separated from by a gift from a bored demon on All Hallows Eve two souls connected

by the power of love have been searching through time for each other and incarnated as both men and women.

Over time, the gift became a curse and a game for the demons.

Now the souls have finally met again, and they must fight for a life together.

Will love prevail? Will they finally be able to live together again for a lifetime? They have one night to figure out the riddle and get it right to break the curse.

NOTE: 18+ Lesbian Romance. Some light erotic moments.

C.L. Cattano

Available on Amazon <u>Cursed Hearts</u>

Salvaggio's Light Series
Available on Amazon
<u>Shattered Paradise</u> – Book One
<u>Blue Inferno</u> – Book Two
<u>Secrets & Rivalry</u> – Book Three
<u>Wildling's Claim</u> – Book Four
<u>Sowers of Discord</u> – Book Five
Fire of Wrath – Book Six

REQUEST FOR REVIEW

Thank you for reading **Salvaggio's Light** — *An Epic Contemporary Romance Serial.*

I hope you enjoyed book six, **Fire of Wrath**, and will consider leaving an honest review. It only takes a few minutes, so I encourage you to go now and leave a review!

Check out the Salvaggio's Light Facebook page to join in the discussions and fun! www.facebook.com/pg/SalvaggiosLight

Join the CL Cattano Mailing List www.clcattano.com

I love getting fan mail, and you can contact me at clc@clcattano.com